MW01242941

Milestones

Samira Armin Hodges

Milestones

Samira Armin Hodges

An imprint of Gauthier Publications

1st Edition
Proudly printed and bound in the USA
Hungry Goat Press is an Imprint of Gauthier Publications
www.EATaBOOK.com
Cover image by Daniel J. Gauthier/
Cover design and layout by Elizabeth Gauthier

ISBN 13: 978-0-9820812-3-5
Library of Congress Number: 2009920144

Recycled
Supporting responsible use
of forest resources
FSC www.fsc.org Cert no. SW-COC-002283
© 1996 Forest Stewardship Council

100%

First and most importantly, I dedicate this book to my wonderful parents; any success of mine is only a reflection of your endless attributes (the one thing I could never quantify in writing). Thank you for "dreaming big" for me and for always putting my needs before your own. With much appreciation and gratitude to my beloved extended family and my two best friends, whose love and support are never-ending and unwaivering. And finally, with all my heart, to my husband: my biggest fan and the only person I will always want beside me licking envelopes.

1
Chapter

It all started when I got struck by lightning. I still remember the walk home. I was wet, confused and I smelled like burnt toast. It was a particularly miserable day in Seattle. The sky was unremittingly angry.

Probably at me, I thought as I looked up in fear, willing my knees to unbuckle.

Was that cloud following me?

It was five o'clock and it looked like the dark before dawn. As I was wobbling home unsteadily, I continued to replay the day in my mind. I can honestly say it was the most bizarre and humiliating moment of my life. Part of me wondered if it had even happened. Had I imagined the whole thing? Did I really get hit by lightning and survive to tell the tale? Did these things actually happen to normal people? Or was it all a horrible dream?

"Impossible," I grunted out loud, as I looked down at my scorched shoes.

I'll bet Converse never thought their product could look like latticework. Impressively, they were still somewhat intact, carrying me home as I tried hard not to walk like the bride of Frankenstein. Do you want to know what it felt like to get hit by lightning? It was torturous. My hair was matted to my head like it had been doused in tar, my calves felt like I had unrelenting charley horses and my head was both pounding and spinning simultaneously. I was the poster child for near-death experiences. Yet, I had only one person on my mind: *Benji.*

As I opened the front door to my house, I knew I was still far from normal. Think lightheaded, with a touch of nausea and tinnitus. I was so abnormal that I still don't remember exactly what my parents said when they saw me. I just remember barely answering them.

"Huh?" I asked in a daze. My thoughts were lost in a fog.

My mother repeated herself. Again, it was all so hazy. I really don't know what she said, or if it even registered, but it sounded a lot like:

"You're getting a postage stamp this summer."

"Oh. That's nice," I replied flatly. I glanced over at my dad, who was peering at me from above his bifocals.

Wait.

Why hadn't they said anything about my appearance? Or that I was noticeably late from school? I wondered but I also didn't really care. My head was throbbing and I felt a certain urge creeping up from the pit of my stomach. Was I going to throw up again? No, that wasn't it.

Oh, I realized. I was getting the urge to start crying. I was thinking about the day again and I wanted to crawl into a hole and cry. And sweet mother, I was in so much pain. I ached. I ached so damn bad. Every ounce of me hurt, from my elbows to my teeth to my heels. Before I could help it, images began to flash in my mind, as if I was watching my life in rewind. Rain, a branch, a shovel, and then Benji ... once more.

"I'm going up to bed," I finally declared, my voice quivering. It was too early to sleep.

My eyes began to well up with tears. I knew my parents

were still looking at me but I didn't want to reciprocate their eye contact. I still don't know why I chose to keep this a secret from them. My parents knew everything about me. My mother was the most intuitive mother on the planet and usually she could read me like a book. But on that day, for the first time in my life, she wasn't in tune with me and I took advantage of it. I wanted to be alone. I blame the high voltage shock. In hindsight, maybe I should have said something. Perhaps a visit to the emergency room wouldn't have been the worst thing. Instead, I turned around and stumbled up to my bedroom.

By the time I stepped into my room, I felt so dizzy I couldn't feel the floor beneath my toes. What I found strange at the time was the sensation of the ground slowly coming closer to my face. Of course, it was me who was leaning — Pisa-style — face first onto the carpeted floor. I let out a groan as my face smashed into the ground.

And that's the last thing that I so poorly remember.

~

I woke up the next day feeling so wonderful, I began to doubt my memories of the previous day. I looked around my bedroom and noticed I was sleeping in my bed.
What the —? How'd I get in bed? I wondered.

I peered under the blankets and saw I was wearing pajamas. A few moments later, I got out of bed and glanced around. Nothing looked odd. Nothing looked out of place. Everything seemed as unaffected by lightning as every other room in the world. I wasn't even in any pain. It was just another Saturday. Heck, it was the first Saturday of summer! And there I had it; it was all a bad dream.

"It was all a bad dream," I repeated, as I walked down the stairs and headed toward the kitchen. I was surprised my muscles weren't aching at all and my gait was flawless. I took a quick peek at myself as I passed a mirror and exclaimed:

"Normal. As always!" Life was OK again.

"Good morning, sweetie," my father said to me as I sat

down at the kitchen table.

We lived in a modest brick house with all the usual amenities. No perks. Kind of like me.

"Hey dad," I answered happily. I poured myself some cereal.

"Feeling better?" he asked me.

"What do you mean?" I wanted to know.

My dad looked taken aback.

"I mean, are you feeling better?" he repeated, slightly confused.

"Uh ... yeah, sure."

Did he know I wasn't feeling well the day before? Or was he just making inane conversation? Suddenly, my mother's voice came from behind me and what she said sent chills down my spine.

"Faye, do you want to pack these ratty shoes for your trip or can I throw them away?"

Feeling slightly paralyzed, I slowly turned my neck to see her holding up my busted Converse.

"Omigod," I hissed under my breath.

My shoes.

My stupid shoes brought me back to reality. It *had* happened. I *did* get hit by lightning and I lived — somehow. It all came rushing back to me like a stampede of wild animals. *Oh, yeah.* I had passed out on my bedroom floor and my mother (my mother!) changed me into my pajamas and put me in my bed later that night. It was all coming back to me. It was real. It had happened. I almost died.

"Faye," my mother said again, snapping me out of my daze, "Keep or throw away?"

"K-keep," I stuttered.

My mom looked at the shoes disapprovingly and shrugged her shoulders. I think my traumatized mind was a bit slow but it was at that moment something finally registered.

"Did you say trip?"

She nodded.

"Wh-what trip? Where are we going?"

So here's what actually happened. As you probably gathered, my parents had actually not informed me the night before that I was getting a "postage stamp this summer." In fact, they had informed me of something much, much worse. So much worse. Let me build this up a little more. It was really, *really* bad.

They had chosen the exact moment after I got hit by lightning to blurt out the most incredible and ridiculous piece of information, like, ever.

"You're sending me to summer camp? But, why?" I choked out after the initial shock wore off.

"Honey, it will be a wonderful experience for you," my mother said without flinching. I snorted.

"A wonderful experience?" I repeated with a touch of attitude.

Did I mention that I was 14 at the time? And although I was wrong, I was convinced I didn't need wonderful experiences. I was quite content being a regular teenager with no experiences at all.

"Faye," my father stepped in, "we're not trying to make your life difficult. Your mother and I feel you need to get away from everyone around you. You've had the same group of friends since kindergarten. You aren't happy. You need a chan—"

"Don't you think that's for me to decide?" I interrupted. My head was throbbing again. "I happen to like my friends, thank you very much!"

Of course, I was lying, but can you blame me? This was ludicrous! I had just been hit by lightning and my parents chose that moment to spring this madness on me. Unfair was the understatement of the century. This was downright embarrassing — and unbelievable! Unfortunately, due to my post-jolt status, I know I remained far from convincing.

"Faye," my mother said, "You're going to camp this summer. This isn't a negotiation."

No. No. No. This isn't happening. I shook my head in frustration.

"Wait, wait. Mom? Dad. I have something to tell you."

I was desperate now. I needed leverage. The room was beginning to spin around me like a merry-go-round. Consider that I'd just had a trillion volts of electricity run through all 5-foot-2 of me. Note that trees get split in half by lightning. Note I almost got split in half by lightning.

"What is it?" my less than enthused dad asked.

"You see, I can't go to camp. Because, well, because, uh, I, um, got hit by lightning yesterday."

"It's OK, honey. You'll be all right," my mother said rather instinctively.

"No, no. I don't think you heard me right. I said I got hit by LIGHTNING."

"We heard you."

I let out a little laugh of disbelief.

"No, like, I mean the kind of lightning that kills people and *trees*."

"Even more reason to go to camp."

My jaw dropped an inch. *Huh*?

"What? How is that more reason for me to go to camp? Are you guys listening? I said I almost died!"

"But you didn't die," my dad said, frowning.

What the hell? Were we even speaking the same language? Was this really happening? They didn't even care. How could they not care? My fiery side quickly took over my astonishment.

"Are you listening to yourselves? You don't care? You don't care that I came home yesterday like a character from *The Night of the Living Dead*? You don't care that I probably needed to go to the hospital and I didn't? That I could have been seriously hurt?"

"Don't be so melodramatic, Faye. You're fine now. These things happen."

These things happen? These things happen? Were they losing it or was I?

"I am not going to camp. I almost died and it's, it's just stupid. I'm not going," I said, feeling like a heel.

11

"Oh, yes you are," was the annoying, firm response I got back.

"No, I'm not."

"Yes, you are."

"NO!"

"Yes."

"Aarrrr!"

We went on in that manner for hours. In the end, I was too tired to argue. I know it's a poor excuse, but it's pretty much why my parents came out victorious in the battle against me and my reputation. It upset me that they were oblivious to my situation, and I just couldn't find the energy to continue on with the losing battle. Plus, I should warn you that back then, I wasn't good at being disobedient.

So there you had it. In a nutshell, I got hit by lightning (in front of Benji — say it wasn't so!) and, somehow, I survived. And now, I was being sent to some summer camp like a 9 year old by my newly heartless and insensible parents. It was so unlike them to act this way. Yet they were so convincing, I doubted everything, including myself.

~

In my defense, I spent the first two weeks of summer coming up with ways to convince my parents to change their minds about sending me to camp.

"Listen, Mom, Dad," I pleaded one morning. "I don't know what is going on with you guys, but you can't be serious. I'm almost fifteen years old! Don't you think you should be pushing me to get a job or something? To learn responsibility? To grow up, earn a living, make some money? People my age don't go to camp, you know. They, like, work there. You guys? Hello?"

Silence.

I felt like a one-man circus with no audience. My parents had a unique way of paying attention to me when I wanted to be left alone and leaving me alone when I craved attention. Take the lightning incident (although, that was a new low, even for them). My parents didn't respond to my pleading (and even begging) at all. Quicker than you can say jolt, my life was taking a turn for the worst. I was going to camp whether I liked it or not. *Not!*

To convince (read: brainwash) me, my parents gave me some background information. I accepted it willingly, seeing as how the camp was virtually nonexistent on the Internet. Camp Milestone supposedly had a wonderful reputation. Apparently, thousands of people from all across the country attempted to get their children admitted year after year, but the camp was very selective. They chose me and it was not an opportunity my parents were willing to let pass. *But it's one I'm willing to pass*, I thought.

One thing was for certain. I made sure the camp was not academic by any means of the word. I wasn't a bad student or anything, but I knew going to some nerd camp for summer would be social suicide. My parents assured me this was not the case.

"Lakes, swimming, activities, sports, and cabins, Faye!"

Apparently, that was Camp Milestone in a nutshell. As if I'd never moved a muscle in my life. Little did they know, I climbed the stairs in our house at least five times a day.

In one last attempt to salvage my former life, I barged in on my parents the day before I was set to leave for camp. I was putting my foot down. I needed a way out.

"Forget it. I'm not going. I don't know what has gotten into you guys, but you need to stop now, because you're scaring me," I huffed in a last desperate effort.

My parents looked at each other and sighed. They were reading on the patio.

"Faye Grace Martin."

Oh lord. It was never a good sign when my mother used my full name. I cleared my throat and adjusted my stance.

"Listen to me," she continued. "Your father and I only have your best interest at heart and you just have to trust us."

"Oh no," I moaned. "Not the best interest speech."

My mother pretended to ignore me. Her glower accentuated the lines on her face.

"All you have done for the past two weeks is complain, whine, and make yourself miserable. You could have made some happy memories in the past two weeks, but instead, you chose to spoil them with your lousy attitude."

"But I don't want to g—"

"Regardless," she interrupted. "Come tomorrow, you are getting on that plane and you are going to this camp. End of discussion."

And with that, she returned her attention to her murder mystery novel.

"Great," I said. "The quintessential parent-laying-down-the-law thing."

Looking at my mother, I was angry and confused. If they were going to be typical absent parents, then I had no choice than to be a classic teenager. With that, I let out a loud irritated sigh, rolled my eyes and stormed off to my room, making sure to stomp my feet with every step.

But all the stomping, the pleading and the eye rolling in the world didn't change their minds. I ended up going to Camp Milestone. And naturally, my parents knew a lot more than they were letting on. They had known very well that I'd gotten hit by lightning that day. And behind closed doors, they had been worried sick about me. What happened to me was not chance. It was part of life's plan. Camp Milestone was my destiny and all the resistance in the world couldn't stop me from fulfilling it.

2
Chapter

The next thing I knew, I was unwillingly standing at the airport, ready to leave home for two months. For summer camp. By myself. I still couldn't believe it. It was like a drawn out nightmare, which had begun with a rusty old shovel. *Ugh*.

"Goodbye, Mom. I'm sure I'll have a great time," I said, trying to muster up some sincerity. It wasn't working. I knew I didn't believe what I was saying, and the whole world knew it. I was that wear-your-heart-on-your-sleeve kind of girl.

Observing my parents, I cocked my head to the side and gave them a weak smile. My mom was crying and my dad had that sheepish grin on his face that I inherited. I hugged them, kissed them goodbye, wished them a good summer, and promised to write often.

"Did you leave your cell phone at home?" my mom asked.

"Yes, though I still don't understand why you would send me on a trip all alone without my cell phone."

"Camp rules," she said as she patted me on the back and pushed me toward the security check line-up. "There will be phones there."

I grunted.

"Be good," my dad said.

"I don't know how else to be," I replied half-serious, sneaking one last glance at their teary eyes.

"I don't have to do this," I reminded them. "It's not too late. I could stay home."

"Nice try," my dad said.

"Why am I doing this again?" I wanted to know.

"Because it's better than the alternative. Now go," he said.

I sighed and made a face. I walked away from my parents, determined not to look back for fear of bursting into tears myself. I admit it, I was scared. I had never been on a plane before and, honestly, I never imagined my first trip would be to a childish sleep-over summer camp. I always had hoped my first trip would be to somewhere exotic like Greece or New Zealand. But as far as clichés go, life doesn't always turn out the way you envision. Mine certainly didn't.

As I gave one last wave to my sobbing mother and smiling father, I couldn't help but notice that they seemed proud of me. I wasn't sure why exactly but there was no mistaking it. Some pride definitely was shining in my general direction. And OK, you caught me. I loved that feeling.

~

At the airport gate, I found a pay phone and called Diane. Diane was the prettiest girl in school and, unfortunately for my confidence level, she was also my oldest friend.

"Well?" I asked her to provoke a reaction.

"Well, what?" she said.

"Well, I'm at the airport." People already were lined up for my flight, waiting to board the plane.

"I don't know what to say, Faye. I think it might be OK. At least you're going somewhere, right?"

"Right," I agreed.

"Personally, I have *no* desire to do anything this summer. But I'd be happy to go if I were you. My parents would never do anything like this, but then again, your parents have always been a little … different."

Although it wasn't something I was proud of, I was easily influenced when it came to certain things. Hearing those words from Diane altered my opinion and made me a little more accepting of what I might soon have to face.

"But I never asked for this, Diane." I secretly wanted more validation. "They can't just wake up one day and say, 'Hey, let's send her to some stupid camp!' I mean, where do they come up with these things? And by the way, I think the word you're looking for is eccentric, not different."

We both chuckled. Diane was my friend since before I could make permanent memories. She was probably the equivalent of a best friend, though we never officially called each other that. We had been through a lot together: boys, girls, rumors, events, moments, triumphs, let downs, bad teachers, you name it. But with each passing trial, it seemed our friendship deteriorated. Maybe it was because we'd both hurt each other so much over the years. Maybe it was because we both expected too much and just felt disappointed all the time. Or maybe it was because we didn't truly understand each other anymore. Our friendship had become shallow; it looked good on paper but didn't hold water in real life. Despite this shrinking factor in our friendship, deep down, I loved Diane. And even though I wouldn't have bet my life on it, I assumed she loved me back. At least, I hoped she did.

"I know," Diane went on, "it is really strange that they sprung this on you the way they did. How long do you think they've known about it? And did they ever tell you how they even found this camp? Camp *Mile-stone.*" She tested the word.

"I know. It's so, uninformative."

"I've never even heard of it. And you were right. There's nothing about it on the Internet. Does it even exist? I mean, why are your parents being so weird? What's up with that?"

"I'm not sure, I don't know, and I have no idea." I sighed in response to her loaded questions. "So what should I do?"

Diane laughed. It's something I could provoke easily. She usually found me amusing. Like a little pet.

"Um, I hate to break it to you, Faye, but you don't seem to have a choice here. Look around you. You're at the airport. You're going to this camp."

"Now you sound like my parents," I groaned.

"I aim to please."

"I really thought this was *the* summer, you know?" I asked her. "The summer that I'd get to go out and have fun and just let loose. Instead, you guys all get to have fun without me."

"Yeah, that's true ..."

That was a typical response from Diane and I had come to expect nothing more from her. She had abandoned her sugar-coating techniques a long time ago.

"Look, I gotta go, Faye. I'm going shopping with Lena," she said.

I groaned again. *I hate my life!* We said a shallow goodbye and hung up.

So to summarize, I had no clue what was in store for me, why it was in store for me and why I agreed to go along with it. Maybe I secretly wished for a miracle.

Or maybe I've come to trust my parents after fourteen years of proving their instincts are always right, I thought. *Or maybe, I could make twenty similar phone calls to twenty similar friends and not one of those phone calls would truly make me feel better. Maybe, I just have nothing to lose. Ugh.*

It was settled. Although I had put up a decent fight against my parents the past few weeks and though I struggled to squeeze out every ounce of information to gain some insight into this rash decision, I couldn't help feeling a little nervous. Or was that excitement?

I took a big breath and ran to the back of the line at the gate.

3
Chapter

The thing is, there was a boy. Deep down, it always comes down to a boy, and in my case his name was Benjamin Parker (Benji, if you will). He was handsome, sweet, shy, smart, and totally not into me. Because boys like Benji don't go for the regular girls.

Let me explain. Imagine the prettiest girl in school. Imagine how she looks, with her perfect features, her long, dark flowing hair and her leggy figure. Imagine her getting ready for school in the morning. Think of how everything falls perfectly into place as she puts herself together in the most flawless manner; every hair in place, every accessory impeccably matching her enviable outfit. Pleased, she takes one look in the mirror and heads off to school. Imagine her walking down the halls, oozing confidence and smiling coolly at those who notice her. Which, of course, is everybody.

Now imagine the other girl. The one who watches the prettiest girl from the sidelines and secretly wishes she could trade places with her. This girl is me. To others, I'm probably pleasant and approachable. I'm basically known to everybody as the pretty girl's best friend. I'm a good sidekick, somebody who always can be counted on, somebody to befriend if you want to get close to the prettiest girl. To myself, I'm flawed. Not to sound really down on myself but most times when I look in the mirror, I find something new to dislike. To my despair, I've always seemed really boring. Plain old blah Faye, you know? Not that I'm ugly or anything. I'm just not *her*.

Therefore, it was no shocker Benji always talked to Diane, who couldn't be bothered with keeping count of how many boys liked her. Benji blended into the sea of teenage suitors who would do anything to please her. For me, his attention to her was absolute torture. Unfortunately, it was absolute silent torture because my crush was a secret I'd kept since fourth grade. Nobody knew how much I liked (OK, loved!) Benji and nobody knew how miserable I would be this summer knowing he'd be alone with Diane while I'd be picking slimy leeches off of myself in the middle of nowhere. Life officially sucked for me.

~

In all the years I'd known (read: loved) Benji, we had actually spoken a total of four times. The first time was in fifth grade. We were all on the school bus, heading home. I was singing some ridiculous song with Diane and the two of us were giggling uncontrollably. Then Benji spoke to me. He told me I had a nice voice. I believe the exact words were: "You have a nice voice."

That was enough to make my heart sink like a ton of bricks. My face turned a bright shade of red and I looked him right in the eyes. They were small and the perfect shade of green. Instead of accepting the compliment like a normal person, my voice raised a few octaves and I had to speak.

"Psha!" I sputtered. "You're crazy. I have a horrible voice!"

I still don't know why I called him crazy. He was clearly stunned and the conversation ended before it even started.

The second time he spoke to me was at the lunch line. It was several years later. He asked me to pass the salt.

Something deep and meaningful, like: "Hey, could you pass the salt please?"

I spent a good year of my life analyzing that particular encounter. I remember justifying in my head that he loved me, too, just because he'd asked me to pass the salt. I actually convinced myself he could have asked anyone to pass the salt but he chose to ask *me*. I must have been nuts.

The third time Benji spoke to me was just a year before the lightning thing. This time, I was standing next to my locker talking to Diane. Benji walked up to Diane and asked her about an assignment we had for our history class. Then he turned to me and said, "Nice shoes," referring to my notorious Converse.

"Thanks," I replied, "Nice, um, socks."

Yes, I know, I'm really bad at this. Irritatingly, in fact. It was the only thing I could think of at the time! Sadly, I'm not even sure if I could see his socks. Actually, whenever Benji and I made eye contact my blinking rate virtually stopped altogether. He grinned uncomfortably and walked away. I've had longer interactions with my tooth brush.

The fourth time Benji spoke to me was the day of the lightning storm. This one is the time I wish I could take back. But it's also the day that started everything. It had been a really dark and dreary morning, and even though my mother reminded me to take an umbrella to school, I still managed to forget it at home. I guess everything really does happen for a reason.

When the last school bell rang, I sprang into the hallway in search of Diane. I wanted to make it home before the rain started, but Diane and I never left school without saying goodbye to each other. Grabbing my bag, I ran outside and spotted her. Only, she wasn't alone.

Like a sickening romantic scene out of a movie, she was standing in front of Benji, looking right at him as he was brushing the hair out of her face. Rapidly, I felt the color drain out of my face and a wave of nausea hit me without forewarning. I had imagined a similar scene in my mind a million times. Only, in my version, Benji was brushing hair out of my face and telling me I was beautiful, or something more original than that. In my version, I was Diane and Diane was me. In my version, I didn't feel like I'd just been bucked by a horse.

Without realizing it, I had walked right up to Diane and was staring at her in disdain. As soon as Benji noticed my presence, he backed off.

"Hey, girl!" she said as if she hadn't just broken my heart.

"I'm going home," I replied, trying not to sound overly transparent.

"So soon? Well, wait, I need to talk to you," she said.

"No, I can see you're busy getting your hair picked at like a baby monkey. I have to go."

"Like a baby monkey?" she said with a chuckle. She thought I was joking. I wasn't. "No, Faye, I have gum in my —"

"Bye," I said, waving stiffly as I walked off.

In all the years I had known Diane, I'd never felt as disgusted with her as I did at that moment. Granted, she had no idea I liked Benji, but still. She had a million guys following her every day! Why couldn't she just stay away from him? Why couldn't she just leave him be? Why did she want to have all of them? How selfish could one person be? And why did she have to flaunt her perfection in my face? It was revolting!

It started storming before I reached the end of the street.

"Typical!" I said out loud. It seemed like the entire world was against me. I looked up briefly and shrugged at the particularly dark cloud that hovered over my head. Normally, it took me less than ten minutes to walk home, but that day, I decided to take the scenic route. At that point, I didn't care if I got wet. All I wanted was to be alone. All I wanted was to cry alone.

Dragging my heavy feet, I slowly headed for the local park. My shoes were squishing in the wet grass. I was probably the only person dumb enough to be walking around during the storm but I just didn't care. I was so upset I didn't even hear the thunder. All I could hear was the sound of my own wretched sniffles.

As I walked past the playground, I entered the wide open field that used to be a drive-in movie theater. The rain poured down on me like a warm shower. It didn't take long for me to get soaked. I was blubbering from head to toe.

I continued to mope until I came face-to-trunk with a big oak tree. Wiping away the mixture of tears and raindrops accumulated on my cheeks, I looked up at the tree for answers. I wondered if I would always feel this way: insecure, heartbroken, bitter. I wondered why these things only seemed to happen to me. Then I wondered how I could turn off my feelings for Benji. I was tired of liking him. Liking him was exhausting. I wanted to stop. If only I could just stop.

Suddenly, a bolt of lightning hit one of the branches, which fell dead a few feet away from me. I'm pretty sure I screamed at that point. The reason I'm only pretty sure and not positive is because I also heard someone screaming out to me simultaneously. I turned to see Benji standing there in the rain, looking directly at me. I frowned, then blinked a few times to make sure I wasn't hallucinating. Yeah, it was definitely him. He looked so good in the rain wearing khakis and a T-shirt, his hair was molded. But I digress. He was there, in the flesh.

"Are you OK?" he asked at the top of his voice, trying to be heard over the roaring thunder.

I nodded. I wondered what he was doing there and blinked again.

"What are you doing here?" he asked, echoing my thoughts.

"I, um, came to …" I stuttered. *Blink, blink.*

I began to look around, looking for an easy way out. What *was* I doing there? I couldn't tell him the truth. The truth was, I had come to cry my eyeballs out after seeing him swoon over my best friend! It wasn't exactly something I could divulge.

Scanning the immediate surroundings, my eyes landed on an old shovel a few feet away. I walked over to it.

"I came to find my shovel," I said, as I picked it up.
And yes. That's when it happened. Here are some quick
words of wisdom I'm sure you've gathered by now.

> *Rule Number 1*: Don't go walking outside
> aimlessly in a thunderstorm.
> *Rule Number 2*: Don't wander into a large,
> deserted field with one giant, isolated tree sitting
> in the middle.
> *Rule Number 3* (and perhaps the most important
> rule): Don't pick up a long piece of metal and
> make yourself a lightning rod.

It was the combination of those three events that
turned me into a human shish-kabob. As soon as I picked up
the shovel, the air filled with a sound like a thousand highly
amplified angry buzzing bumble bees. Suddenly, before I had
time to react — ZZZZZZZAAAAAAAAAPPPPPPPPPP!
The current ran through me, I got knocked out of my shoes and
I was thrown four or five feet forward. Then, all I remember is
darkness.

~

I must have lost consciousness because the next thing I
knew, Benji was leaning over me, shaking me vigorously. An
odor of burned-almonds filled my nostrils. My mind was blank
and my body was numb.
"Hello? Are you OK? Are you OK? Open your eyes.
C'mon, open your eyes. Hello?"
His frantic voice rang deafeningly in my sensitive ears.
I didn't dare open my eyes. For all I knew, I was dreaming. I
suspected something bad had happened, but I wasn't ready to
face that reality yet. Meanwhile, Benji continued to ramble.
"Holy mother of crap! What did you do? What were

you thinking? Please wake up. C'mon, wake up. Open your eyes."

I still couldn't do it. He must have been ready to take me to the hospital just then because he put his arms under me and started to pick me up.

"Am I dead?" I finally managed to choke, as I tried to move. I opened my eyes to meet Benji's wide, distraught eyes gazing back at me.

"No, you're not dead," he answered. He gave me a half-smile and heaved a sigh of relief.

"Am I dreaming?"

"If you are, then make sure to wake me up, too," he said, his kind eyes warming me up like a blanket.

"What happened?" I finally wanted to know.

"You scared the crap out of me, that's what happened. What the hell were you thinking? Who comes into a rain storm looking for an old, rusted shovel?"

"I do," I groaned, trying hard to rise to my feet. I leaned on him for support and he made sure I didn't fall.

"Be careful," he warned.

Just one more thing I loved about him; he was always such a gentleman.

Coming back into my own, my eyes swiveled over to see my burned shoes in one place and the mangled shovel in another. Suddenly, I grasped the magnitude of what had happened. I had been hit by lightning in front of the guy I wanted to marry.

Oh.

My.

GOD.

This was beyond humiliating.

"I, I have to go," I finally said abruptly as I shuddered. Ahhhhhh! What did I even *look* like?

"Wha—? Wait, well, are you OK? I mean, you just had a lightning bolt go through you and out your feet," he yelled, still trying to be heard over the rumble. "You survived something that should've killed you. You got thrown like a pole vaulter without the pole, like —"

"OK, OK, I get it!" I said, wanting to die. "Stop. I get it. I'm fine. Sorry to, uh, scare you. I really have to go. Have a nice summer."

I walked off in a trance, trying not to look wounded and knowing full well my body was shaking violently.

"Don't forget your shoes," he called earnestly after me as I gritted my teeth and whimpered silently.

And that was the extent of our fourth conversation.

4

Chapter

Back on the plane, I was annoyed to discover the trip
to Camp Milestone was a milestone in and of itself. Whoever
heard of flying halfway across the country to go to summer
camp? The plane ride was long and boring, but it gave me
time to further reflect on the past two weeks. I had managed
to get little bits of information from my parents, even though
none of it made any real sense.

First off, Camp Milestone was *far*. It was a seven-
hour plane ride and a three-hour bus ride from Seattle. You'd
think my parents were trying to get rid of me or something.
Nobody could even visit me there. I was literally stuck! And
with no cell phone to boot. Second, the camp was split into
three grades: grades one, two, and three. Very original, right?
Apparently, those in grade one were 14 years old, those in
grade two were 15 years old and the last grade was reserved for
the 16-year-olds.

A couple of days before my departure, I was even sent a
hand-written electric pink "brochure" (if you could call it that)
from the camp's director. Underneath a microscopic picture of
a lake, was scribbled:

Greetings and welcome to Camp Milestone!

Once upon a time, Camp Milestone was founded with the hopes to prepare today's youth with the essential tools to fulfill their incumbent destiny. Ever since that time, it has exceeded its reputation year after year. We look forward to an incredible summer.

Sincerely,

Cecilia Chung,
(Camp director/counselor/
coordinator/ principal/ chief
instructor and executor)

I bet you're wondering what the heck that even means. Your guess is as good as mine. I pondered it for hours as I read the brochure over. Once upon a time? What was this, the first grade? And why did this Cecilia Chung person have so many titles? My frustration was feeding my sarcasm.

While I was examining the brochure on the plane, I got that strange feeling you get when you feel someone is watching you. I quickly scanned the passengers on the plane. Then, my eyes landed on the oddly familiar silhouette of a boy sitting a few seats away from me, across the aisle. The boy put something in his backpack, but not before I noticed what it was: an ugly electric pink brochure. I considered the odds he was going to Camp Milestone as well. *Probably next to none,* I concluded, remembering how obscure it all seemed.

When the boy was distracted by the flight attendant handing out drinks, I snuck a longer peak at him. He was very peculiar looking: dirty blond hair and a perky profile that was somewhat identical to the profile I had been in love with since fourth grade.

But it can't be, I thought, convinced I was officially losing my mind. Now I was turning random strangers into Benji, a new low, even for me. I leaned in to eavesdrop on the conversation, narrowing my eyes into slits. The flight attendant asked the boy where he was heading.

"Camp Milestone," he replied so quietly it was almost a whisper. His voice sent chills down my body. Then, he turned his head and looked directly at me. *Oh my heart.* There was no mistake. It was him.

Of course, being the queen of awkwardness, I gasped so loudly it startled the flight attendant standing over me, causing her to spill the contents of her cart all over my lap.

"Oh, I'm sorry dear," she said as she handed me some napkins. "You shouldn't startle people like that."

"It's OK," I said, stretching my neck even further so I could see and hear the rest of Benji's conversation.

Is it him? Is it really him? Am I dreaming? I could feel the liquid seeping into my pants but I didn't care. Once again, I was in Benji's vicinity and had forgotten the art of blinking.

"Oh, yes, Camp Milestone," another flight attendant chimed into the conversation. "Is this your first year?"

Benji hesitated before he said, "Yes."

He glanced back at me again. This time I was the one to swiftly glance away in that manner that says, '*I was never looking at you.*' These teenage games are mildly absurd, but we all play them in hopes they actually work. I don't know what I was trying to accomplish by withdrawing my gaze from his but I knew I was doing a very good job of it.

I tried to look busy by dabbing my pants with the paper-thin napkins I'd been given. I finally looked down and gasped. The liquid had been some sort of red juice and I, of course, was wearing beige corduroys. Quickly looking around me, I saw that the flight attendant was long gone. I buried my face in my hands.

"This can't be happening!" I screamed internally. "Why do my encounters with Benji keep getting worse and worse?"

Realizing there was nothing I could do, I sank down in my seat feeling defeated. My clothes were in my suitcase and no amount of soap or club soda could rescue me now. I gracelessly covered my pants with the remaining napkins.

Still in shock, I thought about walking over to Benji's seat for a millisecond before quickly deciding against it. I was way too self-conscious for something like that. Not to mention he probably didn't even know who I was. Or if he did know by now, then he'd know me as the girl from school who was stupid enough to get hit by lightning. Not exactly my proudest moment.

5
Chapter

When the plane landed, I had one eye glued on Benji (which in my experience, was not a hard thing to do). I had no idea where I was going and was starting to entertain scary thoughts of getting lost. I promptly decided to stay within twenty feet of him at all times. He seemed confident in his destination.

During luggage claim, I could sense him looking at me. *Should I just go talk to him?* I wondered. *Would he still be annoyed at the whole lightning issue? Does he even remember the lightning issue? What the heck was he doing here anyway? Was I really going to the same camp as Benji?*

Shaking my head over and over at my recent misfortune, I waited impatiently for my suitcase. I'm sure I don't need to tell you it was the last to arrive. As I headed out the door, I made a necessary stop in the bathroom to change my pants. It was only as I was struggling inside the dirty and claustrophobic stall that the feeling of regret poured over me like thick syrup.

"Why did I ever go along with this? What's the matter with me?" I asked myself. "I'm almost fifteen. I should just stand up to my parents. Why am I such a pushover?"

Then it dawned on me. I know you already picked up on this a long time ago: If Benji was going to Camp Milestone, then I would get to spend an entire summer with him. Alone. Away from school. Away from Diane. This scenario is pretty much exactly what I've wanted my entire life. It was not nearly as bad as I was making it out to be. A rush of excitement flowed through my veins and I smacked my lips together in delight.

"I love my parents!" I said aloud, not believing they had actually done something right for a change.

I exited the bathroom stall and looked at myself in the mirror. I smiled and straightened my shirt. I was definitely presentable. Just then, I noticed something odd on my neck. *What is that?* I lifted my shirt to get a better look. I gasped the deepest breath imaginable. Some sort of crazy rash had appeared on my back. It was reddish and feathery. Almost like a tree, with radiating patterns branching outward. It covered my entire back, some of my neck and extended onto part of my torso. I died a little just then.

"What the frig is this?" I screeched in horror.

I touched the rash and was surprised to find it didn't hurt or itch. Petrified, I stood in silence, examining myself. I was panting. I had no idea what to make of it. A million thoughts raced through my mind. *How long had that rash been there? Did I need a doctor? Was it from the lightning bolt? Was it from something else? Was I going to die? Was it contagious?* I urged myself to calm down, swallowed hard and took a deep breath. When my mind finally stopped racing, I decided to pull my shirt back down and forget the rash. For now.

"Let it go, Faye. It's probably just from the lightning. It'll probably go away soon," I said aloud, my voice cracking. I had been talking to myself a lot lately.

Still shaky, I left the bathroom in search of my final destination. I tried to regain my focus and concentration. It was hard, considering how confused I was, but I couldn't afford to miss my bus.

The exterior of the airport looked entirely different than

the one in Seattle. This airport was much smaller and seemed more primitive. Although my parents had told me a bus would be waiting for me outside the airport doors, no vehicles were in sight and the airport looked completely deserted. It looked like a scene from one of those old Western movies, with the tumbleweed rolling across the scene. And accordingly it was really, really hot. I soon noticed a man standing by the exit doors. He looked like an airport employee. He was tall, in a uniform and pacing back and forth while staring at his feet.

"Excuse me, sir," I said as I approached him.

The man didn't acknowledge me. He continued with his pacing. Every time he turned around and took a few steps, the automatic sliding doors opened and closed.

"Excuse me? SIR?" I repeated louder. He twisted his hands uneasily. I took a few steps closer to him. Was he ignoring me?

"Do you know —" I started, but the man kept marching and would have bumped into me had I not jumped out of the way. I rolled my eyes, took a deep breath and started again.

"Do you know where the buses are? I'm supposed to take a bus to —"

"Are you Faye?" he spat out. He stopped dead in his tracks and looked at me. His stare was so intense, it made me exceptionally uncomfortable.

"What?" I couldn't believe what I'd just heard.

The man had the most piercing and clear blue eyes I'd ever seen. Although he looked to be a decade older than me, his eyes seemed like those of a young child.

"Are you Faye?" he persisted.

I didn't answer. With all the horror stories in the world these days, I felt admitting to my name would be like accepting candy from a stranger.

"Well, if you *are* Faye," the man continued, "your bus is leaving without you. You'd better run."

"P-Pardon?" This day was getting worse by the nanosecond.

The man had a sparkle in his eyes. He pointed to

something beyond my shoulder and smirked. I darted around to see a grey coach bus pulling out of the airport parking lot and heading toward the freeway. I glanced back at the man in disbelief.

"Oh no," I whispered.

Swearing internally, I picked up my heavy suitcase with a groan and started running as fast as my weak legs would take me. I remember wondering if my rash was making me feeble as I ran onto the road, chasing after the bus.

"WAIT!" I yelled as I waved my free arm. "Wait! Stop! Wait for me!"

But it was too late. The bus was long gone. I stopped running. With a loud sigh and a few wheezes, I dropped my suitcase and hunched over to catch my breath. I was devastated. Life had been unfortunate to me lately and I was feeling sorry for myself. *How could this happen? How could they leave without me? What am I supposed to do now?*

Dejected, I let out a whimper and sat down on my suitcase. As quickly as I'd been given everything I wanted, it was taken away from me. I couldn't believe my life.
Not knowing what to do, I watched the highway in hopes the bus had somehow seen me and was turning back around to get me. But this is my life. And in my life, the bus never comes back to get me.

Or does it?

6
Chapter

Just then, a loud horn sounded behind me. It was a big, yellow school bus and I was sitting in the middle of the road, blocking its way. I half-heartedly lifted my suitcase and groaned. *Is this thing getting heavier or am I getting weaker?* I moved toward the side of the road to let the school bus pass. The bus inched forward and stopped next to me. The bus driver hurled opened the passenger door.

"Are you Faye?" she growled.

My jaw dropped an inch and a little noise escaped from my mouth. Was this really happening? *OK. Be rational. Maybe Faye is just a common name around here. Maybe everyone is named Faye. Maybe Faye is used around here like the word "senora" is used in Mexico. Right. Maybe the bus driver is just asking me if I'm a lady. Or maybe I'm dreaming. Yeah, I must be dreaming. I never got hit by lightning. I was not on the same plane as Benji. I am not going to Camp Milestone. This is all a nightmare.*

The bus driver continued to stare at me and my open-mouthed, shell-shocked expression. She was clearly wondering if I was mentally capable. She was a middle-aged woman with stereotypical frizzy, sun-dried rusty hair and a big wad of gum in her mouth. I tried to speak, to say anything, but the words were stuck in my throat. Or was that my heart?

A few seconds later, I scanned the school bus and noticed some faces staring at me. Snapping back to reality, I quickly recognized one of them; it was Benji, with his green eyes and sweet face. Before the color had time to reach my face, I realized the mistake I'd made. This bus was the one to Camp Milestone. *Crap.*

"Y-Yes," I managed to sputter, "I'm F-Faye." My mouth felt very dry.

"Well, where in heck have you been? We almost left without ya!" the driver said. She was clearly suppressing a laugh.

"I, well, my suitcase, m-my pants, um, that man!"

I turned to face the man but he was no longer there. The automatic sliding doors were closed and he was nowhere in sight. My mouth hung open. He had tricked me. I'd been fooled. The bus lady barked again.

"Well, come on! You just gonna stand there all day? We've got a long trip ahead of us and ain't any of us gettin' any younger."

I took a deep breath and lifted my suitcase with both hands. I walked toward the bus door and started to climb the stairs. The first two steps were brutal and by the third step, I felt myself falling backward again. *Nightmare! Definitely a nightmare!* Benji quickly got up to my rescue. Like I said, gentleman. Unfortunately, I hated being a damsel in distress. I was one of those self-sufficient girls. Or at least, I tried to be.

A pretty girl with long, straight blonde hair and sparkling green eyes also got up to help. She and Benji each took hold of the suitcase and pulled it onto the bus. Mortified, I followed behind them, but not before I caught the bus driver snickering quietly.

"Thanks," I said as the bus pulled out. Nobody responded. I didn't dare make eye contact with Benji, but I could swear he was chuckling, too.

Five people rode on the big bus, including myself.

Benji sat at the back of the bus next to another blond boy with curly hair who was wearing those funky-frame eyeglasses. The pretty blonde girl who helped me was sitting near the middle of the bus. A brunette was sitting behind her. Trying to act confidently, I picked the first empty seat and sat down, turning my back to Benji.

The blonde girl was one of the prettiest girls I'd ever seen. Another one of those girls who made me feel inadequate. Her hair was extremely long and flat-iron straight, and she'd probably never had a bad hair day in her life. Plus, she had the most attractive dark green eyes and an adorable button nose, which complemented her pleasant profile. Before I could stop myself, I already accepted that Benji would fall head over heels in love with her and I would have to bear more heartbreak in secret.

All right, now is as good of a time as any, I guess. Though I hate to do so, I'll briefly describe myself so you can picture me back then. Let me say I don't look like this anymore. But back when I was 14? Well, let's see. Googly hazel eyes? Check. Previously normal nose with a small bump on it because I broke it playing soccer in fifth grade? Check. (Yup, I'm sure you wouldn't be surprised I got distracted by Benji, but that's another story.) Long wavy hair that extends down my back? Check. Hair color? Well, my friends and family often debated the color of my hair. Some would argue that my hair was auburn. All you need to know is that it's some kind of light brown. Oh. And the only compliment I ever remember receiving in my entire life? Cute. No, that's not true. I also am told often I'm feisty. But I'm not too sure that's a compliment. I have no idea why, but some random boy wrote a weird quote in my yearbook one year about me growing up to be a women's rights leader in the future or something. Whatever that's supposed to mean. So that's me in a nutshell. Cute and feisty.

The dark brunette also was cute. Personally, I hated the word cute. Like I said, any superficial compliments directed toward me always contained the word cute. I often wondered if it was just a cop-out because people didn't believe I was pretty. The brunette, though, defined the word cute. She looked like a little rabbit with almond-shaped eyes (which were encircled with far too much makeup, by the way) and two front teeth a little bigger than the rest. Her hair was dark brown, but it was obvious by her roots she had dyed it much darker than her natural hair color. Just as I was looking in their direction, she leaned over to the pretty blonde.

"It's bad enough we had to wait until her plane landed but she took an hour longer than the other guy," she said. "What a winner."

I turned around and stared, not bothering to respond. This trip, this experience, wasn't starting off very well. I glanced at Benji who, cuter than ever, was looking sleepy. I decided to take my notebook and pen out of my bag and stared at the blank piece of paper. I sighed and started scribbling to my only friend.

Dear Diane,

Well, here I am on the bus and on my way to Camp Milestone. I hope. Things aren't going well so far. I don't know if I'll end up having a good time at all.

At first, I'm sitting on the plane, minding my own business, when the flight attendant decides to christen my voyage by spilling cranberry juice all over my pants. That's always a nice treat. So I end up walking around a foreign airport with an unflattering and suspicious stain on my pants.

Then, because I had to go and change my pants (in order to prevent further humiliation), I almost missed my bus and only find it when it nearly runs me over. Let me tell you, this camp seems weird (read: scary and strange). They know the names of all of their attendees. I know because everyone has been asking me, "Are you

Faye?" It seems to be the question of the day.

Four other people are on the bus with me so far. One girl seems nice enough, but I don't think she likes me very much. OK, fine. Nobody seems to like me yet. Let's just say, I don't think I made a good first impression. If you want a good chuckle, picture me sitting in the middle of the road (on my lead-filled suitcase), almost getting run over by a big yellow school bus. Anyway, I hope things are well with you guys. I'll send this letter to you as soon as I get to camp. Write me soon, OK? I miss home. Hugs,

Faye

I don't know why, but I didn't mention Benji in my letter. She still didn't know he saw me getting struck by lightning. Or that he was sitting behind me and heading toward Camp Milestone too. And she certainly didn't know I had liked him since I was barely literate and that she had broken my heart that rainy day at school. I knew I would have to tell her eventually but I wasn't ready. It didn't feel right. In fact, it felt so wrong.

For the rest of the bus ride, I stared at the countryside and thought about the curveballs life had thrown at me in such a short time. I remembered the airport man with the piercing blue eyes. Why did he tell me to run after the other bus? Was he just playing a nasty trick on me? But if he was, how did he know my name? I looked over at my suitcase. It had a small identification tag on it. Maybe that's how he knew my name. Maybe I was just being naïve and he was a mean guy with nothing better to do than to play a prank on a tourist. Yeah, that was probably it.

What else could it be?

7
Chapter

After what seemed like a decade, the bus got off the freeway. I could tell we were getting closer to the camp. I heard my teeth lock together. All the other passengers looked just as nervous as I was. The bus pulled onto a one-way dirt road and drove for another fifteen minutes. A forest surrounded all the bus windows. I never realized how secluded this camp would be.

After all the fuss my parents had made about Camp Milestone, I started to anticipate something fantastic, something like what was written in books or seen in movies. You know what I'm talking about, right? Those places you've never actually seen but you know deep down they exist? I closed my eyes and pictured large, dark, wooden cabins. I imagined acres of lavish and vast campgrounds, peppered with state-of-the-art facilities and surrounded by rows of green, rustling pine trees. I dreamed of a large, tranquil and gorgeous lake as a centerpiece, where I could spend my time reflecting on the things that mattered to me. Like how to get Benji to notice me. You know, the vital stuff.

The camp would have tennis courts, a giant swimming pool with slides, majestic horses in a stable, kayaks, canoes, maybe even a fencing area! In the mountain setting, we would learn to value the simple joys of nature, the hum of rushing water, and the delight of beautiful and romantic sunsets. There would be a large library with brand new computers where we could use e-mail and webcams with our families. The food would be made by top chefs and closely resemble home cooking. How else would they feed hundreds of campers? My roommate would become my new best friend. We would have so much in common and I finally would feel like I belonged somewhere.

The atmosphere would be laid back, allowing everyone to do whatever they wanted. It would allow us to gain experience in making our own decisions. We were, after all, almost grown-ups. Each week, we would choose from different activities, including horseback riding, pottery, sports, drama, hiking, rock climbing, and white water rafting. My new friends and I would spend our days playing games, swimming, and tanning. We would gain a deeper understanding of ourselves and nature. Everyone at school would be so jealous of me. I would return to school with a great tan — and maybe even a boyfriend? I opened my eyes and smiled. I started to feel a little jumpy with excitement. Slowly, I realized why my parents had sent me to Camp Milestone.

Of course! I realized. *We're almost grown-ups. This camp has got to be amazing. How else could it get this wonderful reputation my parents were so adamant about? And the brochure said something about "building our destiny," so they probably do that by treating us like adults and helping us blossom! That's why my parents have sent me here! Camp Milestone is meant to help me become an adult! Hence the name!*

The bus slowed down and turned into a semi-circular dirt driveway. A split second before the bus had come to a stop, the bus driver flung the doors open and hollered, "OK. Out!"

I was the first to head out. As I took a few steps toward what I assumed was Camp Milestone (there were no signs anywhere), I examined what was surrounding me. The other four passengers followed closely behind me.

My steps slowed down until I came to a stop. The other campers followed my actions until we all stood in line, staring at what was in front of us. For a full five minutes, none of us said a word. We were all thinking the same thing: *You have got to be kidding me.*

8
Chapter

Camp Milestone was the anti-camp. Four cabins were lined up in an L-shape. They seemed like dilapidated little dollhouses, chimneys and all. To the right of the cabins was what could only be a dirty, swampy puddle posing as a lake. A little dock led out to this poor excuse for a natural resource, while in the middle of it a wooden raft floated pitifully. Several old, beaten-up canoes were on the grass. To the left was a small hall. And that was all. That was Camp Milestone.

No, no, no. This can't be Camp Milestone. It can't! I wanted to scream, as I shook my head in disgust.

My heart was beating hard against my chest. I tried to swallow, but the lump in my throat refused to budge. I did a three-sixty several times to make sure I wasn't missing anything.

As I looked around, my eyes round like marbles, I could see the others spreading out and looking just as horrified and unsettled as myself. Aside from the scattered trees that stood tall in the camp and the dark forest that surrounded the campgrounds, this was Camp Milestone, in all its pathetic glory.

A few minutes later, after realizing for the second time this was it, we all stopped dead in our tracks and stared ahead without saying a word. Our mouths were wide open, welcoming the horse flies already buzzing around our heads.

9

Chapter

I couldn't believe what I was facing.

"This can't be Camp Milestone," I tried to convince myself with a hollow laugh. I swatted furiously at a persistent horse fly.

"This is it?" someone next to me said in a scathing tone. Then, "Get away from me! Shoo! SHOO!" The persistent horse flies were getting to him, too.

"This can't be it," another voice echoed. "My parents must have done some research before sending me here. This is disgusting! Look at it! What the hell am I supposed to do here for an entire summer?"

In another dip of my recent roller-coaster emotions, I began losing the little faith I had in my own parents and their absurd decision. I made a mental note to call them and then I cursed them when I remembered they'd made me leave my cell phone at home. Now would have been a perfect time to scream bloody murder right into their foolish ears.

Not willing to accept the status quo, I continued to look around me. Maybe I could spot something else this time around. *Anything* else this time around. Normally, I would have spoken to someone and bonded over our mutual misery, but seeing as how they all still hated me for keeping them waiting, I decided to keep quiet and suffer in silence.

I watched the others as they headed toward a bulletin board in the middle of the tiny "green area." I was about to follow them and read the board when I heard something rustling in the forest beside me. Squinting, I made out the silhouette of a man behind the shadowy trees. I could see he was bending over to pick something up. As he stood up, we made eye contact and I immediately recognized the same piercing blue eyes I had seen a few hours ago. It was the man from the airport. It was the *creep* from the airport. Leaving my luggage behind, I began to march toward him, angry and ready for a confrontation.

"Are you following me?" I yelled. "Are you stalking me?" Unfortunately for me, as soon as he realized I was approaching him, he scurried off, getting lost quickly in the wilderness. I ran faster to catch up with him and called out angrily, "Hey! Wait!"

But he already had disappeared. I approached the edge of the forest and peered inside but didn't dare walk in. It was dark and scary in there and my bravery quickly withered. Confused and frustrated, I turned around and returned to my luggage.

Looking up, I realized the other campers were heading into their cabins. I headed for the bulletin board.

"Camp Milestone Camper List 2009," I read aloud, as I swatted the bugs away again. On it was a list of the campers and next to it, their respective assigned cabins. I scanned the list and noticed there were only about a dozen names in total.

Where were the rest of the names? A dozen names? I couldn't quite fathom that the camp only had twelve campers. I inspected the list once more. The words "Cabin Three" were written next to my name.

"Well, I guess I better go find cabin three," I mumbled. I was not happy.

As I wobbled over to the first cabin directly to my left, I started getting that feeling at the pit of my stomach you get when you're homesick. It hadn't even been an hour and I wanted to leave Camp Milestone. This experience was turning out to be a comedy of errors. I staggered up the steps, opened the screen door, and tried to open the front door. It was locked. I knocked several times and waited. Inspecting the cabin, I couldn't find a sign or engraving anywhere. You can understand the bland nature of this camp by now, right?

Noises were coming from the cabin beside me. I darted toward the racket. As I walked up the stairs to the second identical cabin, I noticed through the screen door that the front door was open. Inside the cabin was a living room with a fireplace on the left. Several boys were sitting on the couch and chairs, and one girl was sitting on the floor beside the fireplace. The girl, who was talking as I came up the wooden steps, became quiet the moment she noticed me. I walked up to the screen door and attempted to open it. It was locked.

"Can we help you?" the girl asked. She hadn't been on the bus.

"Is this cabin three?" I asked, puzzled by the rudeness I'd just received.

"Um, no. This is two," the girl snipped, every syllable filled with rudeness. She turned away from me, faced the boys and said, "Anyway, what was I saying?"

"Um, sorry, can you tell me which cabin is cabin three then?"

The girl pretended to ignore me.

"Gee, thanks a lot," I said under my breath.

Side note: Why are girls so rude to each other? Why do we get a kick out of being mean to each other? Boys don't play these games, so why do we?

Just as I was about to speak up again, I noticed one of the boys pointing to the next cabin in line.

"Thanks," I said, flashing him a quick smile. I peeked at the girl beside the fireplace one last time and walked away.

The sun was shining forcefully with no wind to offset its sharpness. It was much hotter than the weather I'd grown accustomed to in Seattle. The third cabin's door was ajar. I took a deep breath before opening the screen door, let out a sigh of relief when I realized it wasn't locked, and walked in. The interior of this cabin looked identical to the one next door. Benji and the other boy from the bus were sitting on the couch with their feet up on a wooden chest acting as a coffee table. Their luggage was sprawled in front of them. It dawned on me that this cabin wasn't mine either. I was spent. I let out a sigh of desperation.

"Hey," Benji said to me.

"Hi," I replied as casually as I could, conscious of my sweaty forehead. "What cabin is this?" I was trying not to ogle him.

"It's three," both boys informed me in unison. My breathing stopped.

"This is cabin three?" I asked in disbelief.

I was in Benji's cabin? Benji was in my cabin? We were in the *same* cabin?

"Yup. Faye, right?" Benji said, sending a thrill through me as I heard him pronounce my name.

Here we go again with the Faye stuff. I poked my head forward in incredulity and let out a tired laugh.

"Yes. Very good! I am the notorious Faye! You guessed it. You, like everyone else in this crazy place, knows who I am. So tell me, please. How do you know my name?" I demanded, knowing perfectly well my face was flushed and I was belligerent.

"Well," he said, looking a little hurt, "you told the bus driver your name and plus, we go to school together. I mean, we've gone to school together for a long time, right? Aren't you Diane's friend?"

That last sentence irked me like the sound of fingernails dragging on a chalk board. I stayed silent for a minute, trying to sift through what all of this meant. Diane's friend. I hated being Diane's friend. But wait. He knew me. Maybe not just as Diane's friend (gag), but as Diane's friend "Faye." He knew me as *me*. Whether it was because of the lightning strike or not was irrelevant. He knew me like I knew him.

"Um, yeah, right." I could feel the heat radiating from my face.

"Well, uh, because you obviously don't know me, I'm Benjamin. Uh, Benji," he said, misreading the situation entirely, "and this is Calvin."

He pointed to the curly-haired, blond boy with the funky glasses. I grinned as I willed myself to look at the other guy. Benji's hospitality was making me giddy.

"Cal," the boy corrected. "Hey."

"You mean, there are boys and girls in the same cabins?" I asked, not sure whether to be excited or scared. I should've pinched myself. *I get to be in the same cabin as Benji? What is going on with the universe and who should I thank?*

"Looks like it," Cal said.

"We took the only room downstairs," Benji explained, pointing to a hall to the left of the living room.

Trying to act interested in what he was saying (and not how he was looking), I peered around the corner. The kitchen was directly past the living room, and in it sat a kitchen table and four chairs. A bathroom was beside the kitchen, and to the left of that was the bedroom Benji was pointing at.

"There are two bedrooms upstairs," he continued, "the girls are all already there."

"Thanks," I said with an encouraging smile as I straightened my hair.

I didn't want to leave but knew I had to. I had mastered the art of not letting on how much I liked Benji, so I knew it was time to leave. I knew not to linger. Actually, these were the rules I had set for myself in the past when it came to Benji (yup, I'm a rule person):

Rule Number 1: Stare, but only when you know you won't be noticed.

Rule Number 2: Always be the first to say goodbye or the first to leave. I hadn't gotten the chance to use this rule much.

Rule Number 3: I love you! Will you marry me?

Obviously, Rule Number 3 was just a figment of my overactive imagination. Unfortunately, I found myself thinking it way too often for my own good. I admit, I always wondered what would happen if I just blurted it out. Would he scream and run away? Would he laugh at me? Would he say it back? Could he have loved me secretly all along too? *Nah.* Doubtful, right? But was it possible? Is there a one in a million chance I could end up with Benji someday? That chance, however small, was what kept me going on in this pathetic fashion, day after day.

I climbed the steep stairs by the entrance. The second floor was awfully small. Miniature was more like it. One bedroom was to the left of the stairs and one was to the right. I arbitrarily picked the bedroom to the right and walked in. The tiny room contained only two beds and two dressers, one on each side of the room. It fit perfectly the camp's plain motif. The beautiful blonde from the bus sat on the right bed, unpacking her suitcase as impeccably as humanly possible.

"Hi!" she said with a smile as she looked up at me. "Faye, right?"

I clenched my jaw. I had never hated the sound of my name until that moment. Had someone approached me with legal documents and asked me to sign a name-change agreement, I would have done it gladly without even checking if the name was cool or not. I was willing to change my name to Sniffles Poppycock, just so nobody else would ask me that question again. Trying not to look too obvious, I nodded but I knew the nauseating look on my face was in full force.

"I'm Niki. I guess we're roommates," the girl said with a giggle. "I hope you don't mind, but I took this bed. They're identical, I think. Unless, do you want this one?"

"No, no, that's OK. This one's fine," I insisted. I sat down on my bed facing Niki and let out a massive sigh. The trip had been insanely long and I knew I looked exhausted.

"So, where are you from?" I asked her. I couldn't believe how much prettier she was when she smiled. Her teeth obviously had been perfected by an orthodontist. Her hair was pulled up into a perfect bump-less ponytail. Her big green eyes glowed with confidence.

"Oh, I'm from New York. So are Cal and Melaine actually. We all go to school together. You're from Seattle right?"

"Yeah, how did you know that?"

"Benjamin told me. He said you guys go to school together."

You need to know the musings of my 14-year-old mind. At that moment, my internal monologue sounded a lot like this: *Oh, you guys have already started talking? Of course you have. I bet you'll have a nickname for him by the end of the week. I bet you'll be the new Diane. We'll become superficial friends and, because of that, I'll have to watch as you two build a relationship. You'll fall in love, and I'll get to be heartbroken all over again. Wait ... Benji talks about me?*

I smiled at Niki. She had such an inviting and friendly manner, I found it impossible not to like her. I was just about to ask her a question when the last passenger from the bus — the bunny girl — walked into the room. After awkwardly saying hello to me, she asked, "Niki, you coming? Hazel's waiting outside."

"Yeah. OK," Niki said, putting down her clothes. "Mel, this is Faye. Faye, this is Mel. Mel's got her own room across the hall because she's quicker than me."

"That's short for Melaine," the bunny girl amended. "M-E-L-A-I-N-E, Melaine," she said, spelling out her name.

I was perplexed.

"Um, Faye. F-A-Y-E," I said, hoping that was the appropriate response.

Melaine and Niki looked at each other and laughed.

"Don't mind her," Niki said with a giggle. "She's just got a complex because everyone thinks her name is Mela-*nie*. So she feels the need to sound like a walking spelling-bee contestant."

"Oh," I chuckled.

"You have no idea what it's like to grow up with an unusual name. It's traumatizing. Trust me. And she," insisted Melaine, pointing a slender finger to Niki, who was still giggling, "thinks it's funny for some reason. But she and you are lucky. You've never had to worry about that. You've both got common names. Your parents were nice to you. But until you have a name that can be mistaken for every name but your own, you won't know the aggravation that I have had to put up with."

I nodded, knowing I couldn't argue with her.

"Anyway, we're off. Bye, Faye," she said, leaving the room.

"We'll see you soon?" Niki asked me, flashing a bright grin.

"Yeah, definitely."

Finally, I was smiling again.

10
Chapter

I unpacked and poked around my room. I was
disappointed (but not surprised) to learn there wasn't a
phone. The view from our small bedroom window was also
uneventful; a forest surrounded the camp and all you could see
were giant pine trees.

It didn't take me long to consider going downstairs to
see what Benji was up to. In case you hadn't noticed, I liked
to fantasize. I want to lie and tell you that my fantasies were
eclectic and imaginative, and that I was a wild and fascinating
spirit. But I was the epitome of boring. And being boring
meant that most of the time, my fantasies centered on one thing.
OK, one person. OK, Benji. Like you had no idea.

This time, I fantasized I would go downstairs, we
would chat, and somehow, he would profess his undying love
for me. We would spend the rest of the summer entwined in
each other's souls, blissful and in love. Oh, and in my fantasies,
I was never aloof but would always find a clever and loveable
thing to say. Despite my wandering mind, I was chicken, and
that side of me painfully pointed out I didn't have the guts
to go downstairs and talk to Benji. So I decided against it,
convincing myself that it would seem way too desperate.

Sitting on my bed, I looked at a picture of me and Diane taken a few years back. It was the most recent picture I had; one of those self portraits taken at arm's length. Both of us had full, pearly smiles, and we looked happy. Diane, of course, looked beautiful. Ugh, that was so infuriating. Closing my eyes, I remembered the day the picture was taken. We had spent the entire day swimming at the local pool and had talked about everything and nothing. Those days, we never ran out of things to say. Those days life was better somehow, less complicated or something.

I got up, stuck the picture above my bed, and started to write a second letter to her. I described the atrocity that was Camp Milestone and went on to relive my first encounters with my cabin mates. I even wrote, "Coincidentally, Benji from our school is here." As I was formulating the sentence, I found myself wishing I'd told Diane about my feelings for him.

Honestly, I'm not sure why I never told anyone, especially because I hated harboring it. Sometimes, the best part of liking someone is sharing it. It was lonely holding such a big load all the time. I felt I was missing out. Good friends will obsess over your crushes with you. They will encourage you to find the guts to make a move. Good friends will call you at 3 a.m. and tell you they just remembered that your guy asked about you. They will tell you he looks at you when you're not paying attention. Good friends will support you and tell you the guy would be lucky to have you. The problem was, I wasn't sure if Diane was a good friend anymore. A long time ago, she had most definitely been, but those days were gone. She wasn't someone I trusted anymore. I was afraid she was the friend who would stab me in the back and play dumb. Lonely was better than betrayed, I decided, remembering the day of the lightning strike.

I finished my letter the same as the first one, writing, *"Write me soon. I miss home. Hugs, Faye."* Just as I signed my name, I heard a thunderclap, followed by a loud horn. Startled, I walked across the hall and looked out the window. A woman stood on the grass with a loud speaker.

"Attention, campers!" she yelled, her voice amplified. Another rumble sounded above her. The sky looked dark and rainfall seemed imminent. "Attention, campers!" she repeated. "Please gather immediately in the main hall for assembly." The woman reiterated the message several times before disappearing into the hall.

"Finally," I said under my breath as I scratched my first mosquito bites. I needed something to do. Plus, I wanted this dumb camp thing to get started.

I walked down the creepy stairs of the cabin, strolled out the front door and halted on the little porch, realizing I'd missed my window of opportunity. It was pouring rain, and naturally, I had come to hate rain since my near-death experience. My knees wobbled and I held my breath. I couldn't do it; I couldn't make myself go out into the rain. I breathed out through my nose and tried not to panic. Unable to calm down, I began to feel anxious. Remembering the previous lightning storm, I lifted the corner of my shirt and peaked at my rash.

"Oh, no, it looks worse," I mumbled, my eyes popping out of my face.

It still wasn't painful but it was definitely an eyesore. And, was it glowing or was my mind playing tricks on me? I blinked and focused my eyes on it once more. Yes, glowing. It was glowing. *I'm glowing. Like a Christmas tree.* I whimpered. *What the hell is happening to me?* The panic consumed me and before I could help it, that lump began to form at the back of my throat again. *Gulp.* I swallowed again to dislodge it, but it stayed put.

Just then, a figure emerged in front of me. It was Benji, standing at the foot of the porch steps. He blinked hard through the rain, uncaring that he was quickly becoming soaked. I turned to see what he was looking at, only to discover he was looking at me. *Oh, no. Not again.* This scene was all too familiar. I didn't want to say anything. Correction: I didn't dare say anything. We must have stared at each other for an eternity. Him, wet and hopeful; me, dry and petrified. Why did Benji and I keep meeting like this in the rain?

Finally, I spoke.

"What?" I asked, wanting to know why he was standing there, making me more uncomfortable than I already was.

"Nothing," he said, still blinking excessively. God, he looked so sexy in the rain. I was being tortured from every angle.

I knew he was thinking about the lightning, too, but I didn't want to acknowledge it. I wanted to pretend it had never happened. I wasn't proud of what I'd done, and when I recalled that Benji had witnessed it, I wanted to crawl into a hole and die. But not by lightning.

"Are you coming to the assembly?" he asked, breaking the awkward silence.

"Yes," I replied, with a great deal of apprehension.

I was willing my feet to run. Move. Sway. Budge. Ambulate. Anything! If only I could move my feet and run past him toward the hall, this moment would be over. But I couldn't. I was scared stiff. I glanced up at the dark and fear-provoking sky. I wondered if another bolt of lightning was charging up, just waiting for me to run out into the open air.

"No," I moaned, remembering the aftermath of last time.

The memory of the pain paralyzed me even more. That pain was the worst I'd experienced in my life. The little hairs on my body were standing straighter than a hedgehog's needles. Goosebumps materialized on my arms and I began to shiver. How was I going to do this?

Just then, a bolt of lightning hit a tree in the distance and sent a loud crackle into the air. I shuddered as fear overtook the feeling of déjà-vu. Another tree. Next, me. Did the sky want to kill me? Was this going to keep happening until I died? It was, wasn't it?

"Do you want to take my hand?" Benji offered, extending his hand. He was reading my mind.

I wanted to. I wanted to so badly. As soon as I reached out and grabbed his hand, I felt something run through my body again. It was a bolt, yes, but I was relieved to realize it

wasn't lightning — more like a bolt of disbelief. I couldn't
believe I was holding his hand. I was holding *Benji's* hand; this
guy, whom I had watched from afar since, well, since forever!
Butterflies fluttered in my stomach, reminding me just how
hopeless I was when it came to him. To my disappointment,
Benji didn't flinch. He proved the moment was magical only
to me. As soon as I put my hand in his, he turned away and
ripped a hole in my heart. Leading me through the rain, he took
charge and got me from the cabin to the hall. Emboldened by
his self-assurance, I followed closely behind, bracing myself
for impact. The next moment, we reached the hall and his hand
turned limp as he let go of me and walked in without looking
back.

~

The hall was somber inside. Several rows of dark
wooden benches faced a small parquet stage. Shivering and
shaken, I walked inside and sat down next to my cabin mates.
A small woman stood on the stage, facing the spectators who
watched her attentively. Out of the corner of my eye, I saw
Benji sit down next to Cal. Our eyes met and we both smiled
timidly.

I looked back at the woman on the stage. She stared
beyond the audience. I traced her stare to the back of the
hall and noticed a shadow looming in the darkness. I tried to
make out if the shadow was male or female. Was it that man
again? My stalker? I couldn't tell. The woman on stage started
speaking,

"Hello, everyone. My name is Cecilia Chung and I am
the headmistress. You may call me Miss Chung."

I turned back to face the woman. All eyes were on her
and the room grew eerily quiet. Miss Chung cleared her throat
and spoke with a proud smile on her face.

"Welcome, to all of you. And welcome, to Camp
Milestone."

11
Chapter

Miss Chung, in her late 50s, had traces of grey hair. She wore a professional business suit and looked the part of headmistress. I was surprised to discover I was nervous.

"As many of you may be aware," Miss Chung said, bringing me out of my thoughts, "you have been carefully chosen to attend this camp. It is a great honor and you should be proud of yourselves."

Niki and Melaine exchanged a strange look, which I deciphered quickly because I had the same thoughts. What do we have to be proud of exactly? We hadn't done anything. All I did was let my parents send me to camp. Judging by their faces, the others were just as perplexed. Miss Chung seemed to take note of the confusion that filled the room.

"Please take a moment to look around. There are twelve of you here. Seven of you are in your second year at this camp. Please raise your hands so the rest of the campers know who you are."

Afraid to move, I watched attentively, my eyes round like saucers. This camp was getting stranger by the minute. All of the members of cabin two (including the girl who'd been rude to me), raised their hands reluctantly. Most of them were looking at the floor with embarrassment. I was officially confused. So they were in grade two? If our cabin was in grade one and their cabin was in grade two, who was in grade three? Miss Chung pressed on.

"This means that each year, only a handful of you are selected to attend this camp and we are honored to be in your presence. Camp Milestone has a special purpose you will come to know by the time you graduate. This is no ordinary camp. You can consider us to be like a covert society, but it's only covert because it cannot be any other way. But, I'm getting ahead of myself. You will learn all that and more during your stay here."

I grasped at Miss Chung's every word. I found myself almost afraid to breathe. Breathing might have caused me to miss vital information. Suddenly, Cal's hand jumped up and he waved it around to get Miss Chung's attention. The headmistress looked at Cal and spoke calmly.

"Yes, Calvin Spellman. You have a question?"

Cal stood quiet for a moment. The surprised expression on his face confirmed to me they knew all of our names in this crazy place.

"Yes, sorry, Miss Chung, but I just don't understand," he blurted out. "Why are we here exactly? What kind of camp is this? You say we were chosen," he was being condescending now. "How were we chosen? Why did you choose us? I mean, I don't think I applied for this camp. I don't think I've ever even heard of this camp. I don't think anyone has ever heard of this camp!

"Or, is it just me? Has anyone here ever heard of this camp?" he challenged, gaining more confidence with every word.

We all shook our heads and Benji let out a little chuckle, which I recognized without even looking. I loved his chuckle. Still looking up at the stage, I studied Miss Chung's reaction. Although it comforted me slightly to hear Cal's little outburst and discover I wasn't the only one who'd come here without a clue, I also found this realization disconcerting.

"Nobody knows what we're doing here," I heard someone mutter. "We're all clueless."

It was evident we were all confused and mystified. Miss Chung stayed as composed as ever.

"Well, Cal," she said, with a hint of delight. "That was more than one question, but I'll do my best to answer them. First, you must know there is no application process for Camp Milestone. It's not like every other camp. In fact, we seek you out and then we wait until —"

"Cecilia!" a voice called from the back of the hall. A young woman entered from behind us.

"Oh, Cecilia!" the voice said again. "Chester wants to see you. I'll take over from here."

The woman began walking toward the stage. She was in her 30s, had dark red, fine hair and beady black eyes. As she walked by the first row, she flashed us a toothy smile and waved. There was something about her; I couldn't quite put my finger on it, but it wasn't good.

"Hello, everyone!" she said in an irritatingly enthusiastic tone. "My name is Galiana Moore and —"

"Galiana," Miss Chung interjected. "Galiana, I wasn't finished. And I wasn't about to say anything about —"

Galiana flashed Miss Chung a threatening glare and continued with her sentence, which turned out to be less like a sentence and more like a bomb.

"My name is Galiana Moore and I am Camp Milestone's new headmistress."

What. The. Hell.

A heavy silence fell over the crowd and a chill spread over us. Soon, the other campers started whispering and I found myself sitting at the edge of my seat. This was absurd. My formerly normal life was now completely ridiculous. I shook my head and caught a glimpse of Benji rolling his eyes. This was my life.

Miss Chung no longer smiled and her face looked ghost white.

"Galiana ..." she urged again, but Galiana didn't care. She began talking over her again.

"Campers, Miss Chung has been a key asset to Camp Milestone's development in the past few years, but she is now moving on to another project and I will be taking her place."

Her smile was so big, it almost prevented her from enunciating her words. Miss Chung glared at Galiana. If looks could kill, Galiana would have been six feet under at that moment. Nobody else dared say a word. Although the hall was as quiet as a classroom during a brutal exam, Galiana's massive smile almost screamed at us. After what seemed like an eternity, Miss Chung cut through the silence with her icy words.

"Well, I must say, I'm disappointed I won't get to know all of you." She turned her gaze toward me. She seemed genuinely regretful. "But I know Galiana will do a wonderful job and I'm sure you will be very supportive and will make her feel at home. And Galiana, in turn, will always be someone you can go to if you have any concerns or questions," she almost demanded of her. "I'll leave you all to become better acquainted now."

"Thank yo-uu!" Galiana barked.

"Before I go," Miss Chung persisted, "I would like to say one last thing. If at any point, you feel lost, the answers are not far away. Just look to yourself. You know more than you think."

Miss Chung continued to look at me. I began to feel a little paranoid. It was almost as if she had directed her comments only to me. Niki turned to catch my reaction. I made eye contact with her and tried to convey a look of confusion. Instead, I think what came out was a look of disgust. I had no idea why Miss Chung was staring at me so intensely.

Miss Chung began to walk off the stage, but not before she gave me a small wink on her way down.

"Did she just wink at you?" Niki whispered.

"I don't know," I answered truthfully. I watched the former headmistress as she walked off the stage and then in front of us. Just as she passed me, she stopped dead in her tracks. Turning around, she came back and faced me.

"Faye," she said matter-of-factly. It wasn't a question.

"Yes?"

"May I see it?"

"See what?" I gulped.

Miss Chung leaned over and gestured with her eyes. I immediately understood. She wanted to see my rash. I didn't answer her, hoping she would see the desperation in my eyes. I could sense everyone in the hall focusing on me. I hated (hated!) being at the center of attention that way. You could have cut the tension in that room with a butter knife.

"May I?" she repeated.

"I don't know what you're talking about," I lied. I doubt I sounded convincing. I was usually a pretty crappy liar.

Please go away. Please go away. Miss Chung and I were caught in an intense stare-down. I prayed for her to leave me be. I pleaded with my eyes, hoping she had an ounce of mercy in her soul, hoping she would let this thing go and move on.

"Kids," interrupted Galiana. She clapped as if gathering a class of first graders. "Kids, let's take a five minute break, shall we?"

I finally let out a long-awaited breath, thanking the world Galiana rescued me.

"Cecilia," Galiana called out.

Miss Chung continued her interchange with me, her eyes kindly asking me to consider her request. Stubbornly, I shook my head.

"Cecilia," Galiana hissed again.

Miss Chung finally straightened up. I swallowed again loudly. Defeated, she smiled and walked away.

"What was that all about?" Niki asked as everyone continued to stare at me.

"I have no idea," I lied. "She's obviously way past her retirement days."

12
Chapter

The break lasted longer than five minutes. Thankfully, everyone's attention veered away from me the moment Galiana pointed out the juice and snacks for us at the back of the room.

Drinking my juice, I continued to observe Galiana and Cecilia on the other side of the hall, clearly in an intense discussion. Galiana used her arms wildly while Cecilia stood immobile, her lips barely moving as she retorted. Most of the campers gathered around the food while I stood a little farther out, intent on finding out about the squabble on the other side of the room.

"I'm starving," I heard Cal say. "Don't they have anything else here but cheese and crackers?"

"How do you think I feel?" another voice asked. "I'm lactose intolerant."

"There's some dried up, stale cookies over here," someone else said.

I couldn't make out any of the conversation across the hall, but I was convinced it centered on me. This theory was validated every time both of them would pause and look over at me.

"How do you feel?" a pleasant voice came from beside me. It was Benji.

"Good, how are you?" I said, forgetting right away about Galiana and Miss Chung. Heck, I usually forgot my own name at the sound of his voice.

I gave him the once over. He looked so handsome and I loved that I could talk to him more and more. *Home, schmome,* I thought in a quick change of heart. This place was awesome.

"That's not what I asked," he remarked coyly.

"What did you ask?" I discretely wiped my sweaty palms on my pants. My heart fluttered uncontrollably.

"I asked how you're feeling," he said. He stood much taller than me, so I had to look up at him when we spoke.

"I'm feeling fine," I answered defensively. "How are you feeling?"

What was with that tone?

"Fine, but I don't have a reason to feel not-fine. You do."

There was that tone again. I didn't know what he was getting at. Was he talking about the lightning or just making conversation? Either way, I didn't like it one bit.

"How about this crazy weather," I said, attempting poorly to shift the conversation.

"Are you trying to change the subject?" he asked, trying not to smile. It was the longest we'd ever made eye contact.

"No, I am merely commenting on the weather. It's become a lost art, really. Commenting on the weather is not what it used to be back in our grandparents' day. Nowadays, what do we talk about? Filth, really. We're a filthy generation."

I was rambling and I didn't even know what I was rambling about. I had just called my generation filthy and I didn't even know why. For the first time in my life, I withdrew my gaze from him and looked to the ground.

"The weather," he humored me. "Yeah, the weather's pretty crazy. It actually reminds me a lot of the weather on the last day of school."

I swiftly looked up and shot him a dagger. That sneaky, sneaky guy. He *was* trying to talk about the lightning storm.

"I don't remember that day," I challenged savagely.

I pulled my lips tight and stared at him now, unafraid and unamused.

"No?" he said, raising one eyebrow. "Seems to me like you remember it quite well."

His expression was difficult to read. On one hand, he looked like he was trying not to smile, on the other, he looked annoyed. Or angry. I had never seen that side of him. But then again, until now, my interactions with him had been rather minimal.

"No, I don't remember it at all," I persisted, my heart racing.

"Would you like me to refresh your memory?" His eyes seemed to glitter with that last comment.

I grimaced in confusion. I couldn't believe it. We were fighting. Passive-aggressively, but still, fighting.

"I don't appreciate you," I blurted. "I mean, I don't appreciate what you're trying to do. Or insinuate," I corrected.

Benji was frustrated. I could see it clearly — his eyes turned hard and he clenched his teeth tightly.

"I don't appreciate you either," he said.

Ooo-Kay. What the heck was that supposed to mean?

"Are you mad at me or something?" I asked.

"Why would I be mad at you? Are you actually admitting to something now?"

I was beyond lost. Did we know each other well enough for this conversation? His voice seemed distorted by anguish, yet he oozed with accusation.

"Admitting to what? Am I missing something?" My forehead creased.

"Do you honestly have no clue or do I need to spell it out here?"

"Spell it out, puh-lease!" a voice interjected. It was Cal.

Benji and I turned to see everybody, including Galiana, staring at us, listening fixedly to our head-butting. Busted, we backed off of each other. Somehow, we had managed to move closer and closer to each other, leaving only inches between our faces.

"Wow," one of the campers from cabin two remarked. "You guys had, like, an entire conversation of questions."

I looked at Benji, who sighed loudly through his nose. He remained irritated. I didn't understand what he wanted me to admit. Did he want me to thank him for that day? Why did we have to talk about that day? Didn't he know I wanted to block it out of my mind? Why couldn't he do the same? Why couldn't we just erase that stupid day and start fresh?

"Shall we continue with the assembly, kids?" Galiana asked. I looked at her and smiled.

"Yes, that would be divine," I answered for everyone, wondering when was the last time I'd used the word divine.

Benji still stared at me. I wasn't sure why he was so peeved, and in all my years of loving him, I had never envisioned us bickering. It wasn't something I enjoyed.

The other campers headed back to their seats. I stood back, looking at Benji, trying not to let emotion overshadow my expression. Hoping he would make a friendly gesture, I smiled as I passed him. He reacted in a way that felt like a blade stabbed me in my side.

"Thank you," I said quietly.

"You're welcome," he snarled as he walked off.

13
Chapter

Galiana waited for a few seconds after we had all sat down to start addressing us.

"Well!" she said. "I like the idea of getting to know each other better, don't you? I'm sure you all have a ton of questions for me, so let's call this *Getting to Know Galiana Time*. So fire away! Anything you want to know about me?"

Everyone in the room exchanged glances. The overt enthusiasm wasn't pretty.

Melaine was the only one brave enough to raise her arm timidly.

"Yes ..." Galiana said, pulling out a folded piece of paper from her pocket and scanning it. "Mela-*nie* Jacobs, is it?"

I could feel Melaine tensing up.

"It's *Melaine*, actually," she said.

Galiana made no acknowledgement of her mistake. Melaine continued uneasily.

"Uh, well, Miss Chung was just answering some of Cal's questions about what we are doing here and why we were chosen to attend this camp. It seems none of us knew anything before we came, and frankly, we're a bit confused."

Thank you, I thought as I sighed in relief. *Finally*.

Galiana's smile, although pasted onto her face, seemed to lose its genuineness. Despite that, her facial expression stayed consistent. She started pacing on the stage like one of those important public speakers.

"I believe what Mela-nie is really asking me, is how did I become the new headmistress?"

Huh? Actually, no. That's not what she asked at all. Galiana continued.

"And *I* can answer that easily. You see, *I* have worked hard my entire life. *I* am a go-getter and *I* won't let anything get in the way of what *I* deserve. Next question, please."

Melaine looked to Niki and me. She was just as speechless as we were.

"Please, go ahead with your other questions," Galiana said. "Remember to keep them focused on me. It's not a hard task." She rolled her eyes.

The rude girl from cabin two raised her hand.

"Yes!" Galiana said with glee. "Name please?"

"Hazel Lane," the girl answered. "Can you please tell us what a typical day will be like here? Will it be like last year? Or will it be different? What are we going to do everyday?"

What was it like last year? Galiana didn't seem to like those questions much either. Although she had not altered her plastic smile since she cantered into the hall, I found it easy to read her emotions; she was annoyed.

Galiana was tall, thin, and not pretty. Her black, beady eyes looked cold and unfriendly and her teeth appeared much too big for her mouth. Her mannerisms came across as harsh and ugly, but nevertheless, she projected an overly confident attitude that made her intriguing to watch.

"A typical day at Milestone," she sighed, "will consist of me waking you up in the morning, games, meals, and some, uh, play time later on. As for *me*, I'm the headmistress! I will run the entire camp, manage, and supervise all of you."

"Uh, thank you," said Hazel, who obviously wasn't satisfied with the answer.

"Next question, please," Galiana ordered, as if standing

in an assembly line. She scanned the audience but everyone was baffled into silence. Nobody spoke.

"Well, one thing that will have to change soon is how shy you all are," she said. "That is completely unacceptable here, especially considering the circumstances. That will be first on my to-do list."

She pulled out a pen from inside her jacket and scribbled on the paper in her hand.

"In the meantime, why don't I tell you a little about myself, hm?"

A low rumble filled the room. Galiana rambled on about herself for two painful hours. It was even more boring than school. By the end of her excruciating soliloquy, I had serious trouble keeping my eyes open. Although I had hoped she would reveal more vital camp information, she didn't. All that talk and nothing even remotely useful.

Benji also looked bored to tears. His head kept dropping down every few minutes; he seemed to be unsuccessfully fighting the urge to fall asleep. Thanks to the encounter we'd had during the break, I was able to tune Galiana out and focus on him.

Why was he so angry with me? Did he hate me now? I couldn't think of anything I'd done wrong.

"OK!" Galiana finally shrieked so loudly it caused Benji and the rest of the campers to sit up straight. "Time sure flies when you're having fun, doesn't it? Let's conclude this gathering, shall we?"

Galiana liked to ask questions, but she never waited long enough for the answers.

"You need to leave now and return in an hour for dinner. Please make sure you are on time. After dinner, you're free to do as you please. I will see you all tomorrow morning."

My legs had fallen asleep. The rest of the campers struggled, too; some stretched, others yawned. Most blinked their eyes repeatedly, attempting to wake themselves up. As we started to clear out of the hall, I heard my name.

"Faye Martin? Faye? Could you stay behind, please? I'd

like to have a word with you," Galiana said.

I stared blankly ahead. Not only was this delay unexpected, but the sight of my cabin mates exchanging looks at my expense again made me edgy. I shrugged my shoulders at Niki to convey that I knew nothing. She replied with a half-smile.

I had been singled out now by both headmistresses and I had no inkling as to why. Watching the others leave the hall, I stood back, perplexed. More questions began filling my thoughts. What could Galiana possibly want to talk to me about? Why did they switch headmistresses in the middle of the first camp assembly? Where were the rest of the campers?

I fixed my shirt and found myself hoping it had nothing to do with my dreaded rash.

14

Chapter

"Well, well," Galiana said. "Faye Martin. *The* Faye Martin. So, how are you finding camp so far?"

"Good, thank you," I said politely. *Did she just say,* the *Faye Martin?*

"Um, I'm sorry, but why did you just say *the* —"

"Did you like the question-and-answer period we just had?" she interrupted.

I paused. Although I was tempted to tell the truth, I decided against it, sparing her feelings.

"Yes, it was very interesting. You've had a nice life."

"Why, thank you! Aren't you sweet? Well, I'm sure we'll get to know each other much better in the days to come. Now, tell me," she said, pulling out her pen and paper again. "What do you think I did well and what could I have done differently in the assembly?"

I felt like a deer caught in headlights. I had no clue what this woman was talking about. Was she asking me for advice? Granted, we probably witnessed her first assembly and her first five minutes as headmistress, but still, what could I possibly contribute?

"I, um, I ..." I struggled to say something that sounded

remotely intelligent. "I think it was fine just the way it was," I managed, trying hard to smile.

Galiana wrote furiously on her paper. I tried to read what she was writing, but her handwriting was atrocious.

"Uh-huh, uh-huh, tell me more," she urged.

She continued writing obsessively. I laughed quietly, wondering what the heck she was scribbling.

"I, um, liked how you, uh, talked about yoursel— " I stumbled. "I mean, your experiences. It really was all fine. Nothing to do differently."

Galiana kept writing passionately.

"OK, good, good. Now, tell me, Faye. How is it going so far for *you*?"

She finally looked up from her pad.

"Here?"

"Yes, at Milestone, Faye."

"Uh, well, I've only just arrived. But, so far, I guess it's going, um, fine?" I said, hoping that was an acceptable answer. Galiana nodded her head. She set down her pen, her eyes wandering between her pad and myself.

Seeing an opportunity, I decided to seize it and get some information. *OK*, I thought. *Now's the time. Here I go.*

"It's just that, I'm a little confu— "

"I have a favor to ask you, Faye," she intruded again. "Can you do some investigating for me tonight, Faye?"

Why did she keep saying my name like that?

"Investigating?"

"I would like you to interrogate the people in your cabin. Can you do that for me, Faye?"

"Why?"

"Can you write down all of their names and get a quick biography of each person? That would be great. I'll obtain the results from you tomorrow. Thanks!"

She didn't even wait for me to say yes. It was more of a demand than a request.

"You want me to interview them?" I asked, suddenly aware of how little I had smiled since she had come into my life.

"Interview. Interview," Galiana said as if she were testing the word. "Let's use the word interrogate instead, shall we?"

I blinked in shock as my mouth fell open. What was the difference?

"Interrogate?" I repeated annoyed, in hopes she would hear how stupid it was that she corrected me.

"Yes, perfect!"

Oh, forget it. Unsure of why I was doing this, I took down the rest of Galiana's explicit instructions and got up to leave the hall.

By the way, let me share something I learned the year I was 14 years old: It's almost guaranteed that if you hate attention, you will most definitely be the person to attract it. While I'm at it, let me tell you something else, too. As you can probably already tell, I was a bit of a goody-goody back then. I ended up growing out of that, and the main reason was none other than Galiana.

"I'll do my best," I said, looking back at Galiana on my way out of the hall.

"Do better than that," she called back, smiling in a manner so friendly, I almost didn't realize what the woman had just said.

15
Chapter

Walking back into the cabin was awkward. My four cabin mates were sitting around the kitchen table. *Oh*, I thought. *There are only four chairs. How convenient.* Everyone laughed as I approached the kitchen and I found myself wishing the subject of laughter wasn't me.

"Hi," I said gawkily, as I walked in. They all reciprocated.

I hoped one of them would be curious enough to ask me what Galiana had wanted, but none of them said a word.

"I've been asked to interro— no, interview you all," I said.

"Interview?" Melaine asked.

I explained what Galiana had asked me to do. Benji, Cal, Melaine and Niki exchanged looks while I looked nervously at the floor. It had taken three minutes and I was already teacher's pet. And I didn't even like the teacher!

"I guess I'll go first," Benji said.

I smiled warmly at him. Was he calling a truce? Were we done fighting? Yet another reason to love him. He was a good person.

We walked into the living room and sat on the couch

facing each other. It didn't take me long to realize we were about to have our first real conversation since I laid eyes on him in fourth grade.

"So, what's this all about?" he asked.

His expression was hard to read again. I wished he would warm up to me.

"This conversation will be a lot different than our last one," I said, wanting to set ground rules.

He stayed quiet, examining me. His eyes moved from my eyes to my forehead and then down to my wringing hands. I felt self-conscious as I tried, unsuccessfully, to not seem tense. God, he was so perfect. Not a flaw in sight. Nothing that I would change.

"I'm sorry about our last conversation," he finally said, his voice softening. The regret in his tone elated me. I wanted to lunge across the space between us and hug him. It was crazy how much I craved physical contact with him. I fought the urge and replaced it with a genuinely goofy grin.

"That's OK." The delight in my voice gave me away and I caught myself looking at him longingly and pathetically. Trying to unscramble my thoughts, I looked down at my blank paper and pen. *Focus. Focus, you love-sick idiot!*

"So, what's this interview business all about?" he asked, breaking the silence.

"I'm sorry. I'm so sorry," I said. "I really don't want to do this, I promise. I don't know why she asked me to do this. I don't even know why I'm here."

He smiled again. I noted he had been doing that a lot lately.

"It's OK, don't worry. I'm sure we'll all have to do something at some point," he reassured me. "Galiana is new. She just needs to settle in."

I felt better already. I looked at him again, noticed my reflection in the greenish hue of his eyes and quickly realized I had lingered a moment too long.

"So, do you know *anything* about this camp?" I asked him.

"Is that what you're supposed to ask me?"

He was startled, yet I didn't understand the edge in his voice. I shook my head.

"Are we doing that thing where we keep asking each other questions again?" I asked.

We both laughed at yet another question. I made sure to store the moment in my memory for future dissection. We already had an inside joke and it made me feel a little giddy.

"Oh. Well, to answer your question, no, actually. I don't know a thing. I'm totally lost. Do you?"

"No," I replied in mild disappointment.

Benji was just as clueless about the camp as I was. Neither of us had been told anything by our parents, and to my dismay, our parents didn't even know each other.

"So, do you have any questions you're supposed to ask me for this interview?"

He was confusing me now. Was he trying to end this conversation?

"No, not really. I'm supposed to write down your biography," I explained apologetically, even though I secretly was dying to know everything about him. Well, everything I didn't already know, that is.

"Well, I'm not sure how much of this will be interesting to you, but here goes."

I had to clench every muscle in my body not to shout, "HAH!" Interesting was not the word. This was the stuff that kept me daydreaming every day. If only he knew how much I adored him.

"Go ahead," I said through my teeth, suppressing my instinct to confess my interest in him.

I noticed his preppy outfit. He struck me as one of those boys who had no clue when it came to clothes but always ended up looking amazing.

Benji's last name was Parker (duh). Like me, he was 14 years old (double duh). His birthday was in October (triple duh). He had a younger sister who, "used to be a pain in my side until we both became teenagers. Then we just started getting along."

I know, I thought over and over as I pretended to hear these things for the first time. He liked baseball, hockey, soccer and pretty much any sport except golf. All things I knew already. He loved music. Again, something I had known for a long time.

His mom stayed at home and his dad worked, which I didn't know. Benji looked sad when describing how his dad worked in a large company. For the past few years, he had been unlucky enough to have the boss from hell. Benji's dad had to work so hard, he barely had time to see his family anymore.

"I miss him," he said in a low voice. "Sometimes, I feel like he's dead. But my dad's boss threatens to fire him almost every day and dangles bribes in his face. My dad is just too scared to stand up to him, he — "

His voice broke off and he took a deep breath.

"Wow," I said. "That's horrible. Why doesn't he quit and find another job?"

"I ask him that every time I see him. He just won't do it. I don't get it. We fight about it all the time," he said.

He flinched and looked up at me solemnly.

"So, did you write all that down?" he asked me apprehensively.

It was clear he didn't want me to write down the personal details he had shared about his dad, not knowing I would never do that.

"Let's see," I said, reading my notes back to him. "Here's what I've got. Benjamin Parker. Fourteen years old. Loves math. Younger sister. Sports. No golf. Has a mom, a dad. And loves music. That's all I wrote!"

He laughed at my excitable attitude.

"Thanks," he said and then, "did I tell you I love math?"

Shoot! I looked down at my hands, realizing I'd been caught. That was one piece of information he hadn't mentioned. It was something I knew based on all my years of professional Benji crushing.

"Um, yeah," I lied, hoping he'd believe me.

He looked at me for a few seconds, and gradually, his look turned concerned.

"What?" I questioned, hoping he couldn't hear my heart thumping.

"Nothing." He got up. "Nothing at all. I'll go get the next candidate."

To my surprise, he patted me on the head as he walked into the kitchen and let Niki know she had been "summoned." In the moment after Benji left the room, I felt hopeless. The head pat sealed the deal for me. Could it be a more condescending gesture? I had been on such a high during the whole conversation, that his abrupt exit felt like my balloon had been deflated.

He'll never like me, I thought. *I should give up and move on.*

But that wasn't an easy thing to do. I would have done it a long time ago if I'd known how.

"Hey, Faye," he said, sticking his head back in the room.

"Hmm?"

"Do you, um, have a boyfriend?"

And just like that, my emotions flip-flopped and I felt a rush. I was euphoric, excited, giddy — I died a little just then. I knew I looked completely stunned but I didn't care. Never in my wildest dreams did I think Benji would be so bold as to ask me about my status. And in such a forward fashion! Could something finally happen?

Think fast, I ordered myself. *Say something clever. Say something intriguing. What would Diane say?*

"N-no, I don't," I finally uttered, trying not to look too transparent.

"Oh, OK, because, um, well, Cal wanted to know. So, good. OK," he said and walked out.

And there you had it. Balloon deflated again. *Cal* wanted to know. He was just the messenger. And I was just the idiot of the century, gutlessly loving this guy from afar.

"Well, make sure to tell Cal that I'm taken — by you," I

mouthed quietly to myself, feeling like I had to vomit. Back to square one. *Ugh.*

16
Chapter

Swallowing my Benji-induced distress, I spent the next hour learning about my other cabin mates. Although I enjoyed getting to know them better, I felt awkward and nosy asking them to divulge so much personal information. Even though each one of them had been nice and cooperative, I felt alienated from the group. Like the odd one out. What else was new, right? And maybe it wasn't her fault, but I blamed Galiana — and Miss Chung, too. What was all that wanting-to-see-my-rash business?

So here's what I learned from the stupid assignment. In hindsight, I wish I had told Galiana to take her assignment and shove it. But I didn't know her very well back then and my desire to be obedient consumed me. Niki, Melaine, Cal, and Hazel all lived in New York City and attended the same school. Melaine and Hazel were best friends. They had grown especially close when both their mothers died recently. Melaine took it hardest. Apparently, she had been a sweet, lovely and bright person before her mother died. Afterward, although she remained all of those things, nuances began to emerge. Her sense of style morphed into a darker version of herself. Her hair turned darker, her makeup became more prominent and gloomier, and she stayed away from bright colors in general. She was one step shy of being Goth.

Niki's friends and family called her "Giggles." It didn't take a genius to figure out why. Cal also didn't have a mother. His uncle had adopted him. I didn't know what had happened to Cal's birth parents and I didn't dare ask.

I also asked each of my cabin mates what they knew about Camp Milestone. Unfortunately, none of them knew anything. Their parents told all of them "they needed to get away," which I considered an eerie coincidence. Melaine explained to me that the prior year, Hazel and her six cabin mates (who were all boys) were in their first year at Camp Milestone, just like me.

"Cecilia Chung was their headmistress and she left them completely unsupervised for the entire summer," Melaine said. "Hazel had the time of her life for the first month. But then she noticed a change during the second month."

"How so?" I inquired, captivated.

"Well, there were fourteen campers that year," Melaine explained. "In the second month, the seven campers in the other cabin became secretive and anti-social. Hazel and her cabin mates felt confused. Although they tried their best to approach the other campers, the others kept shutting them out. They just didn't seem to want to talk to them anymore. It was all really strange."

"Wow," I said.

"By the last week of the summer, Hazel and her roommates were sent home and told to come back the following year. The other seven campers stayed for an extra week, and no matter how much Hazel protested, she never found out why they were told to leave."

"So she still doesn't know?"

Melaine shook her head.

"Hazel spent the entire school year trying to track down the lost camp members, but none of them returned her phone calls or wrote her back. It was like they had disappeared off the face of the planet."

"That's so freaky," I said. "What does she make of it?"

"Well," she confided, "Hazel told me she thinks there's another section to Camp Milestone where the rest of the campers were living. Hazel has this theory that Camp Milestone let's you 'graduate' somehow into the other section. She thinks the other campers discovered something, some secret, and because of that, they graduated last year. But because Hazel and her cabin mates had no clue, they stayed behind or something."

It made sense.

"We'll have to figure it out," I said, surprising myself with my confidence.

Melaine nodded in agreement.

Another good thing that came out of my interviews with my cabin mates was the discussion that followed during dinner. We all headed back to the main hall, where some sloppy macaroni and cheese was waiting for us on the table. To our surprise, nobody was around to supervise. It didn't take long for us to talk about the noticeable secrecy surrounding the camp.

"So, we're all in the same boat. No one knows what we're doing here," Benji concluded. His voice sent my heart into flutters.

I had a hard time looking at him. He had showered and put on a green shirt that made him look a hundred times more irresistible. Plus, I could smell him from afar. I loved his smell. He didn't wear cologne or anything, but he always smelled clean, like soap.

"It's safe to say there's more to Camp Milestone than we know. Something doesn't add up. This isn't an ordinary summer camp," Melaine said.

"Maybe it's a boot camp," Cal suggested.

"I don't know about you, Cal, but I haven't done anything that would require rehabilitation," said Melaine, half-joking.

"See, but I know my parents know more than they are letting on," I said. "They wouldn't just send me somewhere they've never heard of. Plus, they've been acting strange lately."

Everyone agreed. We all felt our parents had been unusually secretive.

"How do you think I feel?" Hazel asked the group. It had been almost a full day and she still hadn't acknowledged me. "I've been here before and I still have no clue. And when I found out Mel, Niki and Cal were coming here, too, I honestly couldn't believe it."

"I know. I have a feeling that's not a coincidence," Cal said.

"Well, it's probably also not a coincidence that we all go to the same school," another boy interjected.

"Oh, you all know each other?" I asked the remainder of the campers.

They all nodded.

"As do we," Benji said, referring to the two of us.

I nodded, trying hard not to seem like a crazy fan who had just seen her favorite rock star for the first time. I still couldn't believe we were actually talking. Who needed fantasies when the real thing was just as good?

"One thing's for sure," another boy said. "We need to stick together. I am not repeating last year's mistake. There will be no secrets this time. Agreed?"

"Agreed," we all said in unison.

"We definitely need to stick together," I repeated. "We have got to tell each other everything and do this thing as a team."

We decided our first mission would be to find a phone, call our parents and clobber them with questions until we got some answers.

"Just to let you guys know," Hazel said, "I doubt there's a phone anywhere. We looked for one last year and couldn't find one. Mind you, we were having the time of our lives and weren't exactly worried about calling our parents, but still."

"We have to try," Cal said.

"Um, also," Hazel added snobbishly, "the guys and I

have been hammering our parents for a year now. Maybe you guys will have better luck, but ours are harder to penetrate than a steel door. They won't budge."

"So, do you think it will be the same this year?" I asked her, trying to get her to acknowledge me.

"Whatever. I don't know," she replied rudely, turning away from me.

Wow, I thought, catching Benji's glare. She does not like me. By the time we finished comparing stories, it was late and I was exhausted. We didn't know what was in store for us the following day, especially with the new camp headmistress, but we knew we would have to pool our efforts if we wanted some answers.

Back at the cabin, I reluctantly said goodnight to Benji and Cal. No amount of time spent with him was enough to satisfy me, I'd discovered. Now that I'd tasted this new type of relationship with Benji, I had become greedy, craving more and more. Up in our room, Niki and I got to talking. After we turned off the lights and got into bed, she opened up to me a little more.

"Faye?" she asked, "I'm sorry I didn't tell you much about myself today. It felt weird."

"Don't worry, Niki. I should feel weird for agreeing to do something so absurd for Miss Perma-smile."

Niki giggled. I had hoped to get that reaction out of her. Her giggle was sweet and comforting. She had a lot in common with Diane.

"I'm looking forward to tomorrow. Especially if our parents cooperate with us and tell us what the heck we're all doing here," Niki said with a yawn.

"I know what you mean. I really think we must all have something in common to be here, don't you?"

"Yeah. If we're chosen, then there is something about us that made us, um, worthy or whatever."

"Exactly. Plus, I am really starting to think there's much more to this camp than we give it credit for."

"That sounds scary," she said in a low voice.

I tried to reassure her and told her we had nothing to worry about. I reminded her that our parents were all rational adults and they had our best interests at heart. Even though I sounded confident, I was scared, too. And the more I tried to calm down, the more questions continued to eat at me. Why were we sent to this camp? Why all the secrecy? Why were we special? Who was that man at the airport? Why did Miss Chung get fired? Why did Galiana want me to interrogate everybody? What were we going to do tomorrow? And more than anything: Why were we here?

My mind raced. Then, like what always happens before I fall asleep, my thoughts changed and focused on something else. Why did I love Benji so much? Why was I tortured so badly? Why was he so obsessed with the day of the lightning strike? And finally, remembering the pat on my head, the awkward goodbye, and the lack of any reciprocation on his part: How, oh how, could I get over him?

17
Chapter

I woke up the next morning to the repeated sound of my name. Galiana was standing directly over me, scowling. At first, I had no idea where I was or even who I was. Then, as I came out of my disoriented fog, it all came rushing back to me. I was Faye Grace Martin, the girl who'd been struck by lightning in front of her love and who'd subsequently been sent off to "camp crazy" with a handful of unsuspecting teenagers. Right. *That story.*

And now, it was 5 a.m. and Galiana and her scary teeth demanded I get my butt in gear. I moaned.

"You have five minutes to get ready," she ordered. "This is the only time I'm going to wake you up. From now on, you're on your own. I will expect you outside your cabin at this time every morning. If you sleep in, you'll have to answer to me."

Slightly frightened, I forced myself out of bed. It was cold outside the covers. I went over to wake Niki up when Galiana spoke again.

"Do not wake her up," she growled. "Mind your own business and leave her alone. There's no need to wake her up."

OK. She was full-on scary now. Afraid to disobey the

new and creepy Galiana, I left Niki snoring as I got ready and headed downstairs. Puzzled and groggy, I stepped outside my cabin within minutes and found Cal, Benji and Melaine. Their faces were transparent; none of them knew what to expect either.

"Good morning!" Galiana said when the seven members of cabin two joined us. "I'm sure you all know that a good leader is an excellent navigator. And a navigator has mastered the art of preparation."

"Huh?" Benji whispered in my ear. I snickered quietly, partly because whispering was a new thing for us and partly because what he'd said was so true. Galiana's sentences made zero sense.

"I'm testing your mental and physical endurance today. While I prepare your first activity, you will all sit in a circle near the lake and none of you are to say a word."

Galiana explained further. She ordered us not to talk until her return. Talking would have severe consequences. She also took all of our watches. We were not supposed to have watches at Camp Milestone.

"Fun has no time constraints!"

No cell phones, and now, no watches. This sucked! We were supposed to "reflect on our lives," whatever that meant. Falling asleep also would have severe consequences. Of course, this information was instructed with a blinding smile.

We obeyed Galiana's orders. None of us wanted to know what consequences she could deliver. She didn't seem like the most sensible person on the planet. With many bitter, sidelong looks and some sullen muttering, we sat in a circle, silently awaiting her return. The first few minutes were the hardest. Sitting in a circle meant we were all facing each other. Benji was the first to crack a smile. I was awful at the "don't laugh" game. I could never stop myself from laughing, especially when it was taboo. Soon, Melaine, Hazel and the rest of the boys were trying not to laugh as well.

Don't laugh, don't laugh, don't laugh, don't laugh, I repeated in my head, biting down hard on my lip. After ten minutes or so, boredom took over and the smiles faded. It seemed like Galiana had been gone for an eternity. I examined everyone's faces. I named all the boys I didn't know from cabin two.

Guy who looks angry.

Optimist guy.

Bookworm guy.

Guy who blushes whenever we make eye contact.

Guy who is fighting a really, really bad cold.

I looked at Benji. Guy who stole my heart and tore it into pieces again and again. Guy who I really needed to get over!

I tried thinking of things I didn't like about him. I didn't like the backpack he took to school. I didn't like that he was so clueless sometimes. I didn't like the way he made me feel most days. That was all I came up with at the time. Next, I tried to picture what the other campers were thinking. This entire time, I also kept a watchful eye on our cabin in case Niki came out. The weather was getting warmer. The bugs were starting to buzz around and the birds were chirping. Although I had no idea how long we had been sitting there, it felt like it had been at least several hours.

There was still no sign of Niki. Benji looked like he might have trouble keeping his eyes open again. Not that I blamed him. Five o'clock was an inhumane time to start the day. Melaine played with a blade of grass. Hazel appeared obviously restless; she kept rolling her eyes and sighing heavily. Another one of Hazel's cabin members kept trying to blow monster-sized bubbles with his gum. Guy with the most creativity? Or guy with the gigantic chewing gum?

"OK. Where the heck is she?" Hazel finally blurted, exasperated. "Did she just forget about us? And where the heck is Niki? How come she's not here? How long are we gonna just sit here? We're tired, we're hungry, and Cyrus, you've got some gum on your nose and —"

"Well, well, well!"

That fake enthusiasm was easy to recognize anywhere.

Galiana stood directly behind Hazel. She had a clipboard in her hand and a pen in the other.

"Hazel Lane. Not too much to reflect on, I gather?"

Hazel didn't respond. Instead she gave Melaine a meaningful look.

This can't be good, I thought.

"Gha-ha-ha! Now you have nothing to say?" Galiana said, laughing.

Her laugh was as fake as her enthusiasm; it was forced and sounded like it started in the depths of her gut. Nobody else cracked a smile, even though it was obvious Galiana had hoped to elicit that reaction.

"Hazel, you didn't follow instructions. And I can't say I'm surprised." Hazel's eyes grew wide. Galiana continued. "I warned you of the consequences. And a good leader always follows through with her promises. I'll be easy on you this time because it's your first punishment."

"Punishment?" Hazel grimaced.

"Hmmm, let me think for a moment. What should your punishment be?" She stopped briefly. "What do you think it should be, Faye?"

I choked on my own saliva. *Me? Why me?*

"I, uh, I don't know," I answered, coughing.

Why the hell was she asking me? Like I would contribute anything to her twisted plans! Galiana examined me for a moment.

"You don't *know*?"

Scared, I looked into her eyes as she returned my glare. I blinked uncomfortably but I didn't dare look away. It felt like we were locked in an intense staring contest. A few moments later, Galiana's face broke out into another awful smile.

"Oh, Faye, that's quite OK. You have the entire summer to work on that. That's what you're here for! As for you, Hazel," she added gloomily, "you said you were hungry, didn't you?"

Hazel's eyes grew even larger, but Galiana hardly noticed. Content, she led Hazel to a lonely picnic table a few feet away. It was broken, and when Hazel sat down, the table jolted and almost broke her nose. Next, Galiana fetched fifteen apples, put them in a basket, and gave them to a pale Hazel.

"Eat!" she ordered.

"Um, what?"

"Eat them!" she growled.

"All of them?"

"Every single one. That's your punishment. Eat 'em!" she barked.

The rest of the campers went inside the hall and ate runny eggs and toast while Galiana sat outside, across from Hazel, watching her every bite, and writing zealously on her clipboard. Sitting in the dining hall, we could see poor Hazel from the window, munching away; she looked absolutely miserable.

18

Chapter

After breakfast, I found myself standing on a raft on the lake. The others were there as well. The raft was square and we were all lined up along the four sides. We were ordered to stand there indefinitely, facing the water, with our backs to each other, until the first person fell in. We were told the first to fall in would get their punishment and the day would subsequently be over. This was so *not* how I pictured my summer, by the way.

Even Niki was there this time. She had wandered out groggily after breakfast, only to find Hazel sitting on a slanted bench, gagging on a bunch of apples. She had no idea what was going on or why she'd been left to sleep in while all the others were called out at the crack of dawn. I felt selfish, but I secretly was a little happy Niki got some special treatment from Galiana. At least I wasn't the only one. Thankfully, this time Galiana had allowed us to talk while we stood standing on the raft.

"After all," she predicted before she left, "it will take you well into the afternoon to finish this task."

"Oh God," I mused. "She's probably right. I don't think any of us want to eat fifteen apples for dinner."

"At least I like apples," Hazel said to Melaine once Galiana had left.

"Yeah, and at least you're not allergic or anything. I have a feeling I'll be the one to lose this time. I don't have great balance. Hopefully I'll be hungry enough to scarf down a dozen apples," Melaine said.

"They're really filling," said Hazel, rubbing her stomach uneasily.

"Can we discuss that this woman is a psychopath, please? Who makes people eat apples as punishment for talking? What kind of a crazy place is this?" Cyrus interjected from his corner of the raft.

A few of his cabin mates responded with vague harmonizing answers. Meanwhile, Niki and I tried to figure out why she had been allowed to sleep in while the rest of us had been yanked out of bed.

"Maybe it's because you're diabetic," I suggested, remembering the insulin I'd seen on her bed. Diane was also diabetic, so I was familiar with the disorder.

"Do you think Galiana knows I'm diabetic?" Niki asked.

"I have a feeling there isn't much Galiana doesn't know about us," I said.

Niki giggled nervously. Her long hair blew sideways in the wind and the scent of her fruity shampoo momentarily filled the air. I wondered why my hair never smelled that potent. Was it in their perfect genetic code or something? Or did I just not get the memo?

"Faye, what do you think?" said Benji from across the raft. He had been talking to the rest of the boys.

"About what?" I asked, my heart pattering at the realization he was asking for my opinion on something.

"I'm pretty sure I saw a phone in the corner of the dining hall this morning. We can use it to call our parents tonight."

"Sounds great —" I replied as my voice broke off. It had been one day and already, I'd had more contact with Benji than in the past five years.

"Anyone else think that we've been sent here for punishment?" Cyrus asked.

"Not particularly," replied another. "What makes you say that?"

"Oh, gee, let me think. Maybe because we're doing these impossibly boring tasks and being force-fed apples as punishment? Do you really think you'd be here if you were a good boy this year, Asher?"

"I already told you," Melaine said. "I have done nothing that deserves punishment. My dad would tell me."

"You sure about that?" Hazel asked her.

Melaine didn't answer because she was beginning to doubt it. We were all beginning to doubt it. Heck, we were beginning to doubt everything by this point. We weren't taking very long to crack. Something was up and rehabilitation seemed the only logical answer.

The conversations went on for hours and helped fill our time. This task was physically more difficult than the first, but mentally, it was much easier. The gift of conversation was a blessing. For one, I found out more about my cabin mates.

Melaine's dad was getting remarried to a woman who also had children. She was trying not to act heartbroken, but she was having issues adjusting to her new life. She wasn't even asked to be a bridesmaid at the wedding. Her future stepmother had given her some bogus excuse about not having enough room at the altar. Melaine would be an usher at her father's wedding. Thankfully, the engagement was set to be a long one, so there was plenty of time for the plans to fall through.

Hazel had spent the entire school year trying to find out more about Camp Milestone but she wasn't able to track down any of the previous campers. She was upset they had gotten special treatment the year before and she hadn't.

Benji's dad worked in the coffee industry. Benji hated to admit he liked coffee because he hated his dad's company. But in his spare time, when he wasn't busy being perfect, Benji had invented these caramel-covered coffee beans and had become addicted to them. He was going to let us try some later that night. He insisted our life would never be the same after tasting them.

Guy who looks angry — Sterne — really was angry most of the time. He complained the most. He was the only one who was content to keep grumbling about our circumstances. He bellyached about everything from the hot weather to Galiana to our uncomfortable mattresses to the tasteless food.

Guy fighting a bad cold — Thomas — explained the cold was actually allergies. He was allergic to almost everything. He was particularly upset with his parents for sending him here two years in a row when they knew how miserable he was in the woods.

"What about you, Faye?" Cal wanted to know, several minutes later.

"What about me?" I echoed.

"You just gonna stand there in silence while we all talk? Or is there anything you want to share about yourself?" Hazel clarified, in a tone filled with contempt.

I still didn't know why, but I was clearly not her favorite person and she made it no secret. She didn't mind putting me on the spot. Heck, she probably even enjoyed it. Thinking she was exposing me, that she was doing them all a favor by showing them I had nothing to contribute, she gave a devilish laugh.

To my dismay, my mind drew a blank. I couldn't think of anything to contribute. Both my parents were alive, I had no siblings, no quarrels with anybody; I felt as though I was riffling through the pages of a blank book. *Think, think.* What could I possibly share of any consequence? My life was so pathetic and lonely.

"Nothing to say?" Hazel was pleased.

"Of course," I said. "Well, let's see. I am an only child. I live in Seattle. My dog died a year ago. I, um ..."

I was losing them. I knew their interest wouldn't last much longer and I could feel Hazel's eyes rolling. Closing my eyes, I took a deep breath and continued.

"Nobody I know has ever died, so I can't comment on that. But what I can tell you is I'm sickeningly plain. To a fault. I hate it. It's a curse." I cleared my throat. "And my best friend at school, Diane," I pursed my lips, "is the person I have slowly come to secretly hate the most. She's perfect. She lives the life I wish I could have. I never asked to be her common sidekick. But that's how I see myself. I'm just there to make her look good."

I winced and opened my eyes, shocked by my own honesty. Was that really something I wanted to say? I was torn between feeling guilty and relieved for saying those things out loud. Maybe I was a secretive person after all. It was the first time I realized how closed off and introverted I'd been. Even my best friend didn't truly know me.

The raft rocked under a small wave. It was painfully hot, the sun was alone in the sky, and its reflection on the water was burning our exposed skin. Bemused, I stared down at the water, catching my own reflection in the deep green lake. It looked a little different. A tan started to show up, my hair glowed in the sun and my eyes looked brighter. But it was more than that. It was the first time I'd seen my reflection and had noticed something different. I smirked at the realization that Camp Milestone already was changing me. Somehow I felt kind of special and free.

Silence followed my confession. Had I said too much? Did I sound like a horrible person? A horrible friend? Apprehensive, I turned my neck to look behind me, half expecting them all to be staring at me in disdain. Instead, they were all in the same positions, standing tall as if nothing had happened. As if I hadn't said a thing. All except for one person, who had turned around, like me, clearly stunned by what he'd heard. Clearly wanting to know more. Clearly perplexed by this news.

With both of us now turned, looking into the empty center of the raft, I locked eyes with Benji. We held it for a few seconds while I wondered what he was thinking. For all I knew, I might have been talking about his crush. Most times, he seemed to really like Diane. Then, he made a sudden motion with his arm, as though to reach out to me, but thought better of it. A few seconds later, he opened his mouth as if to say something.

"You're not plain anymore, Faye," a voice came from beside me. It was an attitude-ridden Hazel. "Actually, you're finally kind of interesting." It was the most back-handed compliment I'd ever received.

Benji flinched and turned around. I followed suit and turned back to face the water, willing myself to breathe again.

"Yeah," Melaine added. "You're at Camp Milestone with eleven other clueless teenagers. It's not a good thing but at least it's not ordinary."

"That's true," I agreed, hoping Benji felt the same way.

After that, we stood in silence, having exhausted our first round of intimacy. The task became more challenging with each minute. Occasionally, a random wave would form and rock the raft, leaving everyone fighting for their balance. Random exclamations of "whoa!" and "yikes!" would get thrown out, and we'd all widen our stance and ride out the wave in fear.

The most challenging moment came when we were least expecting it.

"What's that?" called out Niki, pointing to something floating a few feet away from us in the water.

"It's, it's a log, I think," I replied hesitantly.

"It's not a log, it's moving."

The object was brown and had no discernable features. We stared in curiosity as it floated through the water leisurely.

"It's moving toward us," Melaine said.

"What the heck is it?" one of the guys asked from behind us.

"Oh my God, it's some sort of an-i-mal!" screeched Hazel.

Just then, the beaver disappeared, diving into the water. Before we could say anything, his tail reappeared, splashing loudly and forcefully on the surface of the water.

"Ahhh!" we all screamed as we got soaked by his splash. The raft rocked violently on the waves and I closed my eyes, trying my best not to fall off.

"Hang on!" a voice called out.

Hazel let out another scream and we all did whatever we could to stay on the raft. The desire to avoid eating a bucket of apples gave us unusual strength and determination.

"It's over. The worst is over," Cal said. "We made it."

I opened my eyes to see the lake water returning to its previous calm, with only a few ripples left behind as evidence of the disturbance.

"Wow," Niki said with a giggle as her body relaxed. "That was close."

Too close for comfort, we agreed. We all sighed in relief, not yet realizing that we couldn't go on like this forever.

A few hours later, in the heat of the blazing sun, Hazel joked she wanted to push me into the water to put us out of our misery.

"Ha ha," I said bitterly. "Very funny."

Ignoring my tone, she joked she had "taken one for the team" in the morning with the apples, so it was my turn. Believe it or not, I actually considered the proposed kamikaze. For starters, my legs ached and my skin burned. Holding this position was harder than it sounded. Plus, the water seemed so cool and refreshing, and the temptation to dive in was becoming harder to fight. Finally, I was insanely thirsty and even the thought of eating apples had become mildly appealing.

"Thomas!" Hazel snapped. "Can you please stop sneezing? You're rocking the raft."

"Sorry, I can't help it," Thomas replied with another sneeze and a sniffle.

"Can't you take medicine or something? It's really distracting and it's not fair. How would you like it if I did this every minute?" Hazel barked as she jumped up and down to rock the raft.

What happened next took less than a second. From the

corner of my eye, I caught a glimpse of Melaine losing her balance. Instinctively, I tried to grab her arm to steady her but it was too late. She fell in and I followed. We lost.

"I hope you like apples," Melaine said after we emerged from the water and we all laughed nervously.

~

We had been on the raft for six hours, Galiana explained, apparently something to be ashamed of. We should have lasted until dark at least. Yeah, until dark! She was totally serious. Lucky for me (sorta), only one loser was declared. Poor Melaine technically fell in the water first. Galiana was going to think about her punishment. Melaine wouldn't have to eat apples. Galiana had something else in mind.

"Why doesn't anyone else have to eat apples?" accused Hazel.

"When you figure that out, you'll know everything," Galiana chanted mysteriously as she walked off.

"It's not Melaine's fault," Cal said, jumping to her defense. "It's mine. I did it. I pushed her into the water. Punish me."

Nobody said a word. Galiana stopped as if she'd just hit an invisible wall. "You pushed her in?" she asked, narrowing her dark, hollow eyes.

"Yes."

"And why would you do that?"

"Because, uh, I was bored. So, punish me. Not Melaine."

I smiled listening to him stick up for her. *So sweet*, I thought. Did he like her? I looked at Melaine, who was smiling at Cal. Her hopeful eyes gave her away. She wanted to get out of the punishment. She was scared of Galiana.

"So you're telling me you arbitrarily decided to push her in because you were *bored*?" Galiana asked, raising her voice a few octaves on the last word.

Cal nodded.

"That's really interesting Calvin."

"It's not interesting. It's the truth."

"The truth? So, you're sure Melaine didn't fall in when Hazel rocked the raft because she got annoyed at Thomas? And you're also sure Faye didn't fall in because she tried to hang on to Melaine, who lost her balance?"

Nobody spoke. Galiana's words hit us like cold water; it was clear she had watched us. For six hours, she had been hiding somewhere out there, watching us, waiting for us to falter. We stood in silence, anticipating her explanation.

"Yes, that's what I thought," she continued smugly. "You are so funny, Cal! I love it. But let me explain something to you, OK? Rocking the raft isn't going to get you anywhere in life. I have always excelled on my own," she preached. She loved to put the emphasis on the word "I." "But taking the blame for something you didn't do is also a sign of weakness. You better absorb what I'm saying. All of you. Otherwise, you won't amount to anything."

"But —"

"But nothing!" she said with a bogus smile. "I know you're lying, Cal, but nice try. I'm impressed."

"I'm not trying to impress you!" Cal said, outraged.

"You did anyway."

She turned to Hazel, gave her an evil glare, and then followed the gaze to each of us individually. Hazel frowned. Cal huffed. Benji glowered. Niki giggled fretfully. Melaine looked scared and I sat there, observing everyone's reactions; this pattern would become a trend throughout the summer.

19
Chapter

The first day at Camp Milestone proved disappointing and infuriating. Conveniently for Galiana, a storm supposedly destroyed the phone lines about a month ago. Baloney, right? Yeah, we thought so, too. We were advised the lines would be fixed soon, but in the meantime, the only form of communication with our parents would be by mail. Can you believe it? Like we were were in the 1800s or something. There was a mailbox in the camp's driveway; so much for my fantasy of e-mailing and web-caming with my family. This camp was anything but state-of-the-art or modern. Really, it was atrocious.

The weather was hot, the food was bland and Galiana was beginning to show signs of a double personality. One personality seemed phony and overly chipper; the other could be harsh, uncooperative and unforgiving. Both were difficult.

Not knowing what else to do, we decided unanimously to give Galiana more time to adapt to her new role as headmistress. We figured she might be overwhelmed and trying to prove her authority. One of Hazel's cabin mates, Asher — *optimist guy* —suggested we kill her with kindness. We all agreed it was a good plan.

When Galiana read my notes from the previous night's mandated interrogation, she mumbled something about me being useless.

"What?" I asked, shocked at her forwardness.

"How do you get straight A's with this unorganized and careless attitude?" She shook her head as she skimmed through the notes I'd taken.

I went rigid.

"How do you know I get straight A's?" Galiana rolled her eyes.

"Please, I know these things, Faye. I do my homework, unlike you. Now listen, go tell Melaine I've decided on her punishment for falling off the raft. Tell her I want her to polish the floors of the dining hall. Tell her to apply three coats. I also want her to wash the windows."

"Wha— ? Why do I have to tell her?"

"Gha-ha-ha! You're pretty ungrateful for someone who was given mercy. In case you don't recall, you also fell off the raft."

"Then punish me, too," I dared her. "I'm, I'm not scared of you." She chuckled.

"You could have fooled me. Now go and tell Melaine about her punishment. I don't have time for this."

I didn't know why, but like most of the campers, I actually was quite frightened of Galiana. Something about her was creepy, like she had a dark side she couldn't wait to unleash on us.

"That's a really harsh punishment for Melaine," I tried again, trying to hide the quiver in my voice.

She paused. I tried to maintain my gaze as she looked at me incredulously. My face went paper white and my eyes grew huge, fixated on her unforgiving glare and unwilling to blink.

"I disagree. But fine, have it your way. Forget about the windows. Have her do the rest. Now go!"

It was more than easy to dislike Galiana. I found myself rolling my eyes a lot whenever she was around. With my fists in little balls, I got up and left. Upset, I was reluctant to deliver the news, but to my surprise, Melaine took it rather well. She muttered something about Galiana hating her already, leaving me feeling alienated again. It was obvious Galiana treated me differently than the others. I couldn't deny it. After all, she even lessened Melaine's punishment because I asked. What was I supposed to make of that?

~

That night, the twelve of us collectively decided to write letters to our parents. Hazel showed us the camp's library, which was in cabin one, the first cabin I had seen. The front door was nailed shut, so we crawled in through the window.

"Are we allowed in here?" I whispered once we were all inside.

"Ugh. For Pete's sake, stop being such a goody-goody," Hazel snipped. *Strike three.*

The library was dim and dusty; it had not been used recently. It was small, yet somewhat cozy. Some large leather chairs sat in the corners of the room, the old comfortable kind. Antique mahogany bookshelves covered the walls from floor to ceiling and gave the room a musty scent. Young children's books filled the shelves. I recognized multiple editions of my favorite childhood tales.

"Wow, this camp must have been a kids camp at one time," Melaine observed.

"Yeah, no kidding."

We walked around, running our hands on the dark wood and smooth leather, taking in the strange ambience that filled the room.

"I think this library is our first clue about this camp," Benji said.

I nodded in agreement. It was no coincidence this library was locked up; something in here was not meant for our eyes.

"Let's get to work," Hazel ordered, after we'd worn out our senses.

This pleased me. I loved writing and writing with a purpose was even more appealing. We sat around in the leather chairs and scribbled letters to our parents, friends, and siblings.

Dear Mom and Dad,
Dad,
Dear Bobby,
Dear Diane,
Hi Terrence,
.... I am writing you a letter because I am in misery ...
.... Why, in the name of Benadryl did you ever send me to this allergy hell?
.... You know more than you're letting on. Spill it!
... You have to do something for me, please. Try and find out what the deal is with this camp. Mom and Dad are acting really weird and I'm being tortured ...
... We don't have a phone here. Doesn't that worry you?
.... What do you know that you're not telling me?
... Did you pay for this camp? Because you're really getting ripped off ...
... It's only fair I should know why I'm spending my summer here ...
... Look, go into Mom's room and look inside her dresser. Let me know if you find anything. I'll give you half my allowance when I come home ...
... They are making us eat dozens of apples and wash floors ...
... Please tell me, did I do something wrong this year? I'm so sorry if I did. I learned my lesson. Now come get me!
... Please just be honest. I won't get mad, I promise ...
... You can wear my clothes for the next year if you can squeeze information from Mom and Dad. This is beyond important. I need you on my side. I am suffering here ...

... I promise I will never throw another tantrum ...
... Can you help me, please? Can you find out anything
for me?
... I still love you even though you've clearly lost it ...
... Love always.
... Write back NOW.
... Faye/Melaine/Hazel/Benji/Cal/Niki/Cyrus/J.J./
Thomas/ Asher/Cary/Sterne

By the end of the night, I had three separate letters to Diane and one to my parents. We placed our letters in the mailbox without saying a word. Through the silence, it was obvious we all thought the same thing. If our parents wouldn't open up to us, our fate would be up to us. Somehow, we would have to find answers on our own, a scary thought. Deep down, we knew regrettably our answers could only come from one other source: *Galiana*.

20

Chapter

We decided to give our parents and friends two weeks to reply to our letters. For two weeks, we collectively and unhappily agreed to do what was asked of us wholeheartedly. Maybe if we did everything we were supposed to do, Galiana would soften up and relax. It was the hardest thing most of us had ever done. The more obedient we were, the more this would upset Galiana. Though she didn't tolerate rebellion, she didn't seem happy with our obliging attitudes either. She consistently made comments about the gang "being up to something."

"You're all a bunch of amateurs!" she often said. Naturally, we got a kick out of irritating her.

Our activities varied daily. They were random, unorganized, and ridiculous. The most difficult activity was when we had to form a human pyramid. We only lasted for an hour before I fell off the top. It *really* hurt. It wasn't as bad as the lightning strike, but I thought I'd broken my leg. And what was my punishment? Well, strangely, Galiana was inconsistently consistent with her punishments. Each person was stuck with the same punishment, yet most people had different punishments. I know, it didn't make any sense to me at the time either.

Poor Hazel had to eat more and more apples each time she faltered. She began to hate apples by the third day. Melaine always was forced to clean. By the end of the first week, the camp looked as clean as a whistle, though still disgustingly bland and decrepit. Benji had an unusual and dangerous punishment — he was made to climb up the highest tree in the forest and carry down dozens of pinecones at a time. The first time he did it was by far the worst.

"Be careful!" we warned him, as he looked down at us from what seemed like a hundred feet up.

"Holy crap, she's psycho!" he yelled, trying hard to keep his voice even.

I could feel his knees shaking. OK, they were my knees knocking, but still. Although he was a strong boy — sigh — he found his punishment draining and terrifying. The tree Galiana had picked stood at least thirty feet tall. Whenever he'd be at the top, I would be at the bottom, looking up in fear and praying he wouldn't fall. My life as I knew it would be over if he got hurt.

Cal and Niki were the luckiest. Every time there was a challenge and somebody lost, Cal jumped to his or her defense and lied for them. Galiana loved this for some reason, and in general, she seemed to love Cal. She never gave him a punishment and applauded him for continuously trying to fool her.

"Gha-ha-ha! You are too much, Cal. Way to go! Keep it up! "

"Keep what up?" His frustration made his dislike for her obvious.

"Keep everything up. You are the only one who gets the point of all this!"

"There's a point to all of this?"

"Gha-ha-ha! You kill me."

We all found this confusing, annoying, frustrating; you name it, we thought it. Cal wanted a punishment so he could prove he wasn't Galiana's favorite (even though everyone knew I was her favorite). We teased him about his lying ways and he would get irritated, insisting he didn't do it on purpose. Before every challenge he would publicly swear to us he wouldn't lie — but then he did it anyway. It was just the way he was. Ironically, the first time he actually lost an activity, Galiana didn't believe him. He had become the boy who cried wolf. Even to us.

Niki was another strange case. She was allowed to sleep in every day while the rest of us had to wake up at the crack of dawn. Oddly enough, anytime she lost an activity, her punishment was to return to her room and sleep until the next day. She wasn't allowed to leave her room and Galiana would check on her to make sure she was actually sleeping (and not faking). No matter what time of day it was, if Niki lost, she was sent to go sleep. One afternoon, I made the mistake of trying to wake Niki while she was sound asleep. Somehow, Galiana found out and lost her temper. Nobody was allowed to wake Niki. This was of dire importance.

Cyrus, Thomas, Asher, Sterne, Cary and Alex shared the same punishment. They first lost a task during a game of tug of war against the rest of us. Their punishment called for carrying Hazel around piggyback for hours. Although Hazel was slim, she was taller than most of us, and this task proved difficult for her cabin mates. Whenever one person tired of carrying her, he had to pass her to the next person and so forth.

Depending on how you looked at it, I had the best or worst punishment. For reasons I couldn't understand, somehow I had become Galiana's assistant; she had managed to gradually alienate me from the rest of the group. At first, she was conniving and demanded everything of me. But with time, our relationship shifted and I stopped fearing her. For some odd reason, she began to care more about my opinion and wanted my approval on almost everything. I dreaded hearing, "Faye, tell me which tree Benji should climb," or "Faye, I need to know who will be at the top of the pyramid."

To my disgust, I basically had become her personal assistant for my punishment. It was my personal hell. Because of her, in the first few weeks at Camp Milestone, I had interviewed all the campers, made lists of their belongings, delivered bad news to everybody and had to be in charge when Galiana was not around. I was "lucky," I suppose, in the sense that I never had to do anything physically demanding, but being Galiana's assistant wasn't fun. I tried hard to like her, but I couldn't shake my gut feeling. I didn't trust that wretched woman.

~

The strangest part of the first weeks at Camp Milestone was having to learn the camp song. Yes, a camp song. Are you cringing yet? We were.

We were in the dining hall one evening after dinner when Galiana forced us to learn it. She recited the song once and expected the rest of us to learn it immediately. The song wasn't even a song. It didn't have a melody or anything, it's more of a chant. It made us feel as though we were part of a cult or something. When we struggled to learn the song, Galiana got angry; she was getting more and more angry by the day.

"Arrggh," she groaned, stomping her feet. "Why does everything have to be a struggle for you guys? You aren't making my job easy. Fine, let's do this the hard way. We are going to turn this into a challenge. I am going to recite the song until you all learn it. The last to learn it will have their worst punishment yet. Is that clear?"

Nobody said a word.

"Is that clear?" she said louder, springing to her feet, causing all of us to jump.

"Yes," we mumbled. Galiana's red face morphed into a fake, toothy smile.

"Great!" She shrieked. "Now repeat after me:

> *It all begins with what,*
> *What holds us all together,*

It all will end with Leah,
It doesn't get much better,

What's between is ours to find,
We'll do no good to worry,
Take time to find our way,
What's done and Leah's in no hurry."

We repeated the song over and over, but we just couldn't memorize it. Can you blame us? It sounded like a string of words, randomly beaded together. It didn't make any sense! I was learning it the quickest, followed by Benji; but we both kept mixing up the lines.

"This is really pathetic," Galiana said after an hour, her eyes bulging with fury. "There are only eight lines!"

"Galiana," Benji breathed in frustration, "I have a really good memory, but I can't learn something if I have no idea what it means. *It all begins with what?* I don't get it. What does that even mean? And who's Leah?"

"Yeah!" Hazel said. "And this isn't the song we learned last year. How come the song has changed? That song was much easier to —"

"Stop!" yelled Galiana in a tone filled with contempt.

She stared at Hazel with her beady eyes. She pressed her lips together into a thin line and her jaw became more defined, making it clear she was clenching her teeth. She was fuming. Hazel had said something wrong. The silence consumed the dining hall. Finally, Sterne, *guy who looks angry*, spoke up.

"Both songs were stupid," he said. This statement only angered the beast more. Galiana turned her icy glare onto Sterne.

Omigod, I feared. *She's going to kill the poor guy.*

True to her kind heart, Melaine tried to remedy the situation.

"Galiana, it would really help us, or at least myself, if

we could see the song in writing. I'm a visual person and I'm sure I'd learn it ten times faster if I saw it written down."

Galiana's expression transformed immediately. It was hard to decipher which personality would emerge. After a few seconds, she marched slowly over to Melaine and positioned herself opposite her.

"You're visual?" she asked, with a snaky smile.

"Y- yes."

"You're visual?" she repeated, making us all exchange looks. Melaine's smile was strained and I saw, fleetingly, a look of panic.

"Y-yes."

"How's this, then?"

Violently, she grabbed her pen and scribbled on her notepad. The sound of her chewed-up pen scratching on the paper filled the hushed room. Ripping the paper off the pad, she handed it to Melaine and urged her to read it. Melaine read it out loud: "Shut up and learn the song?"

Melaine looked to the ground and her eyes swelled with tears. Nobody dared say a word. We were shocked and in silent agreement that all of Galiana's personalities were evil. I memorized the song soon after. Benji was next and the rest of the gang followed. Hazel and Melaine remained. Melaine obviously had trouble retaining information due to how mean Galiana had been to her.

"It all begins with what," she recited. "What holds us all together … It all will end with, um, um ..."

She continued to struggle and I wanted to cry for her. I hated seeing her that way. Hazel had become angry with Galiana for being rude to Melaine. But even though she was upset, Hazel learned the song in its entirety soon after. Things just weren't going well for Melaine.

21
Chapter

"She hates me," Melaine said, as we walked into our cabin that evening, exhausted.

I didn't know what to say. Unwavering in her absurdity, Galiana had ordered me to tell Melaine her punishment. *Again.* I hated this assignment.

"She doesn't hate you," I replied with a warm smile, trying to hide my displeasure. Benji, Cal and Niki were sitting in the living room, waiting for our arrival.

"She hates me. I always get the worst punishments. Look at my hands, I have calluses." She paused. "Gosh, I'm becoming so paranoid. I'm not usually like this."

Niki giggled in agreement. I sat down next to Benji and accidentally brushed against his hand. Another tiny shock ran through me and I sighed surreptitiously.

In the past several weeks, I had come to know Benji better and had found even more reasons to like him. My crush was officially all-consuming, although I was convinced he didn't reciprocate my feelings. Despite my intuitions, he would do something every day — however little — that kept me wondering about his feelings, always enough to keep me going. Always enough to give me that extra bounce in my step.

Always enough to excite me. Always enough to make waking up at 5 a.m. easy. Always enough to secretly love being at the horror that was Camp Milestone.

"So, what's the damage?" Melaine asked me, looking quite stricken. I sighed. I really didn't know how to break the news to her again. This burden I had received wasn't getting any lighter.

"It's, um, more cleaning," I told her. Benji, Cal, and Niki all scrutinized me.

"Did you tell her that I forgot the song after I learned it?" Cal blurted. "Did you tell her that I should get the punishment instead of Melaine?"

"Yes. Cal," I said, trying to stem my smile. "She didn't believe me. I thought you said you were going to stop doing this."

"Oh, yeah, right. It's just, I, I can't help it."

Benji and I exchanged a look. We did that a lot lately and I loved it.

"You always do this, Cal," Niki said, with a giggle. "She's never going to believe you now."

"Give it up, my friend," Melaine told him as she patted him on the back. "I appreciate what you're trying to do, but it's a lost cause. I'm a lost cause."

"So what does Melaine have to do now?" Benji asked, bringing the focus back to me.

"Um, she has to clean our cabin. And Hazel's, too. And she also has to clean the library and ..."

"There's more?" Benji asked.

"Yeah, you have to do all our laundry, Mel ..."

Everyone stared at me. *Stop looking at me please*, I pleaded.

"Uh-oh," said Benji with a grimace.

"What?" Niki asked.

"I have a lot of laundry and it's all really dirty." Silence filled the room. "We've been here for almost two weeks!" he added defensively.

112

"Keep going, Faye," Melaine instructed as she grinned forgivingly at Benji.

"There's more?"

I took a breath and continued, "And you're sort of in charge of making our beds from now on, but, obviously, that's not gonna happen because we'll all keep making our beds every day. I mean, I shouldn't even have mentioned that one. Just disregard that last part. It's not like Galiana would ever know the diff— "

"Anything else?" Melaine interrupted. She pressed her lips together; she had tried to be brave but I wasn't fooled. She was crushed. I shouldn't have rambled like that.

"No. That's all."

That's all? As if that isn't enough! Melaine got up from her seat and walked over to Niki. She reached out her hand and made a small gesture.

"Hello. My name is Melaine and I'll be your new maid. Nice to meet you."

Niki, Benji, and Cal laughed. I forced a smile. Although Melaine was joking, I knew she was anything but happy.

~

Later that night, I had trouble sleeping. Niki's snoring kept me up and my hatred of Galiana, coupled with my love of Benji, overwhelmed my thoughts. I got up and headed downstairs to the kitchen. I tried to be quiet as I walked across the creaky kitchen floor to fetch a glass of water.

"Nice pajamas," an all-too-familiar voice came from behind me.

I gasped for two reasons. First, he genuinely startled me. Second, usually my heart skipped a beat when that voice made its way to my ears and headed straight toward my thumping heart. I turned around to see him standing in the kitchen with a smirk on his face.

"You scared me," I said, immediately wanting to take that back. I don't know why I became such a Captain Obvious around him.

"Sorry," he said, still smirking. He didn't seem sorry. "Do you like bananas?" he asked, referring to the banana-ridden pajamas I was wearing.

"Yes, they're a wonderful fruit." *Ugh*. Why did I sound like such a dork around him?

Benji was wearing a grey T-shirt and some old shorts.

"More wonderful than say — apples?" he teased.

"Certainly for Hazel," I joked. We laughed as we sat down at the kitchen table, facing each other.

"Couldn't sleep?" he asked.

"Nuh uh. You?"

"No," he answered, though his bed-head seemed to show otherwise. I found him increasingly irresistible. "Can I ask you something?"

"Sure," I said, trying hard to wipe away the ridiculous grin on my face. I was not even slightly challenging to interpret.

"Did you mean what you said that day on the raft?"

I looked at my glass of water. He was referring to what I'd said about Diane. I didn't know how to answer his question. Part of me wanted to lie to him and pretend my friendship with Diane was perfect; I wanted him to think I was perfect, not a flawed and envious person. The other part of me felt comfortable with him, like maybe he would be receptive to my true feelings. I couldn't decide what to do.

"What did I say again?" I stalled.

"You know, about feeling second-best to Diane. You don't have to talk about it if you don't want to."

He picked up on my unease. I had a dozen arguments with myself in the seconds that passed. His green eyes fastened upon mine and I tensed up.

"Can I ask you something?" I bounced back. His lips curled into a half-smile and my pulse quickened.

"Of course, but only after I remind you that we're doing that thing again."

"What thing?"

"That thing where we have a conversation of questions."

That ridiculous smirk of mine popped up again. I pinched myself in hopes that it would ground me a little. It didn't.

"Oh yeah," I laughed.

"You have a great laugh," he said.

I froze. That's when I learned the words required to get rid of that ridiculous grin on my face. Five words. *You have a great laugh.* Yup. Those words sent chills down my spine. I was shocked. He complimented me. Even a romance-moron like me could understand that. I made a mental note to file the comment away for future replay. Nope, too late. I already was replaying it in my mind, like a broken record. You have a great laugh. *I do?* You have a great laugh. Was he flirting with me?

I quickly scanned my brain for a witty response.

"I like laughing at you. With you! With you!" I corrected, smacking myself in the forehead.

Grrrr! Why was I so brainless? He didn't take offense. He chuckled again and so did I.

"There's that laugh again," he said.

Omigod.

Oh. My. God.

EEEK! I was dying.

"Now you're making me self-conscious," I said, biting my lip.

"Not my intention, sorry," he blushed as he broke off his gaze and looked down. "So what was your question?"

"Well," I cleared my throat. "You asked me about what I'd said earlier, on the raft that day. I want to know why. Why do you want to know? Why do you care?"

"I guess it just surprised me to learn that about you. I wanted clarification. Details," he explained.

I had hoped for more. I had gotten a little hint of flirtation from him and I was getting greedy. I wanted him to tell me he liked me. I wanted him to confess his feelings for me, to tell me I wasn't just Diane's sidekick. I knew exactly how I wanted the conversation to play. I just needed him to know, too. I'd never had as much hope as I did in that moment.

"Is that all?" I pressed, leaning forward in anticipation. Benji blinked a few times.

"Well, no ..."

We sat there in silence for an undefined amount of time. *He is so my type*, I confirmed. His dirty blond, disheveled hair. His green eyes. His perfect nose. His hands. God, I loved his hands. They were always clean, his nails neatly clipped. I wondered what it would feel like to hold them again.

"What?" I begged him, ecstasy floating out of me.

"I also, um, care a great deal, um, about, well, I care about Diane."

I blinked.

"What?" I couldn't hide how appalled I was. My face went completely bloodless.

"What?" He was confused.

"You care about *Diane*? That's why you want to know?"

I couldn't believe it. He did love her. Like every other teenage clone at our bogus school, he wanted to be with her, too. He wasn't resistant to her beauty, to her body, to her magnetic properties. He was just like the rest of them. He just wanted to talk about her, to learn about her. From me! He was using me to get to her. That's why he wanted to know. That's why he talked to me.

"Well, yeah, Faye. Why is that so hard to believe?"

"It's not!" I wasn't trying to be cordial and or to mince my words now. I was hurt, but more so, I was angry. "That's exactly my point. Join the club, Benji. Take a number. You're not the only one who loves her, you know."

"I didn't say I loved her, Faye," he said frowning.

"You didn't have to Ben-*ji*."

I wasn't trying to act like a baby but I couldn't help it. I couldn't believe I had spent all this time pining after him, only to have him be another drone in the I-love-Diane saga.

"Why did you say my name like that?" he asked defensively. He was getting angry, too, I could tell. His fingernails were digging into the wooden table.

116

"I'm sorry, do you prefer Benjamin?" I got up and stared down at him, perfectly aware that my sarcasm was ugly.

"Wow, you can be really mean sometimes," he said, looking up at me and shaking his head.

I laughed unbelievingly.

"Mean? Mean?"

I was mean? Me? He's the one who made me like him all this time. I was in fourth grade, for crying out loud! What the hell did I know in fourth grade? Nothing! It was all him! He's the one who made me languish after him. He's the one who made me suffer in silence all these years. And now, he had the gall to tell me I was being mean? After he clearly was using me to get to my best friend? The nerve!

"Yes, mean! The same way you were mean the day of the lightning storm when you called Diane and I monkeys!"

"Hah!" I cried out, slightly surprised he remembered that.

"Do you remember the day of the lightning storm, Faye, or do I still need to shut up about that?"

"Oh, my God! What is your obsession with that day? It happened. So what? Why do we need to talk about it?"

"Why? Why NOT?" He stood up now, towering over me. "I have never seen or experienced anything like that. That's sort of a big deal! You don't just get hit by lightning and go on with your life as if it never happened. I mean, holy crap, Faye. You should have died! And then, you never even talked to me about it. You just vanished. I thought I dreamed it. You acted like a professional out there!"

"What?" I yelled. "You cannot even *begin* to understand what I felt that day. It was not fun getting hit by lightning. It was the worst day of my life! I didn't ask for you to be there, Ben-*ji*. If I'd had it my way, you wouldn't have been there and I could suppress this horrid memory in peace!"

"Be my guest!"

We were nose to nose again. I could feel his breath huffing.

"What were you doing there anyway?" I demanded.

"Did you run after me to make me apologize to your future wife for calling her a monkey?"

"You are unbelievable," Benji said.

"What the h-e-double-hockey-sticks is going on in here?"

Cal was standing at the kitchen door, groggily fixing his glasses onto his face.

"Are you guys fighting?"

"NO!" we both barked.

"Oh, yeah, that's convincing," he said. "What's going on, you guys? What are you so upset about?"

"NOTHING!" we both snapped again.

"OK, then," Cal said. "Glad we got that figured out. If it's nothing, maybe you could do nothing a little quieter. Some of us are trying to sleep."

"Not to worry, Cal," Benji said, backing away from me. "I was just about to head back to bed. This conversation is beyond over."

"Pfff. You're telling me," I said.

"Goodnight," Benji said as they both walked out of the kitchen.

"Not really," I said, all alone.

I headed upstairs in a fury. How dare he tell me I was mean? I was not mean. I was just unwilling to tolerate him loving Diane. Why was that so awful? I'd had enough of guys swooning over her. Any person would crack. I was only human!

It took me several hours to fall sleep. I tossed and turned (and cried) as I tried to unravel my thoughts. I hated loving him, I hated it. I buried my head in my pillow and let out a little yelp.

It was settled.

As of tomorrow, I was going to be over Benjamin Parker. Enough was enough.

22
Chapter

Hazel summoned a secret meeting on the night of our two-week anniversary at Camp Milestone. She had become our leader, mainly because most of us were mildly scared of her. She could be intimidating and malicious. It was always better to stay on Hazel's good side.

The night before our secret meeting, while Niki and I were in bed talking about movies, we heard the door of the cabin slam shut a few times and voices in our living room. We looked at each other briefly before scrambling out of bed and running down the stairs two at a time.

Hazel, Cyrus, Thomas, Asher, Sterne, Cary and Alex were standing in the living room, each trembling. Melaine, Cal and Benji emerged from their rooms shortly after us. Everybody was in their pajamas. Cyrus had the goofiest pajamas — one of those one-piece suits with pictures of cartoon characters on them. He looked like a giant 5 year old.

"What's going on?" Benji asked tiredly as we made eye contact.

We hadn't talked since the previous night. I was working hard to get over him, and to my astonishment, I was slowly getting the job done. The more the day went on, the

119

less I thought about him. Every time I found myself falling back into old habits, I replayed the fight in my head, reminding myself he was just another of Diane's boyfriend replicas. He wasn't different or special. He was boy-toy number sixty-seven. *Disgusting.*

"There's a ghost in our cabin," Hazel said in her nasal voice.

"A ghost?" Cal asked skeptically. An eruption of giggles filled the room.

"A ghost, you guys! I swear. Tell them," she ordered her cabin mates.

"Well, we think it's a ghost," Thomas said as he blew his nose. His allergies were acting up again.

"It's probably not a ghost. Don't worry, everyone," Asher said with a huge grin on his face. *Optimist guy.*

"Look, it can't be a ghost. Ghosts don't exist. They are just figments of our imagination. Illusions. Our minds are playing tricks on us," Alex added. *Bookworm guy.*

"Oh, yeah?" Hazel challenged, "Well, how come we all heard it then? Our minds can't play the same trick on all of us. That's impossible and you know it."

"Heard what?" I asked.

Hazel explained she'd been sleeping when she awoke to the sound of footsteps in her room. Petrified, she jumped up and turned on the lights, only nobody was there. Cyrus, Thomas, Asher, Sterne, Cary and Alex heard a whimper from Hazel's room and ran to her rescue, where they all confirmed the sound of footsteps. To them, it sounded like someone was walking in Hazel's room, yet they couldn't see anything. The floors indisputably creaked. Terrified, Hazel panicked and ran to our cabin, with the boys closely behind her.

"I want to hear this ghost!" Benji said.

His bravery would have sent me swooning before, but not now. *I am so over it*, I convinced myself.

"Great, I'm never going to sleep. This camp sucks. I'm going to sleep in your room, OK, Benji?" Sterne said.

Benji nodded and gave Sterne a small wink. He

summoned Cal and they headed next door to hear the ghost for themselves. Waiting for their return, Niki and I got some blankets for the rest of the boys so they could sleep in the living room. Hazel planned to sleep in Melaine's room. Though none of them admitted they were scared, it was obvious they didn't feel comfortable sleeping in a haunted cabin.

"Tomorrow night we're going to have to come up with a plan," I said as we all made ourselves comfortable.

"I'm going to be exhausted tomorrow night," Melaine said with a yawn.

She turned to Hazel to explain the punishment Galiana had given her for not learning the camp song quickly enough. Hazel glared at me, making it quite clear she blamed me for everything. *They think it's my fault,* I thought.

"It's not Faye's fault," Melaine said.

"Sure it's not," Hazel said sarcastically, her eyes fixed on mine.

Benji and Cal ran back into our cabin shortly after. Their faces looked white and their expressions frozen as if they had actually seen a ghost.

"We heard it clearing its throat," Cal said with a shiver.

Even Alex, the bookworm, didn't have a reasonable explanation for what was going on. Later that night, Niki and I stuck our beds together so that we could sleep closer together.

"What if the ghost can leave the cabin and make his way over here?" Niki hypothesized. "That can't happen, right?"

I shuddered at the thought. Channeling my inner bravery, I tried to make Niki laugh by telling stupid jokes until we fell asleep. Ghost or no ghost, Camp Milestone was getting more mysterious by the day.

23
Chapter

On the night of our secret meeting, the campers gathered in our rearranged living room. We put sleeping bags on the floor and sat around in our pajamas. Cary and Cyrus roasted marshmallows by the fireplace and Benji passed around his giant bag of caramel-covered coffee beans. By the way, he wasn't kidding; those things were tasty and totally addictive. Too bad I didn't like him anymore.

Though Hazel declared herself the leader of the meeting, she quickly ran out of things to say and quit. No one else volunteered to take her place, so I started speaking.

"It's been two weeks and none of us have received any replies to our letters. I've written quite a few letters to my parents and even more to my friend Diane. I've mailed her at least twenty letters."

Benji cleared his throat. I looked at him and glowered.

"Well, maybe, she's having too much fun without you, did you think of that?" Sterne quipped.

"Ouch," Melaine said. "That's harsh, Sterne."

He's probably right, I recognized. What made me think Diane would want to write back? She probably didn't miss me at all. She'd probably found a new group of best friends by now. Plus, I'd been such a bad friend to her lately. OK, I had been a bad friend in general. I had been selfish and jealous. I shouldn't have blamed her for all the attention she attracted. She was just being herself. Jealousy didn't suit me, I realized. So what if I was the sidekick in her life? Was that really the worst thing? I shook my head, disappointed and answering my own questions.

"Sorry, Faye," Sterne said, "I just hate this place."

I turned my eyes to Benji. *How did he react to Diane's name?* I wondered. His feelings were impenetrable.

"You hate everything," Hazel said with a laugh. Niki giggled and I tried to force a smile. "But he might be right, Faye," Hazel continued, "I mean, are you popular at school or is Diane your only friend?"

All eyes suddenly fixed on me. I sighed, aware of their glares.

"I'm actually kind of glad you brought that up, Hazel," I croaked diplomatically. "We should try to figure out what we all have in common. Because we must have something in common if we were 'chosen' to attend Camp Milestone."

The nods that filled the room validated that I was making sense.

"So to answer your question," I continued, "I'm not very popular. I hang out with the popular people at my school, but I'm not popular, per se. And Diane, who's the most popular girl in school, is my closest friend. But not too many people know me, I think."

Benji flinched. He was so hard to read. Everyone else had grown quiet. I knew they were surprised by my candidness. Surprisingly, I wasn't; I had become a little more confident in the past two weeks. I cleared my throat.

"So, uh, what about you guys?" I asked, even though I already knew the answer.

Popularity is often very obvious. A person gives off a certain vibe if they're popular. It's like a secret code, something to do with confidence. Melaine, Cal, Niki, and Hazel were all popular. Obviously, Hazel was the most popular person in their entire school. She was tall, dark-skinned, naturally thin, pretty and quite intimidating — a recipe for popularity. Hazel also had a stylish aura about her. Her clothes were brand name and she was aware of what was in fashion. I had seen her scowl at my outfit several times. She particularly disapproved of my outdoorsy outfits, you know, like hiking shoes, khakis, that kind of thing.

Cyrus was the class clown and I suspected a few girls at his school crushed after him the way I did with Benji. Cyrus was tall, dark-haired with olive skin and prominent eyebrows. He was like a chameleon, always molding his hair and choosing his outfits according to his mood that day.

Benji — I knew all too well — was the quiet popular type. He was handsome in an unconventional way. Not too preppy, not too sporty, not too anything really. He preferred to wear a polo shirt and a baseball cap most days. I shook my head in an attempt to kick out the unwanted thoughts of him. *You're over him, remember?* I reminded myself.

Sterne, Asher, and Thomas were not popular. Sterne suffered from a bad case of acne and his temper prevented him from being approachable. Asher and Thomas were definitely in the awkward and gangly part of their teenage years. Alex and Cary also were wildly unpopular. Alex was a stereotypical bookworm (or nerd, if you will) and Cary was painfully shy, which at times, was easily mistaken for being standoffish. In fact, that night, every time he handed me a marshmallow, he would blush and look at the ground. I tried hard to give him a warm smile so he didn't feel uncomfortable, but my attempts proved futile. He was who he was.

"Well," I said after we had exchanged information. "Obviously, our popularity, or lack thereof, isn't something we all have in common. Let's keep trying."

We spent the night comparing life stories. None of us slept a wink; Benji's caramel-covered coffee beans kept us up all night. We had moments of laughter followed by moments of sadness and then laughter again. We laughed when comparing our grades in school. Alex, Cal and I were amongst the smartest in our schools. The rest varied. Cyrus had the worst grades. He made us all laugh by explaining his theory about grades.

"Only losers get good grades," he joked.

Most of us cried when Melaine and Hazel shared how their mothers had died. Both of them had cancer and died after long struggles with their respective illnesses. It was heartbreaking to hear how much Melaine and Hazel missed their mothers. Coincidentally, both of their fathers planned to remarry. Although Melaine and Hazel were angry when they found out their fathers were considering marriage again, they turned to each other for support and helped each other realize their new stepmothers might fill a void in their lives. No one would ever replace their moms, but perhaps it would be nice to have a family again.

Benji confided to everyone about his father and his boss. He felt like he was the man of the house because his dad was never there. His sister and mother depended on him. He promised himself he would never abandon his family the way his father had. Benji vowed he would never work for anybody when he grew up; he was going to start his own business. Torn between my old love for him and my new mission to distance myself from him emotionally, I found myself admiring his attitude.

We continued comparing stories all night. One by one, we asked each other questions and took turns answering.

"Has anyone ever cheated in school?"

"Anyone won any prizes?"

"What kind of dreams do you have?"

"What sports do you play?"

"What's your favorite movie? Color? Song? Person? TV show?"

"What do you want to be when you grow up?"

"Where are your parents from?"

"We have to spill secrets!" Hazel finally bellowed. "It's probably something we've never told anybody."

Cal went first, telling us about his past. His parents

passed away in a car accident when he was young. Cal was in the car as well, but he had miraculously survived. Sadly, he lived in foster homes until he turned 12 years old. Then he finally got to testify in court and tell the judge he wanted to live with his uncle, who had been fighting for custody for years. Although he loved his uncle and was glad he didn't have to live in foster homes anymore, Cal wasn't happy. He often got the urge to run away from home. He wanted the impossible; he wanted his parents back.

"I don't even remember them anymore," he said.

After hearing Cal's story, the girls got up one by one to hug him. Inadvertently, I made eye contact with Benji while I was hugging Cal. He looked away as soon as he caught my eye. I rolled my eyes in frustration. *Get over it, Faye!*

Niki explained she had a good relationship with her parents. Nothing out of the ordinary had ever happened to her.

"So far, this summer is the most exciting thing that has happened to me," she confessed. We all exchanged looks after that comment, knowing very well that this summer was the most exciting experience for all of us.

"Any other secrets?" Hazel wanted to know.

Nobody answered. I racked my brain to think of something else that might be beneficial to bring up.

"Nothing?" Niki asked. I was startled to see her directing her question at me.

"Me?" I asked.

"You have nothing else to add, Faye?"

"Uh, what would I have to add, Nik?"

What was she getting at?

"I don't know, Faye. You tell me. Is there absolutely nothing else you want to talk about?"

"Um, I don't think so," I replied honestly. She sighed and then gave me a meaningful glance. I raised my eyebrows and attempted to convey a look of uncertainty.

"Not even anything about, say, a *rash*?"

I paused. What did she know? And how did she know it?

"A rash?" I asked, as my voice cracked.

"A rash?" Melaine's voice echoed from beside me.

Niki gestured to me with her eyes. I sighed, realizing she wasn't going to let it go. Perhaps it was time to stop being so secretive. What was the big deal, right? These were my friends now and we had promised we wouldn't keep secrets. I didn't want to be a hypocrite and I knew I could trust them.

"I saw it," Niki said in a low voice.

"Saw what?" Hazel inquired.

"OK, OK," I confessed, glancing around. "A few weeks before camp, I, um, I, uh ... "

"It's OK, go ahead," Benji urged kindly.

"I, I got hit by lightning," I blurted. "There, I said it." I let out a giant sigh and leaned back in my seat. Immediately, I felt as though a giant weight had been lifted from my burdened shoulders.

"You did?" a puzzled Melaine asked.

"Lightning?" Cyrus repeated.

Hazel, Niki and Cal exchanged a look I found difficult to decipher.

"What? What am I missing?" I asked.

"What a coincidence," Melaine's sweet voice interjected. "I've been struck by lightning, too."

"So have I," Hazel said.

"And so have I," Cyrus said.

24
Chapter

"Wait a minute," I said after the initial shock had worn off. "You guys have been struck by lightning, too?"

I couldn't believe my ears. Never in a million years did I see *this* one coming. To think, I wasn't the only one. It was unfathomable to me. Yet, it made perfect sense. In a brief moment of clarity, I scolded myself for alienating myself from the world. Why had it taken me so long to get here?

"Tell me," Melaine inquired calmly. "Does your rash look anything like this?"

She pulled up her sleeve to reveal a familiar image. Like me, she had a rash, though it was no bigger than a coaster. Cyrus and I each took in a loud breath simultaneously.

"Holy crap!" he shouted. "Check out mine." He turned around and began to pull down his pants. I winced and someone else screeched.

"Omigod, where is it?" Niki asked, as she shielded her eyes.

"Relax, my prude little counterpart. I'm not going to show you anything that you haven't already seen," he paused, "I hope."

He had pulled down his pants a few inches to reveal

a similar image on his lower back. I tried not to stare, but my fascination got the best of me. Our rashes all looked similar yet different, like snowflakes. They were all red, tree-like patterns with radiating branches, but each one was unique and easily distinguishable from the next.

"Those are Lichtenberg figures!" Alex said, walking up to Melaine.

"What?" Hazel asked.

"Lichtenberg figures. They are branching electric discharges that appear on the skin of people who have been hit by lightning. They are named after the German physicist, Georg Lichtenberg, who discovered them."

He was fascinated, running his hand along Melaine's scar.

"Wow! These are so rare! I can't believe I get to see so many of them!"

"You're such a nerd, Alex," Hazel remarked. Mincing words was not her forte.

He didn't care. That was his comfort zone.

"Do you have one, Hazel?" Cyrus asked.

"I don't think so," she said, hesitating. "I haven't looked. Mel never told me about her rash before."

We scanned over Hazel's arms and legs, and then Melaine lifted up her hair. She could see the edges of a red fern shape starting at the top of Hazel's neck, the rest of it obscured by her hair.

"Now show them yours, Faye," Niki said.

"Mine?" My heart skipped a beat.

"You have one, too?" Benji asked me. I made a small nod and turned my eyes to the ground. Why was it still so difficult for me?

"Go on," Niki insisted. "It's all right. We're all friends here."

Reluctantly, I turned my back to them, took a deep breath, and lifted the back of my shirt. A flurry of gasps erupted, and a chilly breeze seemed to emanate from the ground and fill the room. A hush followed and I cringed, hoping they weren't too horrified.

"Wh-When did y-you get th-that?" Benji stuttered as I pulled down my shirt and faced them again. His face was red and his knees were locked.

"I don't know," I answered. "I noticed it in the airport after the plane ride."

"Are you hurt?" he asked genuinely. The worry in his voice was obvious, but another emotion also was hidden in there that I couldn't discern. He walked over to me and put his hand firmly on my arm.

"No, Lichtenberg figures are harmless," Alex answered from behind him.

"I'm fine," I reassured him with a crooked smile. This getting-over-him thing was becoming difficult. I'd barely made it a day.

"I'm so sorry," he whispered to me. "I didn't know." He tightened his grip on my arm.

"It's OK," I whispered back, fighting the instinct to like (*love!*) him again.

His hand hadn't budged. He grasped my arm tightly without any intention of letting go. As a consequence, I felt suffocated, smothered, like I was gasping for air; yet I didn't want him to let go.

"Why is Faye's rash glowing?" one of the boys asked.

"You noticed that, too?" I asked. "I thought I'd just imagined that."

"No, your rash is definitely different. It's like it's *alive* or something."

I shrugged my shoulders. The way he said the word "alive" sent chills down my spine.

"How long do these licking bird things last, Alex?" Hazel asked in a nasal voice, causing a few of us to chuckle.

"I don't know," Alex said defensively. He wasn't used to not knowing things. "They are extremely rare. Not many people get hit by lightning. In fact, statistically, it's nearly impossible to get hit at all."

"Yet, somehow four of us have. And we lived," Melaine

said. "That's got to mean something."

"Definitely," Niki added.

"So, Faye, if you don't mind my asking, how did it happen?" Cary asked, still timid in his demeanor.

"Well ... " I started, looking to Benji, who finally broke his clutch as we both sat down. I paused at the realization that my arm felt cold after he had withdrawn his grasp.

"Do you want me to tell it?" he asked me, misreading the situation. Surprised and curious, I nodded.

"How do you know, Benji?" Cyrus asked, raising an eyebrow.

"I was there."

"Interesting," Alex said.

"Why is that interesting?" I wanted to know.

"I'll explain later. Continue, Benjamin." He was taking his problem-solving role seriously.

"Well, um, it was the last day of school," Benji started. "Faye walked up to Diane and I, and she said goodbye to us." He edited the content of his story and I loved him for it.

"I noticed that she looked upset so I, uh, followed her."

"Wait, what?" The question fell from my lips before I could stop it. He followed me? Why? I opened my mouth to say something else but he continued to speak.

"It was raining pretty hard by the time I found her. Actually, I'd never seen a storm like that in my life. It was almost like a hurricane or a monsoon. The storm clouds hovered over us, almost as though they had followed us. The rain struck me from every angle and I struggled to see. Faye was walking in a park close to where we live. As I approached her, lightning hit a tree she was standing right under. I screamed out to her because, from my point of view, it looked like the lightning was heading right for her." Benji straightened in his seat and adjusted his pants. "Then she, well, she picked up a shovel and that's when it happened."

His gaze hadn't left mine and I could see a glisten in his eyes; this was painful for him to recall. I also couldn't help but wonder if I'd been a complete moron this entire time. He had followed me willingly?

"Why on earth would you pick up a shovel during a rainstorm?" Alex asked condescendingly, snapping us out of our silent exchange.

"Temporary insanity," I replied automatically, still staring at Benji. The words escaped me without my volition. He raised his eyebrows at me and I looked away, fully aware that I was smiling.

"That's, er, really similar to our experience," said Melaine, cautiously. "Only, there was no shovel."

"What happened?" I asked.

"Basically, it was Niki, Cal, Hazel, and I. We were hanging out after school and it started raining, so we took shelter under a tree, oblivious to what was about to happen. The tree got hit by lightning, and I guess Hazel and I were too close to it or something because the current went through the tree, and somehow, into us."

"It was awful," Niki shivered, reliving the memory.

"Yeah, they got thrown into the air like rag dolls," Cal said with a shudder. "I thought they died."

"With me," Cyrus started, "it was a little different."

"What happened to you?" I asked

"Uh, I got hit by lightning," he joked. "Isn't that what we're talking about?"

"Be serious, Cyrus," Hazel snipped. "We're finally getting somewhere." He made a face and continued.

"Well, we — all the guys from my cabin and I — we were going to a soccer game and got lost. Naturally, it was raining. The driver had me call our coach for directions. I had to use one of those old phone booth things 'cause our cell phones weren't getting reception. I have nightmares about those stupid things now. I swear, I dream that they're following me," he laughed, and a few of us snickered at his impression of a scary phone booth. "I guess the lightning went through the phone line or something. I don't really remember it. I blacked out."

"Me, too," Melaine said.

"Me, three," I added.

"Wow, this is pretty freaky," Niki said. "This coincidence has got to mean something."

"It does," Alex said. "And it's not a coincidence. Are you ready for my observations?"

We nodded.

"Not everyone here was hit by lightning, but we all witnessed it. It's like we were all part of something, um, for lack of a better word, *magical*, or something."

"That's true," I said.

"OK, so maybe that's how we were chosen for this camp?" Benji asked.

"Maybe," I said.

"But what does it mean?" Hazel asked. "So what if we were hit by lightning? Why does that make us special, other than making us part of the elite few to have experienced the horror of it?" Hazel clearly felt the same way about the experience as I did.

"Not everyone survives it," Alex said.

"I know," Melaine said, looking to the ground. Her expression made me wonder if she secretly had wanted to die by the lightning strike. I suspected she was thinking of her mother and my heart silently broke for her.

"Actually, not many survive at all. It's practically a miracle that you all did. That has got to have something to do with it."

"Something made you all survive the impact," Benji said. "And by us being there, we got sucked into it."

"I don't have super powers or anything, Benji, if that's what you're getting at," Hazel informed him. I laughed quietly, wondering if she'd tested that theory in private.

"I know," he smiled, indicating he was thinking the same thing.

"Maybe it's all a dream," Thomas suggested.

"It's not a dream, Thomas," Hazel said.

"How do you know?"

"How do you know? If it's a dream, whose dream is it?"

she said, thinking she had outsmarted him.

"It's mine! It's my dream! I call it! You guys are all figments of my imagination!" Cyrus teased.

"I doubt it's a dream, Thomas," I said. "This all feels pretty real to me."

"Yeah, let's be realistic here," Cal added. "This is as real as it gets."

"So what does it all mean?" Niki asked.

We all looked to each other for answers.

"Beats me," someone's quiet voice answered.

"Hazel," I said. "Tell us more about last year."

Hazel liked that request. She liked being the center of attention. She still wasn't nice to me, but she definitely wasn't as rude anymore. Somehow, she had warmed up to me a little.

According to her, Cecilia Chung let them do whatever they wanted all summer. They thought Camp Milestone was just a regular summer camp. Some factors they definitely found odd, but they never thought much of it. They certainly never discovered the lightning factor, especially because Melaine and the others weren't at camp with them. Hazel and her cabin mates saw no indication that Camp Milestone held a secret until the other campers started ignoring them.

In the last week of camp, Hazel and the others were sent home a week early and the other campers were told to stay. This action was what got them all thinking they had missed out on something. Confused and irritated, Hazel became convinced the other campers had somehow discovered a secret that allowed them to stay.

"Think about it," she explained. "The brochure we got this year said Camp Milestone has three grades. You guys are in grade one, we are in grade two. And the rest must be somewhere, right?"

"It makes sense," Melaine said.

"So the question is, where are they?"

No one knew the answer, but we decided it would be our next mission to find out. We would have to find where the others were hiding.

By the time the sun rose, we had learned a lot but didn't feel much wiser. We came from different parts of North America. We had different family lives, different school stories, different hobbies and passions. None of us had received any letters from our families or friends. A few of us had been hit by lightning and the rest of us had witnessed the event. The same few had a weird rash as a remnant of the experience. Mine was by far the biggest one and it freaking glowed for some strange reason.

As we got up to face the day ahead, we divided ourselves into small teams and decided to spend every spare, unsupervised minute exploring the campgrounds, starting with the forest, the library and the cabins. Every inch would have to be combed over. Benji even suggested we follow Galiana at night to see if she would lead us anywhere interesting. It was a scary thought, but we knew it had to be done. We now understood we had been among the lucky few to have survived a lightning strike and we had to find out why. Camp Milestone finally started to make sense.

"Now we're getting somewhere," I said, as a few of us gave each other high fives.

25
Chapter

*D*ear Diane,

This must be my twentieth letter to you. Since nobody else has received any letters either, I'm concluding something's wrong with the mail system here, which doesn't surprise me one bit. But let me tell you, it's hard not to think you're ignoring me. I hope you're not. Are you?

How is everything back home? Who are you hanging out with? What are you doing? Are you working? Have you talked to my parents? What are they doing? I miss you. I miss my parents. But things are finally looking up here. I am making some good friends. My roommate is as sweet as pie. Everyone trusts each other a little more, and sometimes, it feels as though we have known each other forever. They're all so different from the people I'm used to. I really like it. Hazel is starting to warm up to me, thank God. You know how I hate confrontation. And she's the queen of confrontation, it seems. Melaine makes me laugh. She has this witty sense of humor that's only starting to come out. She has come up with some clever nicknames for Galiana. My favorite is The Big G. Get it? Last week we had a sleepover in my cabin. Then again,

I guess you can't call it a sleepover if nobody sleeps, huh? Benji has these caramel-covered coffee beans that are to die for. He makes them himself. Can you believe it? He makes a ton of stuff, actually. But if you eat enough of them, you don't feel the urge to sleep. So we stayed up all night talking. It was really fun. But this camp is bittersweet. I'm either miserable or I'm having a blast. Nothing in between. Mostly, I'm miserable when Galiana is ordering us around.

In case you were wondering, the ghost in Hazel's cabin still roams around at night. We go into their cabin regularly to check if the ghost is there. I'm pretty scared of it. Benji puts on a brave face and protects me, but I can tell he gets scared, too. I always tease him about it. Needless to say, Hazel and her cabin mates (Cyrus, Thomas, Asher, Sterne, Cary, and Alex) all still sleep in our cabin. I wouldn't want to sleep with a ghost either. Galiana hasn't found out about that. We make sure to be outside every morning before she meets us. Otherwise, I think she'd punish us until next summer. She wants to know <u>everything</u> about <u>everyone</u> all the time. She doesn't like secrets. To me, that is so hypocritical of her, but whatever. I don't pretend to understand her.

Ever since the sleepover, Benji and I have started sneaking out at night to explore. Despite all of our sneaking around, we haven't found anything useful. The forest is really dark and scary at night, and even though some of us were smart enough to bring flashlights to camp, we still can't see much. I chicken out every time. Plus, the forest seems never-ending, and half the time, I wonder what we're actually looking for in there. I guess we'll know when we see it. Oh, and there's the library, filled to the brim with kids' books. We've practically read each one of them, trying to see if we can find any clues, inscriptions, anything. Cinderella, Snow White, Rapunzel, you name it, it's there. It's crazy how many books are in that tiny space, Diane.

The days are getting more bearable. Our challenges are getting tougher (try treading water for eight hours in a swampy lake with a beaver inhabitant), but we are getting better at them. Galiana still has no mercy. To her, we are pathetic, useless and sad. She was never this weak. She always did the right thing. That's why she's the leader. If she were a real leader, she'd stop talking so much and do something productive. And if she were a real leader, we'd look up to her and respect her. Which we don't. We actually sort of hate her.

Because of her, Melaine has become our new maid, the poor girl. Niki is tired of sleeping (I know, oxymoron). But it's crazy how much that girl is forced to sleep. Most times, she just can't sleep anymore, so she pretends. I had to teach her to snore in a way that sounds authentic. Hazel has probably eaten a whole apple orchard by now. Benji has become quite the tree climber. He's really athletic. But he tried to cheat once and Galiana doubled his punishment. She wasn't around, so Benji just got to the top of the tree and started throwing the pinecones to the ground (instead of climbing back down and putting them in the basket a dozen at a time). Galiana was furious. I don't know how she finds out about these things. It feels like someone is watching us, like she has a sidekick or something. Maybe it's Cecilia Chung or maybe it's — Hey! Do you think it's that man with the piercing blue eyes I told you about in my seventh letter? I saw him lurking in the woods on the first day. It totally could be him, right?

Cal still hasn't gotten a punishment. The poor guy tries so hard to take the blame for things. He even purposely loses activities, but nothing works. Galiana loves him. Oh, and the boys in the other cabin have carried Hazel around everywhere by now. She's much taller than they are, so it's a tough task. They take it in stride, though. We outnumber Galiana but we're deathly scared of her. I can't explain it, I know it sounds asinine, but it's the truth. It's as though we don't want to know what she's capable of.

And finally there's me. I've broken difficult news to all of the campers. I've snooped in everyone's suitcases (don't worry, I warned all of them I was ordered to do it). I've interviewed, interrogated, and tested them. I'm not sure if I told you about the tests. I had to figure out who's the smartest, who's the fastest, who's the best at math, etc. I don't know why Galiana makes me do her dirty work. But just in case you're curious, Alex is the "smartest," Benji is the "quickest," Melaine is the most "meticulous," and Cyrus? Well, he failed at everything miserably.

Oh, I almost forgot! One time, Galiana let me supervise Melaine while she was cleaning. So naturally, I helped her (who wouldn't?) and when Galiana found out (no really, how does she find this out? She's always in two places at once!), I was given solitary confinement. I guess that's the worst punishment I've gotten so far. But it's not the typical solitary confinement you hear about in the movies (no dark hole and starvation, or anything). I was allowed to roam free; I was just ordered not to talk to anybody or be within a 50-yard radius of anyone for the entire day. I canoed in the teeny tiny lake by myself (really, this lake is pathetic) and nearly died of boredom. But after talking to Benji that night, we realized it's a great chance for me to investigate the forest and the camp in broad daylight. So in the latest plan, I'm supposed to sabotage an activity somehow so I can have another day of solitary confinement without "The Big G" breathing down my neck.

I have this theory that The Big G wants to alienate me from everyone. Am I being naïve? It must be pretty obvious to you. I can just hear you now: "Gee, Faye, she treats you differently than all of the others, she makes you feel like you're too fragile for physical labor, she always seeks your opinion and tries to make you look bad in front of the others, she's trying to turn the others against you, and to top it all off, she makes you miss quality time with them by punishing you to solitary confinement."

Diane, why couldn't you be here to help me? I know something is going on here, but I just can't seem to put my finger on it. I don't even know how the lightning thing factors into the whole picture. I need your opinion. Do you think that blue-eyed man has anything to do with all of this? I haven't told anyone about him because part of me thinks he's a figment of my imagination. I can't tell what's real and what's not anymore! What have I become?

OK, I'd better run. But before I go, I'm gonna write you our "camp song." Please tell me, does this mean anything to you? I miss you.

Hugs,
Faye

It all begins with what,
What holds us all together,
It all will end with Leah,
It doesn't get much better,

What's between is ours to find,
We'll do no good to worry,
Take time to find our way,
What's done and Leah's in no hurry."

26
Chapter

A few days later, Hazel, Melaine, and I were sitting in the dining hall facing Galiana and her horse teeth. She had ordered a meeting with us and she was all smiles, as usual. *Ugh, sickening.* The purpose of the meeting was to "gain some insight into Hazel's and Melaine's lives." We weren't sure what that meant or why. I was told to attend the meeting and take notes. Again, I had no idea why I had to take notes when Galiana scribbled frantically on her notepad 24-7. If you're wondering why we didn't stand up to her more often, we really had no recourse. It's insanely difficult to argue with a person who is clearly crazy and irrational. Plus, as you'll soon see, we finally stood up to her — and the consequences proved more devastating than we could have anticipated.

The meeting started off immediately on the wrong foot. In one swift move, Galiana ordered Melaine and Hazel to talk about themselves; naturally, both were hesitant and reluctant. They gave a brief synopsis of their lives as we all exchanged glares. Galiana pushed further. She was up to something, I could tell.

"So both of your mothers have died," she said coolly with that fake ever-lasting smile on her face. "When did that happen?"

Melaine made eye contact with me. *I can't believe she's asking this*, I thought.

"Almost two years ago," she replied reluctantly.

"I see, OK, uh-huh," said Galiana as she scribbled on her paper. *Scribble, scribble.*

Hazel had an uncompromising look on her face. She did not look pleased and she narrowed her eyes in on Galiana. I was afraid to breathe.

"And how did they die?" Galiana asked. *Holy crap*, I thought, shocked at her aloofness.

"Pardon?" Melaine asked politely. Her voice cracked and I looked off into the distance, upset at my traitorous heart thumping rather loudly against my chest.

"How did they die?" Galiana repeated, clearly abusing her authority. She was on a power trip. I opened my mouth to say something but the words stuck in my throat. I hated myself for being a coward.

"Well, my mom, um, she got very sick and even though the doctors tried to help her, she only lived for about a year after, after ... "

Melaine fought back the sudden tears. The feelings were still raw and she couldn't talk about her mother without rehashing severe pain. Her voice quivered and she looked down at her hands. Hazel's expression remained the same — stone cold, like a marble statue. I could feel the rage building up inside her. *Scribble, scribble.*

"What does sick mean? Why must you be so vague? What was wrong with her, Mela-*nie*?" Galiana continued to push unsympathetically.

Melaine looked up at her, startled by the tone and by the tears now streaming down her face. *She won't make eye contact with me*, I noticed. I couldn't help but feel out of place. *I shouldn't be here. This is none of my business. This is private. This isn't my place.*

"C-cancer," she choked. *Scribble, scribble.*

"And what happened after that?" Galiana prodded.

"I shouldn't be here," I finally said, getting up from my

seat.

"Don't you dare move!" Galiana barked. I looked to Hazel like a child who needed reassurance; she made a gesture for me to sit back down. I obeyed hesitantly, knowing all too well that I'd overstayed my welcome. Galiana continued. "Melaine, what happened after that?"

"Well, she, she died," Melaine replied with a confused look. *Scribble.*

"I'll need more than that. And your dad, what happened to him? Is he happy now? Has he found someone else? Do they have a family? What's going to happen to you? Are you prepared to have siblings? What if your father ignores you?" She pried.

She completely ignored Melaine's emotional state. I became convinced Galiana officially held the title of the worst person on the planet. Feeling sorry for my friends, I sighed heavily and held back my own tears. I couldn't imagine losing my mom, let alone having some lunatic woman make me relive it in such a callous manner.

"Why is this any of your business?" Hazel snapped.

"Excuse me?" Galiana said with an attitude.

"This isn't any of your business," Hazel said again. "You owe us an apology."

"An apology? Gha-ha!" There was that throaty laugh again. I made a face. God, I hated that laugh. It sent shivers through my body.

"On the contrary, Hazel, it is my business. More than you know," Galiana said.

"I don't care," Hazel answered. "You've never told us anything that we want to know, so why should we tell you? You're crazy! And now you owe all of us an apology. You are rude and inconsiderate. Maybe if you had asked nicely, you'd have gotten what you want. But it's too late now. Apologize."

I couldn't believe what I was hearing. *This girl rocks sometimes!* Meanwhile, Galiana was livid; nobody had challenged her like this before.

"Faye, hold this!" she snapped, giving me her notepad.

"No," I said firmly, inspired by Hazel's bravery, who smiled briefly at me. Galiana didn't seem affected by my response. She shoved the notepad in my clammy hands anyway as she continued to stare Hazel down.

"Why you immature little —"

"Apologize!" Hazel interrupted. Melaine and I locked eyes; we had become spectators in this feud.

"*I* am the leader here, Hazel, not you. *I* will not apologize. You have to respect me. *I* am the lead —"

"I don't care what you are!" Hazel screamed. "You owe us an apology and until you say you're sorry, you're not getting anything from us!"

Hazel was getting more and more fired up. She breathed loudly while Galiana stayed silent. Her dark and unforgiving eyes remained focused on Hazel.

"Leave," she finally said.

"What?" Melaine, Hazel and I asked in chorus.

"You don't belong here, Hazel. Leave this camp, now. Pack your things and get out. The bus will take you to the airport. Get out."

"Wait a minute," I pleaded. "This is getting out of hand …"

Galiana turned her glare to me. My silent stare back at her acted like a trigger.

"Who told you to hold that?" she snapped at me, referring to her notepad. *What? You did, you psychopath!*

"Are you feeling, OK?" Hazel said with a scowl. "You just told her to hold it a minute ago."

Galiana snatched her notebook from my hands and gave Hazel a dirty look.

"I'm not talking to you," she said to Hazel. Then, with danger lurking in her smooth voice, "Get out."

"Not until you apologize," Hazel said, unwilling to back down.

Galiana looked at us. Hazel was frowning, Melaine was crying a fresh set of tears and I'm certain I was looking like a deer caught in headlights.

"I'm sorry," Galiana mumbled without emotion. "Now leave." With that, she got up and left.

We all stood still, watching her stomp out of the hall. Hazel waited until the door of the dining hall closed behind Galiana before her hard exterior crumbled like an avalanche and she burst into tears herself.

"What ... the hell ... was that?" Melaine gasped between sobs.

Bewildered, I placed myself between the two girls and put my arms around them. I let them cry for a while and tried to make them feel better. I told them it was horrible and wonderful at the same time. Horrible because of what the Big G had done and horrible because Hazel had to leave, but wonderful because Hazel finally said something to that horrible woman. Wonderful because Hazel stood up for herself and didn't let the Big G stomp all over her for a change. Wonderful because Hazel made the Big G apologize.

"How do you like them apples?" she joked, through sniffles and tears.

"What about her asking me about the notepad? That was a new low, even for the G-factor," I said, trying to make them laugh. They both giggled and blew their noses.

"G-factor," Melaine repeated. "Good one."

"G-Almighty," Hazel added. We giggled again and I tightened my hold on them.

"I'm so sorry I stayed. I shouldn't have stayed here. This was private information," I said.

"It's OK," Melaine said. "It's not your fault. Just please don't tell anybody what went on here today."

"I would never," I promised.

I stayed with the girls until they were ready to go back outside. Hazel packed her bags soon after. What would we do without Hazel? She was a part of us. The thought of losing one of our friends just because she'd been brave enough to stand up to Galiana was beyond infuriating. All this time, we had been too scared to discover what Galiana was capable of and now we finally knew. The consequences of disobedience were far worse than we could have imagined. Eating apples, cleaning floors, and climbing trees had nothing on this. Galiana had hit us right between the eyes; she knew exactly what to do to keep us living in fear for the rest of the summer.

~

A few hours later, we all sat glumly in the camp's gravel driveway, waiting for the school bus to pick Hazel up. What would we do without our Hazel? We were all a big family now. We couldn't function without each other.

"This sucks," Sterne said as he sat down on Hazel's suitcase.

"Big time," Cyrus added, not in his usual comical mood.

"You guys better write and tell me everything," Hazel demanded. She leaned on Melaine's shoulder and tilted her head.

"Hazel, you're in this for life," I told her. "There are no secrets among us. You can still help us from home." We smiled pathetically at each other, knowing it was a load of crap.

"I'm proud of you, Hazel," Benji said, as he patted her on the shoulder. "You showed some real gumption today."

"Gumption?" I said teasingly.

"What? It's a word," he defended.

"Sure, if you're 40."

He gave me a playful punch in the arm and we adjusted ourselves closer to each other.

A few hours later, as the sun moved across the sky, we were still moping around.

"This is torture," Hazel said. "If I'm gonna go, I want to go already. You guys should go do something. Don't just sit here with me."

"We're not moving," Melaine said stubbornly.

"That's right," I agreed, as I tried to make myself more comfortable on the hard gravel.

Even later, Galiana pranced toward us, bright as sunshine, with a confused look on her face.

"What are you all doing here? Dinner's ready."

"Um, aren't I supposed to be leaving?" Hazel asked.

"Oh! Gha-ha-ha! You didn't think I was serious did you? Go on, dinner's ready."

"You mean she doesn't have to leave?" Cyrus wanted to know. Naturally, none of us trusted her.

"No, like I said, go eat your dinner."

Instinctively, the girls hugged while the boys sighed in relief and gave high fives to each other. The bus never came and Hazel — by the grace of someone — was allowed to stay at Camp Milestone. We were so happy, no one questioned Galiana's change of heart. We didn't care about her motives this time; this decision suited us just fine. We were so happy, we barely noticed that our sticky reheated macaroni was cold. I was sure Hazel was prepared to eat nothing but apples for the rest of the summer just so she could stay at Camp Milestone with us.

The day of the meeting with Galiana was crucial to our bond. We discovered someone was watching out for us, whether that person was someone anonymous or Galiana remained to be seen. It was also the day we realized how close we'd grown. We knew we would do just about anything to stay together, knowing we were bound for life. And finally, it was the day we realized we weren't ready to leave Camp Milestone. Rather, we badly wanted to see the summer through.

27
Chapter

Dear Diane,

Although she won't complain about much anymore, I can tell Hazel feels sick just hearing the word "apple." Melaine has turned the camp into a germ-free, spotless environment. Benji's hands have permanent calluses from climbing and Niki is tired of sleeping. Cal still lies to Galiana on a daily basis and the rest of the boys have gotten several nonthreatening injuries from having to carry Hazel everywhere.

I don't think the Big G likes me anymore. She hasn't spoken to me since the incident with Hazel. This is so much better than the alternative. I'd rather have her ignore me than be her sidekick. She's truly evil. Just one of those miserable human beings who loves to bring others down.

It's getting hotter each day. It would be nice if we could cool off in a real lake, but our lake is too small and nasty. We only immerse ourselves in it if we have to (read: if the G-factor makes us).

We're still exploring the never-ending forest, but with no luck. Shoot — sorry Diane, I have to go now. Our next event is starting in a few minutes. It's supposed to be a history quiz.

Snort.

   Write back soon, OK? Just kidding. Write back period!
Where are you?

   Hugs,

   Faye

28

Chapter

It was déjà vu. I was back at school and the scene felt oddly familiar. I looked down. I was wearing a grey T-shirt, frayed jeans, and my favorite Converse shoes. I had worn this outfit before. The last school bell rang and a sea of students streamed into the halls, passing me by as if I barely existed.

"What day is it?" I asked one of the blank faces.

"It's the last day of school," it replied before it disappeared.

I floated outside and caught the view I'd witnessed before. There they were. Diane and Benji. Benji and Diane. He was stroking her hair again. I felt a sharp pain in my heart, the same one I'd felt the first time. I walked up to Benji and Diane, aware I didn't actually want to.

"I'm going home," I said.

I willed myself to play it differently this time. I had been given a second chance. Somehow, I should make things right. Only, Diane looked a little odd to me. Her hair was a different color and her face was turned away. I needed for her to look at me, I needed for her to interact with me. Slowly, I lifted my hand and placed it on her shoulder. She turned around and faced me, exposing her true identity.

"Galiana," I said. Her hard, black eyes immediately caught mine. Even in my dreams she was a shrew.

"Hello, Faye," she jeered, barely enunciating through her gargantuan teeth.

"What are you doing here?"

"You're going to be late," she said, ignoring my question.

"Late for what?"

"The lightning storm," she said. It was then I noticed Benji missing. How did he get away?

This version of my life was disturbing. Would I have to find Benji and save him from the lightning bolt this time? A raindrop hit my forehead and I blinked as I looked up to the sky. Dark clouds swirled above me. Was it so windy the first time?

I started running. I knew where I had to go. I could feel my wet shoes squishing in the grass beneath me, yet the rest of me remained dry. It was as though the raindrops bounced off of me. I wanted to run faster, but the more I wanted it, the slower I moved. I panted as I struggled to move toward my target.

Suddenly, as if a curtain had been pulled away from in front of me, it appeared — the big tree in the middle of the open field. Beside it, a broken branch lay lifeless on the ground. I looked up at the sky once more. In the distance, a bolt of lightning emerged from the clouds, illuminating my surroundings for a second. I spotted the human figure by the tree and made my way toward it.

"Benji?" I asked, knowing it wasn't him.

The figure became more defined as I approached. I struggled to get close as the wind blew me in the opposite direction. The rumble overhead overwhelmed my thoughts.

"Benji?" I asked again.

"No, it's me," a voice answered. Like a blurry vision coming into focus, the image of Cecilia Chung came to life. She looked younger than I remembered, but it was undoubtedly her.

"What are you doing here?"

Miss Chung didn't answer me. I shuddered at the thunderous sound of two clouds colliding. Despite the rainfall, Cecilia Chung and I stayed dry. I reached out for her, trying to protect her from her impending fate; I knew the lightning bolt was imminent.

"Be careful," I instructed her.

"I'm fine," she replied, monotone.

"What are you doing here?" I asked.

Miss Chung looked over at the ground. She gave me a meaningful look, ushering her glance toward the shovel I had come to know all too well. *No,* I thought. I opened my mouth to object but nothing came out. The moment, I knew, was only seconds away.

In slow motion, Miss Chung walked over to the shovel. As she bent down, she looked up at me and said something I knew I would need to remember. Only, instead of committing it to memory, I became focused on her actions. *Don't do it,* I thought. I yearned to verbalize my protests, but I had become paralyzed and mute. Miss Chung repeated the vital sentence and reached over to pick up the shovel.

"No!" I yelped softly, waking up abruptly from my nightmare.

I sat up, looked around and took a moment to reorient myself. I was back in my room and Niki was snoring profusely, undisturbed by my vivid dream. I swallowed hard and tried to calm my panting chest. My heart was pounding so hard, I wondered if it was knocking to get out of my ribcage. Relieved but still shaken up, I sank back down, resting my head on my pillow. *What a strange dream.* I closed my eyes and took a deep breath.

Then, without effort, the sentence that Cecilia Chung had told me materialized in my thoughts.

"Believe in love, believe in loveliness, believe in belief my child," I said aloud.

29
Chapter

It was almost a month before anything exciting would happen at Camp Milestone again. Benji awoke me from another vibrant dream in the middle of the night. It was one of those dreams where I don't remember the content, just that it was deep and I was hard to awaken.

"What? What?" I jolted as Benji whispered my name for the sixth time.

"Shhhhh, don't wake the others."

His face was close to mine but I didn't dare make eye contact. We had grown closer over the past month. Always flirting, but never admitting to anything. I, the eternal chicken, was still afraid he longed for Diane. Some days I thought with certainty I stood a chance with him, but on other days, I was convinced he saw me as no more than a friend.

"Where are we going?" I asked in a low voice, as I jumped over the six bodies sleeping in our living room and stepped outside. It was dark and humid outdoors, and I fixed my hair discretely.

"You'll see," he replied mysteriously. Outside, he led me to the lake. We got in one of the old canoes and he paddled us to the other side of the lake in no more than three minutes.

"Get out," he said, as he tied the canoe to a tree. I could barely see anything. It was pitch black outside.

"What time is it?" I wondered.

"Time to get a watch," he joked.

"Benji!" I hissed. "Come on!" I knew he was smiling but he didn't answer me, intent on staying mum.

We began hiking into the woods. Normally, I was petrified of the woods after dark. But that night, his confidence soothed me. It was obvious he knew where he was heading, that he had been there before. I trusted him. *Sorta. Whimper.*

He continued to lead the way and we walked for miles. My shoes were wet and I was tired, but I didn't care. To me, all of this was a dream come true. A few months ago, I would have died at the opportunity to spend a night alone with Benjamin Parker.

"Where are you taking me? And how did you find this place?" I asked.

We were making lots of turns, leaving me completely disoriented.

"Stop asking so many questions, nosy girl. We're almost there."

Knowing how to shut me up, he took my hand and started walking faster. I tried hard not to look as ecstatic as I felt. *He's holding my hand*, I told myself. I pinched myself to make sure I wasn't dreaming. Not wanting to ruin the moment, I stayed quiet for as long as I could.

"So I'm not allowed to talk at all?" I finally asked.

"No."

I pouted. I grew impatient. This hike was the longest I had gone without talking. Probably ever. It didn't take long for me to try again.

"What's your favorite food?" He looked at me in astonishment.

"You really can't do it, can you?"

"Come on," I pleaded. "I really want to know."

He was bad at saying no to me. It was something I had noticed.

154

"Sandwiches," he said.

"What kind of sandwi— Ahhhh! Omigod, oh my God! That was the biggest freaking spider I've ever seen in my life! Did you see it? Ew, ew!"

I jumped around, swatting at my arms and legs frantically.

"What are you doing?" he chuckled.

"Ew! Ew! Is it on me? I feel like it's on me." I was swatting at my back now, convinced I could feel its legs digging into my skin. Benji sighed and looked at my back; I knew he was humoring me.

"No, it's not on you. Relax, it's just a spider."

"It was not just a spider, Benji. You didn't *see* it! Yuck!" I protested. "That thing was bigger than my shoe! It looked like a small mammal!"

Benji rolled his eyes, took my hand and began dragging me again. Every few seconds or so, I'd shudder from head to toe and yelp out a random remark like "Ew!" or "Gross!" But he did not deter from his mission.

"Turkey," he said a few moments later, after I'd finally fallen silent. "I like turkey sandwiches with bacon and tomato. Maybe even some onions."

"Blech! You like onions?"

"You don't?"

"No way. Onions are gross."

"Not to me," he said matter-of-factly. "So what's your favorite food then, onion-hater?"

"Chicken Fettuccini Alfredo with broccoli," I said.

"Whoa."

"What?"

"Nothing. That's just very precise," he noted.

"What's wrong with being precise? Precise is good. Not being precise is stupid."

What the hell was I saying? Sometimes I wondered why Benji hung out with me at all. I had this awful habit of putting him down for no good reason. Case in point: I actually don't mind onions. And I have no clue if precision is a good thing or not. I just said these things sometimes just for the sake of saying them, I guess. It was insanely irritating and I held back the urge to hit myself.

Grunting quietly, I forced myself to stop being a dork and tried to find a compliment to give him. Have you ever tried to compliment someone you secretly love? It's harder than it sounds. It's hard because you're trying not to sound like you're in love. You're trying to sound matter of fact about it, like you're confident enough to compliment him on a superficial level. Like you have nothing to hide. Only, I had something to hide and I'd been hiding it for years. *C'mon*, I thought, nudging myself. *Just say something nice.*

"Benji," I started.

"We're almost there, Faye, hang on just a few more seconds."

"Benji," I repeated. He kept dragging me, his pace accelerating. "You're really a great per —"

Just then, the trees ended and we exited the forest. I looked around, widening my eyes in an attempt to see better.

"We're here," he said. I continued to stare around me. It was still pitch black and I could barely see anything at all. I looked up at the sky, only to notice the moon wasn't out that night. All I could tell was that I wasn't surrounded by trees anymore and I was standing on soft grass.

"Where?" I asked him. "Where are we? I can't see anything."

"The sun will come up soon," he said. He walked ahead a bit farther. I could hear the sound of water next to us and shifted my gaze in its direction. Nothing. It was still pitch black.

"Let's sit by this tree until the sun comes up. Then you'll see what I'm talking about."

"OK."

Sitting down sounded marvelous. I followed his lead as we sat down on the damp ground and leaned against the large tree. I was exhausted. My bones hurt from the speed hiking we'd just done. Plus, I wasn't getting much sleep lately at camp. We were always exploring, staying up late, comparing notes, talking about Galiana, having fun.

"Relax," Benji said. "I'll wake you up if you fall asleep."

I looked at him and smiled sheepishly. *I'll just close my eyes for a minute*, I thought, knowing all too well I was already half-asleep. Benji woke me up after what seemed like a minute.

"Faye, open your eyes. Look, look!"

"Two more minutes, please," I begged him. I had somehow managed to stretch out on the ground, using his legs as a pillow. Two minutes later, he spoke again.

"The sun's rising, Faye. I really don't want you to miss this."

I opened my eyes slowly and straightened up. A beam of sunlight shone into my tired eyes. I blinked a few times and took in my surroundings. Benji was leaning against the biggest willow tree I had ever seen. It was majestic and graceful. Its dangling leaves shielded us from the outside world, encircling us in a small cocoon. The most stunning landscape imaginable was around us. I rubbed my eyes and let my senses experience the moment.

Acres of perfect grass and rolling mountains surrounded the tree. The grass was a light green that offset the dark forest green in the background. The mountains continued on into the horizon, where the golden sun peeked out from between them, warming our skin. It was phenomenal.

In front of us was a massive, crystal-clear lake with a long dock. The lake was so large, the other side was barely visible. It seemed like an ocean but more peaceful, more tranquil. The sun's rays reflected off of the water like in a painting. I breathed in, enjoying the scent of the dewy grass and flowers intertwined with that distinct clean-lake smell. I closed my eyes and let the sun hit my face, smiling at the warmth. I could hear birds chirping in the distance, waking up the world.

"Oh, wow," I managed to croak, as I opened my eyes again. "It's bee-yoo-ti-ful."

Benji smiled proudly.

"Look at how big the lake is. Look at this area behind us. Look at this tree, Faye. Isn't this tree awesome?"

I was in awe. It really was awesome. I sat up and walked out onto the dock. I was in such a blissful daze, I didn't notice my pants were wet from the dew. I realized it eventually when I heard Benji snicker and follow behind me.

The lake was still. It was as if you couldn't speak loudly, as if you would disturb it. Out in the middle of the water, in the distance, was a small island with tall trees lining the perimeter. I squinted to get a better look; I could see something moving on the island.

"Hey, what is that?" I asked, pointing toward the moving object.

"That's actually what I wanted to show you. Shhh, listen," he said.

I listened closely. At first, I couldn't hear anything other than bugs buzzing in the morning sun. Soon, my ears zoned in and I frowned at the sound of voices.

"There are people on that island," I said.

"Yes."

He was waiting for me to catch on. I looked at him as I listened further. *What were they saying*, I wondered? The voices were a little louder now and I could hear a rhythmic melody. It sounded a lot like a chant. I couldn't make out the words, but I could discern some laughing, and yes, definitely a repetitive chant. *If only I could make out the words*, I thought, concentrating hard.

And then it dawned on me.

"Oh my God, Benji, it's ..."

Benji, grinning from ear to ear, sang along with the chant.

"We'll do no good to worry. Take time to find our way. What's done and Leah's in no hurry," he said, excited I was catching on.

"It's, it's the rest of Camp Milestone!" I shrieked. "I can't believe it! It must be grades two and three, right? They're singing our song, right? Hazel was right! They've been here!

They've been here all along! Oh my God, this is amazing!"

I jumped up and down in excitement and gave Benji a big hug. This was huge! Benji let me have my moment of glee and shared in my enthusiasm. As I calmed down, he spoke again.

"So that was the good news. Want to hear the bad news?" I nodded. "The bad news is, we missed our morning meeting with Galiana and the others. We're going to be in a truck load of trouble when we get back."

"Then we're not going back! We're going to that island!" He was pleasantly surprised.

"Faye, we can't swim that far," he said, grinning. In case you were wondering, my heart still skipped a beat every time he said my name. But you already knew that, didn't you?

"Then we'll get our canoe and drag it back here!"

"You can't be serious. Do you know how far we walked?"

"We have all day!"

"We'll starve," he protested.

"We can live without food for a day. And they will have food on the island! Just look at it! It's beautiful!"

Benji obeyed and looked at the island; his eyes then shifted off into the distant horizon.

"OK, let's do it."

I jumped up and down again.

"Wait," I said, realizing something. "What about the others? Shouldn't we tell them, too?"

"It's better if they don't know anything until we get back tonight. That way, they won't be lying when Galiana questions them. We'll wake them up tonight and tell them what we found out."

"OK," I agreed. It made perfect sense. "Let's go get our canoe."

I started walking away but stopped. I turned around, realizing that Benji wasn't following me.

"What's wrong?" I asked.

"We have all day, right, Faye?" he asked, suspiciously.

"Yes, why do you ask?" I eyed him.

"Because that means we have time for THIS!"

He pushed me into the water. Caught completely off guard, I let out a little yelp as I floated through the air and landed into the water back first. When my head emerged, I looked around and realized he had jumped in after me.

"I can't believe you did that!" I said laughing. Like him, I was totally without inhibition. The water was warm and cool at the same time. It was refreshing but also hugged me closely.

"Sorry," Benji said. "I couldn't resist."

I splashed him. He flinched and splashed me back. Soon, we were goofing around, dunking each other and playing childish games. It was the kind of perfect I didn't know existed outside of my imagination. We swam and played around for what seemed like a lifetime. To me, time stood still.

A rope hung from a branch of the willow. Benji, who had become an expert climber, taught me how to scale the tree properly so we could swing from the rope and fall into the lake. I was hardly elegant on my first try. I forgot to let go of the rope and ended up hitting the tree trunk and falling onto the ground. Benji couldn't stop laughing; he was holding his stomach and cackling. But in a true supportive fashion, he helped me up the tree again and yelled, "LET GO!" the second time around, ensuring I fell into the water.

"Good job," he said as I surfaced. "You're a quick learner."

"And you're perfect," I said, not believing I had just uttered those words out loud.

I smiled awkwardly and submerged myself in the water, allowing the words to sink in even further.

30
Chapter

Our hike to retrieve the canoe drained me. I figured out how Benji knew his way around the forest so well; little landmarks were spread through the woods. He evidently had paved the way in the past.

On the way back to the lake with the willow tree, I felt faint. Begging him to stop, I sat down on the ground to catch my breath. Determined to make it back to the lake before dark, Benji wasn't willing to rest. Instead, he walked over to me, picked me up in one swift motion and plopped me into the canoe, pulling it and me the rest of the way. I was too flabbergasted (and tired) to object. Once we were back at the willow tree, we decided to nap under the shade. We wanted to wait until dark to canoe over to the island. That way, nobody could see us coming. It was the first time all summer I slept peacefully.

~

Canoeing across the giant lake was brutal but we were

too excited to care. Despite our arms turning numb, all we could do was talk about what we were about to discover. Upon our arrival, we hid the canoe and darted toward the ongoing ruckus.

The island was even more beautiful up close. It was larger than it appeared and it was just the way I had imagined Camp Milestone more than a month ago. Lights and music filled the air. The cabins looked dark, wooden and massive, not like the little matchboxes we had. Nature trails slithered around and led into the darkness. I even saw a twisting swimming pool in the distance. I could hear and smell horses huffing. I wondered what other wildlife would be visible in the daylight. As we sneaked around in the bushes, I saw a fencing area and gasped.

"A fencing area!"

Benji looked surprised.

"You fence?"

"Um, well, no, but that's so cool! Don't you think?"

"Sure, if you say so." He shrugged his shoulders.

"This is exactly how I originally pictured Camp Milestone. It looks like a picture backdrop. Look at everything there is to do," I said.

Benji smiled and nodded in agreement. For a moment, our eyes met. It was long enough for my heart to miss a beat, like it had done several times that day. I realized at that moment, more than ever, how much I wanted for him to like me back. It had consumed me again.

"You look different lately," he said. My face froze and I put my hand up to my cheek.

"I do?"

"Yeah. You've changed."

"I have? How?"

"I dunno. You're just more alive or something."

I had no idea what that meant. That was the second time that word had been used to describe me somehow. Was it a compliment or was he saying I looked dead before? I couldn't decide.

Our attention shifted back to the camp. Music came from a large, wooden hall with big windows. Benji and I peered through the window, eavesdropping on the occasion. Inside the hall were a dozen or so people. Some shot pool, others played music, and the rest ate and watched a movie on a big screen TV. A dinner buffet set up on one side spanned the width of the hall; meatloaf, pasta, drumsticks, salads, fries, hamburgers, fruits, and desserts. You name it, it was there. I could feel my stomach grumbling.

"We're going to eat some of that food somehow," Benji insisted. "I'm dying of hunger." He rubbed his stomach and made a face.

We all heard a voice behind us. We turned around to see two girls heading into the dining hall.

"After dinner, we gotta go to the library, Stacy," one of the girls said.

"Stacy!" Benji yelled. I jumped. Did he know her? Stacy stopped and turned to face us. Benji ran toward her and I followed.

"Stacy, can you please get us some food, we're starving," Benji pleaded.

Stacy eyed Benji carefully, trying to place his face.

"Do I know you?" she asked.

"Well, not exactly," Benji said.

The girls shifted their gaze from Benji to me. They examined me from head to toe and gasped.

"Oh my God, *you*! You're not supposed to be here! How did you get here?" she yelled.

"No, listen, wait!" I pleaded. It was too late. Benji grabbed my hand and yanked me toward him. At the same time, one girl ran, and the other opened the door to the hall and yelled.

"Miss Chung! Miss Chung, over here! You have to come right away."

My eyes grew big. What? Miss Chung was here? *I thought she was fired.*

"Shhh!" Benji hissed at them. "Damn, we're busted."

163

"Miss Chung is here?" I asked amidst all the commotion.

Benji didn't answer. He was thinking more clearly and he knew we had to get out fast. Before I could fight it, he grabbed my hand and we started running.

"Faster, Faye!"

I ran as fast as I could, but I was tired, hungry and weak. We sprinted toward the cabins, ducking quietly beneath the lights. Benji slowed down a few minutes later.

"I think we're OK," he said, panting, "We have to go back to our canoe, Faye. They're looking for us now. Damn."

"And whose fault is that?" I snipped.

"I know, I know. Bad move. I'm just so hungry!"

"You couldn't leave it alone, could you?"

"I'm sorry, I'm sorry."

I knew he was. I just couldn't believe he had ruined our entire day's trek for food. I was just about to console him when we heard more voices. We ducked into the bushes; it was dark and we were well camouflaged. I suppressed the urge to cry out as a thorn pricked my side. The voices continued to get closer until they were directly beside us. Nervous, I stopped breathing. Two people approached, a man and a woman. Their silhouettes took shape in the darkness and the woman laughed.

"Gha-ha-ha!"

Ugh, I'd recognize that fake, evil laugh anywhere, I thought. Judging by the disgusted look on Benji's face, Galiana's laugh bothered him just as much as it did me. He pinched my hand.

"Regardless," the man's voice said, "more than a month has gone by and they are none the wiser. Something has got to change, Galiana. Maybe we should let them meet the others. Maybe we've been going about this the wrong way."

"Chester, no," Galiana snarled. "If they aren't smart enough to realize who they are, that isn't our problem."

"What do you suggest, that we pair them up at the other camp with a bunch of new campers next year? It can't be done."

"They can't be spoon-fed. That's not what Camp Milestone is about and that's not what *I* am about. A good leader doesn't tell people what do to and *I'm* not going to tell them what to do!"

"Yeah, right," Benji snorted under his breath. I rolled my eyes in agreement.

"Sure, sure. You never tell us what to do," I whispered.

Galiana and Chester continued their walk in the woods. Benji and I followed them quietly. We knew we were learning something important and wanted to hear as much as possible.

"I am heading back to my cabin now," Chester said. "Let me sleep on this because I'm not convinced, Galiana. And it worries me that those two are out and about with no supervision. They could be anywhere and I don't want anything to happen to them. How did this happen?"

I stopped Benji in his tracks.

"They're talking about us!"

He nodded. His eyes were wide open, like an owl blinking in the twilight.

"What should we do?" he whispered.

"Maybe we should go back, Benji. I didn't even consider they might be worried about us. Melaine and Niki are probably worried sick by now."

"Well, maybe that's something you should consider the next time you go traipsing around in the forest by yourselves," came a nasty, familiar voice from behind us.

We turned around to meet a bright flashlight shining in our faces. We'd been caught. Disappointed, we stayed quiet, shielding our eyes with our hands.

"Where have you been." It was not a question.

I blinked excessively due to the bright and uncomfortable light. Chester lowered the flashlight Galiana was pointing directly at us.

"Thank God you're all right," he said.

I blinked to regain my vision; I was seeing spots and my eyes couldn't focus. As my eyes readjusted, I looked at Chester's face. He was a young man, with brown hair and piercing blue eyes. My jaw dropped as I recognized them as the same blue eyes I had seen at the airport and then in the forest on the first day of camp. Chester was that man! The stalker!

"You!" I called out, finally realizing who Chester was.

"Hello, Faye," he replied considerately. He wasn't denying our previous encounter.

"You almost got me killed at the airport! I almost got run over!"

"You two know each other?" Benji asked, startled.

His face was transparent. He was confused and disappointed in me for not telling him about Chester. I had lied to him. Heaven only knew what he thought of me. I opened my mouth to explain but Chester spoke first.

"Yes, Benjamin. Faye and I met briefly at the airport," he turned his attention to me. "I'm sorry about that, Faye. Believe me, that was not my intention."

"You, you met her at the airport?" Galiana shrieked. "You've, you've never done that before. Not even for me! And I'm, I'm, UGH! Chester, what is this? What's going on?"

For a minute, everyone was silent. Chester was afraid to look at Galiana and I was afraid to look at Benji. *Please don't be mad at me, please don't be mad at me,* I pleaded.

"How did you get here?" Chester asked.

"I went exploring and found it. Faye had nothing to do with it," Benji said.

I tried not to smile, understanding he was defending me. Galiana and Chester exchanged a meaningful look.

"Do you think?" Galiana asked Chester. Chester shook his head.

"What?" we asked simultaneously.

"You must be starving," Chester said, ignoring our question. "No more questions tonight. We'll have a meeting tomorrow night with the others. You can discuss whatever you want then. Galiana will take you back to your cabin now and she'll give you some food. You've had a long day."

Benji and I obeyed. The promise of food was too tempting to pass up and we were both exhausted. Plus, we already had so much to tell the others.

~

Galiana didn't say a word during the trip back to the camp. She had a motorboat waiting for us at the lake and took us back through a different route to a car.

She dropped us off in the driveway and drove off without even saying goodbye. Benji and I took one look at each other and raced all the way to the cabin, where we knew our friends waited anxiously.

31
Chapter

The reunion with our friends was remarkable. While Hazel scolded us for worrying her, Melaine had been the most worried of all. She heaved a huge sigh of relief when we walked into the cabin.

"We thought you guys had been sent home!"

After the lingering hugs and warm welcome, we sat around the kitchen while Benji and I explained our adventure. Rapt, they listened quietly, grasping on to our every word. We made sure not to leave out any details. We explained everything from the island's appearance to Galiana's facial expressions.

Although Galiana didn't give us the food Chester promised, Cyrus had pocketed some dinner for us. Famished, we didn't actually eat the food; it was more like an inhalation. Within seconds, it disappeared and we craved more.

"So is this Chester guy gonna be at this meeting-thing tomorrow?" Cal asked.

"We're not sure," I answered.

"Do you think we're finally going to find out what's going on?" Cary asked.

"Don't count on it," Hazel said. "You don't think it'll be

that easy, do you?"

"Hey, that was not easy!" Benji protested.

"I agree with Hazel," Melaine said. "I think we're in for another disappointment. But way to go, guys! You did great. I'm so proud of you. Did you have fun?"

We both nodded and exchanged a glance.

"I can't believe Galiana," Niki added. "What a slice."

"A slice?" I asked with a chuckle. I'd never heard that expression. Niki shrugged and giggled.

"She's definitely not the slice I asked for," Melaine said. We all laughed.

We continued talking for hours. The girls wanted more details.

"What I don't understand," Benji said, "is when the Big G said, 'If they don't understand who they are.' "

"Are you sure that's what she said, Benji?" Alex asked.

We weren't sure. It seemed like such a blur and we had started to doubt ourselves. The more we found out about our purpose at Camp Milestone, the more confused we became. We had so many questions. What did the G-factor mean about knowing who we are? Why is the rest of the camp separate from us? Why do we get G-Almighty as our headmistress and they get Cecilia Chung? Moreover, who is Chester? What does he do?

Of course we had theories, but none of them made sense. Cyrus suggested maybe we were aliens from another planet. *Yes, I'm sure that's it. I've always thought planet Earth was primitive.* Alex implied we had superpowers that allowed us to survive lightning strikes. We considered it for half a second before realizing it was ludicrous. Everything was more confusing than ever, but at the same time, it felt as though we were so close.

32
Chapter

Galiana and Cecilia Chung were seated on the stage in the lunch hall when we entered the room. It was a mirror image of our first day of camp. Only this time, there were chairs on the stage and we were different, wiser somehow and a little more confident. As usual, Galiana's face had a smile plastered across it, one we had all come to know well. As each of us walked into the hall and found a seat in the front row, Galiana made a point to belt out an exaggeratedly chipper, "Hi." She had something to prove to Miss Chung. A few minutes after we were seated, Galiana spoke.

"Who here has been to a theme park?" She asked us, making quote gestures with her hands as she said theme park.

We looked at each other and a few of us rolled our eyes. Some campers reluctantly raised their arms. *Oh, brother,* I sighed. *Here we go again.*

"I've been as well," she said, again with quote gestures. "But not as a child. I went with some of my friends recently."

"She has friends?" Benji whispered. I bit my lip and tried to keep a straight face, but Niki let out a giggle.

"You will agree with me that it is a *magical* place, right?" continued Galiana. She stood up and pranced around the stage. "When you go to there, what does everyone tell you?"

Galiana enunciated each one of her syllables. Her gestures were grandiose and her tone was exaggerated. Nobody answered her question. We all stared in silence. The excessive use of the quotations-marks gesture each time she said theme-park or magical made her even more annoying than usual.

"Anybody? Gha-ha-ha! It's so easy. Mel, why don't you give it a shot? Take a guess!"

Mel? Since when was it Mel? What was going on with her?

"I don't know," Melaine replied curtly.

Galiana rolled her eyes and sighed. That was more like her.

"She's had an extra helping of her crazy potion today," whispered Cyrus.

"OK, I'll tell you," Galiana continued. "No matter where you go in in the park, everyone always tells you to '*Have a magical day.*' " She waited for a reaction from the crowd. Nobody budged. "Have a magical day! Isn't that wonderful? And you know what the best part is? The best part is you do have a magical day! It's amazing. I wanted to do everything when *I* was there. *I* wanted to ride the roller coasters, *I* wanted cotton candy, *I* wanted souvenirs, *I* wanted to take pictures and … "

Galiana continued for another hour. The theme park was wonderful. We got it. It was all about her. It made her feel special. It was like home to her. Magical this, Wonderful that. *Sigh.* It was pure freaking torture.

Cecilia Chung finally brought Galiana back from Neverland. Despite the evil glares Galiana shot her way, Miss Chung decided to stop the painfully boring monologue and get to more pressing matters.

"Before I say anything of actual importance," she said as she shot a glance toward Galiana, "do any of you have any questions?"

All arms shot in the air at once. Miss Chung didn't seem surprised.

"OK," she said with a brisk smile, "let me explain a few things first and then we'll answer all your questions."

She took a deep breath. I could feel my heart in my throat.

Am I breathing as loudly as I think I am? I could hear Thomas blowing his nose but I didn't dare look his way. My attention was focused on the stage. Miss Chung spoke again.

"You're not going to find out any secrets today," she started. We all groaned. "Galiana and I are not going to reveal anything to you. I'll explain why. As I've mentioned before, and as you know, Camp Milestone is a special camp. You have been chosen to attend. You will not find out today how or why you have been chosen. Most of the campers in grade two don't even know this information yet. You still have a lot you need to learn about Camp Milestone and about yourselves. Our philosophy at Milestone — and we pride ourselves on this — is we do not want to reveal anything to you. We encourage you to find out on your own. We believe you need to find out many things by yourselves. And if we told you everything before you were ready, it would be difficult for you to understand. We don't want to cause you any pain or confusion. We want what's best for you. We all want that." Miss Chung shot another glare in Galiana's path. "So you have to trust us when we say we are here to help you and lead you in the right direction, although we are limited in what we can do. You are all bright young people, and I have no doubt you will find out everything when the time is right." She took a deep breath. "I have one more thing to add. I was glad to learn you have become such close friends. It's up to you to maintain this relationship in the future."

She paused and examined our reactions.

"Now, after hearing my thoughts, are there any remaining questions?" she asked us again, this time more quietly.

Hazel raised her hand first. Miss Chung motioned for her to go ahead.

"Miss Chung, how come all the campers aren't

together?"

Miss Chung cleared her throat.

"When Camp Milestone was founded, it was decided it would be most appropriate to separate the newcomers from the others. That way, you would be inclined to take your time and proceed at your own pace."

Miss Chung turned out to be a good politician. Her answers were mysterious and broad, yet she provided enough information so no one questioned her further.

Cary asked the next question shyly.

"Who is Chester and where is he?"

"That's a very good question, Cary," she replied.

She seemed as proud of him for speaking in public as I was. I caught Benji's eye just as I gave Cary a thumbs-up sign for being brave enough to speak up in public.

"Chester is the owner of Camp Milestone. He apologizes he could not attend our meeting today, but he had urgent matters to attend to."

I gasped. Him, he was the owner? But he looked like an airport employee! How could he be the owner? What was the camp owner doing at the airport talking to *me*? Galiana's prior reaction now seemed a little more justified.

"Miss Chung," Melaine asked, "are we not who we think we are?"

Miss Chung took a moment before she tackled that question.

"That's a difficult question to answer, my dear. I'll try to answer it as best as I can. Deep down, you know who you are. But you may not have learned everything about yourself yet. That is natural. All of you are still young," Miss Chung paused. "I don't want you to worry so much. Some things you can't control. It is your destiny. All of you have a destiny. But don't underestimate your power, either. Although you have a destiny, you are still your own person. You can make many choices."

My head was spinning. I felt even more lost than on the first day of camp. Sometimes, Miss Chung seemed to be speaking a different language. Frustrated, I raised my hand.

"Miss Chung, how do you know this secret? How do you, Galiana and Chester know? How do all of you know something about us that we don't know?"

This question stumped her.

"I'm sorry, Faye, I cannot tell you much on that topic without giving it all away. Just keep in mind, history repeats itself. And like I said, you all have a destiny. We, at Camp Milestone, know part of your destiny because we have seen it with others before. We also know what to expect because we have a source, a source that tells us of things that have happened in the past and guides us to understand matters better. Yes, Benji?"

"You said we have to find out on our own. Well, Faye and I tried to do that, but we were sent back here."

"That's true," said Miss Chung, remorseful. "You have to find out on your own, but you cannot leave the campgrounds. That is unsafe and we do not want you wandering around in some foreign woods without an adult. So please do not go wandering off by yourselves anymore. All the answers you need are here within the campground, I promise you. Believe in it. Believe in belief."

My heart skipped a beat as I remembered immediately where I had heard that last statement before. Miss Chung gave me a look that I quickly deciphered; I frowned at her in retaliation. The campers struggled to dig up more questions, but we came up empty-handed. It was hard to ask questions knowing we weren't going to get answers.

Cecilia Chung adjourned the meeting and we headed back to our cabins. Nobody had much to say that night. Instead, we said goodnight and all fell asleep wondering the same thing: *What do we do now?*

33
Chapter

It was a few days before anyone brought up the idea of going back to the island. Cecilia Chung's speech had left us stumped for ideas. I found myself wishing Cecilia Chung was around more. She seemed to know what she was doing, unlike a certain ridiculous camp headmistress whose throaty laugh was a direct hit to my gag reflex.

Speaking of Galiana, the witch grew more and more suspicious of us each day, and unfortunately, her suspicions made her stricter. It was like she wanted to see how far she could push us before we resisted and started a riot. We were determined, however, not to give her the satisfaction.

We randomly picked a Wednesday night to sneak out and head to the island. Even Thomas decided to join us. He brought a small pillow along in case he had the urge to cough or sneeze. Benji and I led the way. It was much more difficult to coordinate an escape with twelve people. We would have to take two canoes. We put Hazel in charge of telling people to stay quiet. Only, our adventure didn't go quite as planned. A rather large hiccup popped up just as we were about to embark on our canoes and head across our little lake.

Melaine gasped first. Startled, she turned around,

clearly looking for something — but there was nothing but darkness.

"I thought I heard someone," she explained.

Niki heard it next. Like Melaine, she gasped, then turned and pointed to something in the woods.

"I saw it, too. Someone's there!" Hazel insisted.

"Stay here," Benji ordered us girls.

The eight boys disappeared into the forest. We huddled close together as we awaited their return. The sound of rustling leaves and snapping twigs broke the night's silence. As I cringed, I distinguished the characteristic racket of a struggle, then a lengthy and powerful scuffling noise. Our eyes grew wider and our pulses quickened as it became louder and louder until it came to a sudden stop. Melaine, Hazel, Niki, and I held hands, our eyes fixated on the forest. It was pitch black and nearly impossible to see a thing. *Blink, blink.*

A few moments later, some voices escaped from inside the forest. As soon as I recognized Benji's voice, I headed toward the forest in search of him. Niki followed me, but Melaine and Hazel stayed back, holding each other tightly. I walked into the forest and saw the boys huddled together. Sterne and Cal were holding an unfamiliar boy.

"What's going on?" I asked as Niki and I reached the others.

"We found our follower. He's the one who's been spying on us the entire time. This is how Galiana knows everything about us; she's got this guy following us around!" Benji accused.

"No, I promise you, you have it all wrong," the boy said in a foreign accent.

He was tiny. Sterne and Benji towered over him. The boy was of Indian heritage and he looked absolutely harmless. Looks can be deceiving, of course, but it was hard to be afraid of this newbie.

"Who are you?" I asked him.

"My name is Bodhan. Or Bo. I'm a camper here, too."

"You're a camper? What year are you in?" Alex asked.

"I'm in grade one," Bo replied.

"Impossible," Alex chipped back. "We've never seen you before."

"Er, well, it's b-because, um, I sort of live under special c-circumstances," he stuttered.

Special circumstances? I was baffled. I looked to Benji, who spoke next.

"I saw his name, actually, on the first day on the board. I knew there were thirteen names in total."

"Yeah!" Bo said relieved. "That's me! I live in cabin two."

"You can't possibly live in cabin two. We all live in cabin two and you don't live there," Alex jumped in again, hell bent on making Bo feel like an imbecile.

"I have a special entrance in the back," Bo explained. "You see, I have this condition. I live on a twenty-five hour clock. I don't sleep at the same time as everyone else. I'm out of sync with the rest of the world. Most of the time I'm nocturnal, which means I sleep during the day and I am up at night,"

"We know what nocturnal means," Alex said, offended. Bo had insulted his intelligence.

The boy continued to defend his position.

"But then, after a while, I'm back to a normal sleeping pattern, like you guys. It's a sleeping disorder."

Bo looked at the blank faces surrounding him.

"Ugh," Benji snarled. "Come with me."

He grabbed Bo by the arm and led us back to the lake. He explained Bo's story to Hazel and Melaine. Naturally, Hazel also was cynical.

"That cabin?" Benji asked as he pointed to cabin two. "You live in that one?"

Bo nodded.

"Why do you get a secret entrance?" Hazel demanded to know.

"I've always wanted to go to camp," Bo continued. He was scared, poor thing, and pleading for acceptance. He was so small. So frail-looking. So harmless. "My parents found Camp Milestone for me. It's the only camp that allowed for my special circumstances. I can't be around you guys when I'm nocturnal. My sleep is a sensitive issue and until I can coordinate my sleep pattern with yours, I need to be — "

"He's the ghost." I said quietly. Though I was the first one to realize it, everyone knew I was right.

"P-pardon?" Bo asked.

"We thought you were a ghost. You've been walking around at night in the cabin, and we could hear you but we couldn't see you."

Nobody was sure how to react. It was almost funny. Should we laugh at ourselves for believing in ghosts or get upset with Bo for scaring us to death? I decided on the former and laughed.

"You scared us half to death, you know," I informed him.

"I'm so sorry," Bo said. A few of the others chuckled uneasily.

"I knew it! I told you guys! Scientifically, there is no such thing as a ghost!" Alex claimed. He was relieved he hadn't lost his mind.

"Were you ever hit by lightning?" Cyrus asked.

"No, never," Bo answered.

"Ever seen anyone get hit by lightning?"

"Well, yeah, actually. A girl at school. Last year. Er, how did you know that?"

We all exchanged looks as a few of us erupted with cheers.

"We'll explain it to you later," I assured him, as I patted him on the back.

"But I don't understand," Hazel said in the midst of the laughter and confusion. "Why didn't Galiana tell us? I mean, it's not like we would have disturbed you or your precious sleep. Instead, we've been sleeping on the floor because of you!"

"I'm sorry to have caused you any troubles," Bo said.

He was genuinely sorry for what he'd put us through.

He was also clueless about what was going on, and we told him we would have to fill him in later. We explained to him we were on a mission and he was stalling us. We had a long trip ahead of us and plenty of time to get to know Bo better later. At this stage, he was either with us or against us.

"Definitely with you. I would hate to be against you," he decided, looking at Hazel in fear.

Although the mystery of the camp ghost was resolved, it only raised more question marks. We all agreed Bo's presence was just a minor obstacle. He would have to come along.

No matter what, tonight was the night.

34
Chapter

Niki took a liking to Bo right away. Although she didn't have a sleeping disorder, she could relate to his sleep stories. On our long hike, she filled him in on everything that had happened at Camp Milestone from the first day. She didn't leave out a single detail. She referred to me as "my smart and talented friend." I was flattered and a little surprised.

Hazel complained the entire hike there. She made us laugh with her continuous whining.

"I'm gonna have a heart attack," she moaned. "I'm seriously gonna pass out, right here, right now."

"You're more than welcome to stop, Hazel. We'll just come and get you on our way back," Benji joked.

"Ha-ha. Very funny, Benji," she said. "But I don't feel like being a feast for the wolves tonight. Plus, I wasn't the one who was scared of the wind a few minutes ago."

"Hey!" Cyrus shouted, realizing she was referring to him. "I told you guys already, I thought I heard howling. Sheesh! Let it go."

"No way," Melaine laughed. "That was priceless."

"Not as priceless as when Faye freaked out over the giant spider," Cyrus said, trying to divert the scrutiny to me.

"The spiders in this forest are mutants!" I defended.

"I know, yick," Niki said. "I feel like they could eat me."

We continued teasing in that fashion while we canoed across the big lake, which we had nicknamed "Momma Lake." Many minutes later, we landed on the island and Benji led us back to where we had been caught previously by Galiana and Chester. He pointed to a cabin in the distance. The lights were on and someone was walking around inside. When we got close, we discovered it was Chester's cabin.

"I have a plan," Benji said. "Bo, you're the guinea pig tonight, I hope you don't mind."

"I know what you're thinking," I said beaming. "And it's brilliant."

~

We explained the plan to the others. It was perfect. Quietly, we approached the cabin and ducked into the bushes. Cyrus gave Bo an encouraging pat on the back and we sent him on his way. It was such a crazy coincidence that he was already coming in handy.

Bo walked up the steps to Chester's cabin, his knees knocking together, and knocked loudly.

"Bo? What are you doing here?" Chester's asked him as he opened the door.

"Huh? Wha— ? Where am I? How did I get here?" Bo faked, as he groggily rubbed his eyes.

"Geez, you must have been sleepwalking. Here," Chester said as he put a blanket around Bo. "This will keep you warm. Let me take you back to your cabin." He closed the door behind him and led Bo back to our camp.

"This is something to worry about, Bo," I could hear Chester saying, as he got further away. "Do your parents know you sleepwalk, too?"

"I don't know," Bo replied. "I'm scared, will you take me back to camp?"

"Yes, don't you worry."

We waited for a few minutes in silence. None of us wanted to say anything until we were sure Chester and Bo were long gone.

"That was too easy," Melaine said after several minutes.

"Let's go," Cal said, as we walked toward the cabin.

~

Chester's cabin was striking. Funky paintings and a slew of framed pictures complemented the rustic wooden interior. We spread out and began snooping around. I could hear the others whispering away while Cary watched the door.

The pictures intrigued me. I looked at each one carefully. It seemed Chester had been at Camp Milestone for a long time. He had taken pictures with many campers. One picture in particular caught my attention. He was standing with his arm around a young girl whose toothy smile was nauseatingly familiar. *Oh, lord.* It wasn't hard to recognize her. "Hey, guys! Check this out," I motioned to the others, wanting to show them my discovery.

I never really considered that Galiana had been a camper, too. Had her headmistress tortured her the way she tortured us? Was that why she was so difficult? Was there a reason behind her madness?

"Oh, my," Melaine said. I turned to see Melaine and Hazel going through some files in a cabinet.

"What?" a few of us asked simultaneously.

"We have files. They've been keeping files on us. Everything about us and — "

"Our letters!" Hazel squealed. "Come look, guys. Our parents, our friends, they wrote us back. Our letters! They're all here. They've been keeping them from us, those jerks!"

We all dashed toward the girls.

"Faye, Benji, Melaine, Cal, Cyrus, Cyrus, Faye, Faye, Faye, Asher, me, Faye, Niki, Niki," Hazel read off the names on the envelopes and handed out the letters.

I had the most. I couldn't believe it, but Diane had

written me back a lot of letters. Benji smiled at me as we cupped our letters with care. This was the first contact we'd had with the outside world in weeks. As we all rejoiced in our discovery, I felt as though time stood still. For a moment, for a small and blissful moment, everything was perfect. I sat there, holding letters from those who loved me, and staring at my new friends, who I had grown to love, too. But moments are impermanent and perfection is only an illusion.

"Oh, no," Melaine said through the commotion. She quietly had started reading our files.

"What is that?" Niki asked her.

"Our files. This is everything Galiana wrote about us on her stupid notepad," Melaine said. She started reading aloud, "Everything is going well. Faye Martin, my assistant, is doing her job well. She is spying on the others and reporting to me consistently. She advised me today that Cal is trying continuously to undermine my authority."

What? I couldn't believe what I was hearing. My jaw dropped and I let out a little cry.

"What? No! That's a lie. What is she doing?"

My stomach began churning and I felt a hot surge of rage. I walked toward Melaine, flabbergasted and reddened. The others remained silent.

"Go on, Melaine," Hazel ordered.

Melaine glanced at me apologetically, flipped the page and continued reading.

"As per Faye's notes, Melaine and Hazel are very sensitive about their mothers," Melaine said, tears accumulating in her eyes. "She suggested I have a meeting with them to toughen them up. I concur and have asked her to join us so she can learn a thing or two from me. I refuse to let her call all the shots. Faye thinks Melaine isn't learning her lesson from the measly cleaning tasks, so I am increasing her chores, effective immediately."

"She's lying! I never said that. I never wrote that!" I pleaded. *This can't be happening.* "She set me up! You guys, you have to believe me. You know there is something wrong with that woman. You don't believe her, do you?"

"Keep reading, Melaine," Hazel said hard-headedly without flinching. Melaine obeyed.

"Benji has been the easiest to win over. He truly believes Faye is his friend. Niki is completely clueless and ... I can't read anymore you guys."

Tears obstructed Melaine's vision. A thousand thoughts raced through my head as I tried hard not to panic. I was desperate. Never in a million years did I think Galiana would set me up this way. I knew she was disturbed, but this was beyond low. Every inch of me wanted to scream out in horror, but I knew I had to stay calm and collected. They would have to believe me. They were my friends and she was the devil.

"Is this true, Faye?"

"What? No way! You guys, you know me. You can't possibly believe this conniving woman. I've been with you guys all along. Look at me. You know me." I could tell my words weren't being received and I couldn't understand why. Everyone was just staring at me in a heart-breaking silence.

"Benji, please ... " I pleaded, turning to him.

You're my only hope. Please, believe me. I gave him the most innocent look I could muster, begging him to see my genuineness. I signaled to him to look into my heart and soul. I was not this person. I was not this monster Galiana accused me of being. They had to know this. They had to know *me*.

"I want to believe you, Faye, but you're so secretive, so private. I mean, is this why you know that Chester guy?" Benji asked, piercing me.

His face looked like an ice sculpture and his hands clutched his letters tightly. His smile had turned into a nasty scowl and his stare felt distant. *He thinks I'm a traitor.*

"Precisely," a snake-like voice came from behind us. It was Galiana. "I see you finally found out the truth."

"Galiana, you lying, horrible weasel of a woman!" I screamed. "Why are you doing this? Tell them you're lying! Do it now!"

Galiana smiled at me. It was a smile so seemingly

genuine, only I could see through it at that moment. Melaine started crying quietly and Hazel put her arm around her protectively. Niki, Cyrus and Cary stared at the ground. They'd had enough of me. They didn't believe me. They actually didn't believe me. Benji, on the other hand, still had his eyes glued on me. His stare made me uncomfortable, but I knew it was because he was having the hardest time letting go. I had never seen him glare at me that way. I was used to his usual warmth, not this frigidness. He wanted to believe me, I could tell. A glimmer of hope remained.

"Let this be a lesson to all of you — you need to be careful who you trust around here," Galiana gloated. "You can keep your letters. Faye is coming with me. The rest of you can find your own way back."

"I'm not going anywhere with you!" I snapped.

"Do you really want to make this worse?"

"It can't possibly get any worse," I said, fighting back tears. I scanned the room, looking for a friendly face. Nobody dared look at me, except for Benji. As our eyes met again, I found myself giving him a look of desperation. A tear rolled down my cheek and I wiped it away aggressively. *Damn.*

"You want to bet on it?" She enjoyed the challenge.

"Benji," I beseeched. "You believe me, right? Right?"

Benji continued to look at me without saying a word. Delirious, I shifted my gaze toward Galiana in frustration. I knew I was being set up for a reason. She wanted this altercation to happen. She was set on alienating me. And me? I wanted to kill her. I *hated* her.

"Benji, don't look at her like that. Feel sorry for her. She doesn't mean to be so secretive and mean."

"Galiana, stop," I demanded, my tone filled with contempt.

"You haven't told him?" Galiana's lips curled into an evil smile. "Don't you know, Benji?" she defied, with a twinkle of evil in her eye.

"Know what?"

Oh, no, no, no, no.

185

"That this poor pathetic mean Faye, this person who's been backstabbing you all along, is actually in love with you?"

It was as if someone had choked me. I opened my mouth to say something but nothing came out. My vision faded and I blinked repetitively to keep from fainting. *This is not happening*, I prayed. But it was. Galiana was set on ruining me.

Benji didn't respond. I knew he continued staring at me but I couldn't bear to reciprocate his gaze. He knew. In one swift, wicked sentence, she'd ruined it for me. It was over. I stayed silent, staring at the ground in defeat. Galiana walked over to Melaine and took one of the papers from her hands.

"What's this?" she asked Melaine.

"It's what you wrote about us in your files," Melaine said. Galiana snickered.

"No, but what *is* it?"

Melaine looked confused.

"Um, it says what you and Faye observed about the rest of us for the past month."

"You're making it too complicated, Mela-nie," Galiana said to annoy her. She waved around the sheet of paper. "What is this?" She asked again, louder.

"Um, it's, um, I'm not sure, what you … "

"Oh, for crying out loud, it's a piece of paper!" Galiana barked. "Right? Am I right, Faye?"

"I don't give a crap," I said, loathing her and finding the courage to speak again.

"Yes, you do. As always, you're making things more complicated than they need to be."

I rolled my eyes, realizing she was trying to teach me a lesson in the midst of all of this.

"I'm going to say this one more time," she said. "The rest of you can leave now and Faye is coming with me."

Without hesitation, the gang started walking away. Back to her roots, Hazel gave me a dirty look on her way out.

"She has this great way of making me feel like a moron," I heard Melaine whisper about Galiana.

"Don't worry," Niki told her. "It's not you. It's them."

186

Them. *Them.* I was a "them." They didn't believe me. And why should they? I should have told them about Chester. I should have told them about the rash right away. I shouldn't have been so secretive. I should have let them see all the notes I wrote because there was never anything there. I never carried out Galiana's task. I never did anything wrong.

"Are you coming?" Galiana asked me.

"You lied about me," I said.

"I did no such thing."

"How can you say that? How can you look me in the eyes and lie? You know I didn't write those horrible things. You know the truth! WHY ARE YOU DOING THIS? WHAT DID I EVER DO TO YOU?" I raised my voice with each word.

"Did I lie about your feelings for Benji?"

"Don't change the subject. YOU LIED AND YOU KNOW IT!" I screamed.

Galiana waited a moment before speaking. She'd lost her smile.

"I hate people who yell," she snarled. I made a protesting noise. *What does that mean? You yell all the time!* Galiana walked out.

"Then you must hate yourself," I muttered, as I followed her outside, stomping my feet in the process.

I noticed Galiana's stride hesitate for a moment, making it clear she had heard me but didn't care. She had won.

35
Chapter

Galiana drove me back to my cabin without uttering a word. When we pulled into the circular driveway, she finally spoke — though I despised the sound of her voice and preferred the silence.

"I'm getting really tired of you following me around everywhere, Faye," she said. "Next time, find your own way home."

I let out an exasperated chuckle. I was too depressed to argue. After all, there was no point. How could I argue with someone who was obviously mad?

"There's a dance at 8 p.m. Sunday," she told me. "Tell the others. Attendance is mandatory. You'll get to meet the rest of the campers. It's in the Great Hall on the island. I trust you all know how to find it."

"Why do *I* have to tell them?" I asked, repulsed by my own words. Was I starting to sound like her? "They all hate me now, thanks to you."

"Stop being so selfish, Faye. All you think about is yourself. Maybe you should think about what *I'm* going through for a change. *I* have it harder than all of you."

I shook my head in aggravation. No, I could never be

like her. Galiana was psychotic. I was just misunderstood.

"It's an obligatory event. Consider it your responsibility. You'll have to pay the consequences if nobody shows up, Faye."

"What could you possibly do to me that you haven't already done?"

"I wouldn't find out, if I were you."

Threats, more freaking threats. I growled and opened the car door. I was leaving when Galiana spoke again.

"And, Faye," she called behind me. "If they were your real friends, they wouldn't hate you over something so trivial. They believed me over you. You obviously don't mean anything to them."

It was as if she had poured salt on a raw wound. I gave her one last callous glare, closed the car door behind me and ran off before she could see the tears streaming down my face.

36
Chapter

Dear Faye/Hi Faye/ Faye/Dearest Faye,

I can't believe how many letters you're writing me! You're the absolute best. You have no idea how much it means to me to hear from you so often ...

... Faye where are you? I don't understand why I keep writing to you, but all of your letters say you haven't heard from me yet ...

... Faye, are you getting these letters? Do I even have the address right?

... Faye, what am I supposed to do? Even if I wanted to help you, how can I possibly do that when you aren't getting any of my letters?

... It sounds like you are having a great time. I am so happy for you, but even happier that you haven't forgotten me. I thought you would have stopped writing me by the second week ...

... Nothing is new here. I'm working with my dad and the gang is not up to much. I don't see them very often. Omigod, Benji is there? How weird is that? That's so awesome for you to have a familiar face there, even though I wish I could be there!

... Faye, I spoke to your parents. They seemed really worried about you. They don't understand why you aren't getting any of our letters, so they wrote to the camp owner. He hasn't written back yet ...

... Faye, I had dinner with your parents last night. That guy, Chester, finally wrote them back. He said you were doing amazing and they felt you guys weren't ready to receive your letters yet. It's supposed to be part of the process, whatever that means. Supposedly, you'll get our letters soon. Don't lose hope, I'm writing you almost daily ...

... Your parents have had me over a few times. I've snooped everywhere, Faye, but I can't find anything! How can I help? They aren't budging. I don't know what else I can do ...

... Faye, once you find out what's going on, do you think you'll be allowed to tell me? What if you're not? It would kill me. I feel like I know all of these people now!

... I'm counting down the days until your return ...

... Faye, don't let the Big G get to you (I love that, by the way). She's not a stable person. She wants to bring you down. I'm not entirely sure why she would want to do that, but there are good and bad people everywhere you go. She's just one of those jealous miserable people. You know what they say, misery loves company ...

... I don't understand! There's an entire island for the others? How is that fair? What kind of camp is this?

... I wish I could meet your friends. Are you allowed to take pictures there? Probably not ...

... The best part of my day is when I open the mailbox and I have a letter from you. I feel like I'm going through this experience with you ...

... Faye, do you remember when your parents would go on business trips and you would stay over at my house? They have been doing that about once a year since I can remember. Do you think that has anything to do with Camp Milestone? I mean, your mom is a nurse and your dad is an optometrist. What could they possibly have to travel for on business? The national nurse and optometrist convention? Yeah, right!

... I miss you so much. Write back soon (why do I even bother writing that? I know you will!)

... I haven't given up. I'm still looking for clues, so don't you give up either! I know you'll find the answer. You're too smart not to!

... Love/Your friend/Your best friend/I could never forget you/Life stinks without you/Have a wonderful time/Hugs back,

Diane

37
Chapter

I had been an idiot in so many ways. I was lucky to have Diane; she was an old friend who had come to rescue me in a new life. She had been loyal and forgiving of my flaws, and I had done nothing but envy her. I also had spent my life pushing people away and wallowing in self-misery. I had kept everything to myself, leaving me as the loneliest, most clueless girl on the planet. I'd learned my lesson. I loved my friends and I never meant to hurt them.

The next day, I had to tell the other campers about the dance. It was a hard task because they continued to ignore me, barely speaking to me and avoiding me. When I told them of the upcoming dance, they barely reacted. Crushed, I realized I didn't know how to act around them anymore. They didn't believe me and nothing was going to change that. My heart broke.

Conveniently, Galiana was missing the next day. Although all of us met outside at the crack of dawn, we just ended up waiting. She never showed up.

"She's obviously not coming," Hazel said. "Faye, are you going to tell us what you know or are you just going to let us wait here all day?"

"I don't know anything, Hazel," I replied.

"Don't you have a bag of apples stashed away somewhere for me? I won't put up a fight, Faye. Just give me the apples and I'll start munching away. Heck, maybe I can make some apple pie with them. Am I allowed to do that or is that against the rules?"

Sigh. I didn't know what to say. No one came to my defense. Instead, they all just stared at the ground like they had the night before. For the first time in more than a month, I wanted to go home. I don't know where I found the strength, but I shrugged it off and answered her.

"I told you, Hazel, I don't know. I hate Galiana just as much as you do."

"We should go then," Melaine said. I didn't want them to leave.

"Uh, wait. Maybe we could see if the other cabins have secret entrances like the one in cabin two," I suggested, hoping this might instigate a better reaction.

"We already did. Last night, after you fell asleep," Sterne said.

"Oh." *Well then. That says it all.* They had done it without me. I should have known.

"We didn't find anything interesting," Benji added coldly. "There's no secret entrance in our cabin. There is one in cabin one, but it's only a small room with a sewing machine and stuff."

"A sewing machine?" I asked.

"Yeah, a dusty room with a sewing machine, tons of fabric and some old dresses and clothes, maybe from a few decades ago. They almost seemed like costumes," Niki explained.

Hazel glared at Niki. She obviously didn't want her to go into too much detail.

"That's so strange," I said.

"Why is that strange?" Alex asked.

"Well, it just doesn't fit into the picture at all. A sewing room? Why would there be a sewing room?"

None of them entertained my questions.

"Why wouldn't there be, Faye? It's Camp Milestone. Nothing should surprise us at this point," Cal said.

"Like we would believe anything you say anyway," Hazel added.

My strength collapsed like quicksand. I fought hard not to cry again. Being strong was harder than I thought. They didn't want me around. They didn't believe anything I had to say. They didn't trust me anymore. Maybe Galiana was right. Maybe they were never my friends. Maybe I'd been kidding myself this entire time.

We went our separate ways shortly after. Nobody talked to me for days. They would always whisper around me, making sure I didn't know what they were doing. Niki moved her stuff out of our room, and then everyone moved into cabin two, leaving me alone in my cabin. Those days were the most miserable of my life. At night, I cried myself to sleep. During the day, I was on my own with nothing to do. Without Galiana around anymore to yell at us and make us do stupid things, I was alone, isolated, and depressed. How pathetic is that? I had been praying for her to magically disappear this entire time, and now that she had, I was lonely.

The worst part was going cold turkey on my fledgling relationship with Benji. He wasn't exactly rude to me, but I knew he didn't want to be around me. He had officially rejected me. He thought I was a mean jerk who was in love with him. Galiana had humiliated me and he had become detached. I couldn't stand his remoteness and I often wished I could turn back time.

~

Desperate and bored, I decided one day to check out the sewing room for myself. The others were right. It was nothing spectacular. It seemed that maybe the cabin had been someone's home a few decades ago and it was their abandoned sewing room.

"Maybe we were all seamstresses in our past lives," I said aloud.

I glanced around and remembered I was by myself. *Sigh*.

"Great. Now I'm talking to myself," I said. "Maybe they're right. Maybe I am turning into Galiana."

For me, it couldn't get any worse.

38
Chapter

Some time later, I went to the small library and read through my letters for the third time. There was still no sign of Galiana. I could see the camp from the small window in front of me. My parents had written me a couple of vague letters and I was almost angry with them for their uncaring attitude. When had they become so smug and secretive? There was one sentence though — only one — that caught my eye.

"Faye, honey, don't worry about anything. You are there to enjoy yourself and to learn valuable lessons. You are trying too hard to control everything and you don't need to. Just be yourself, be your wonderful self, and you will be great. Some things you can't control. History repeats itself. It's all part of fate's plan."

"History repeats itself," I read aloud.

History repeats itself. Cecilia Chung also had said that. But what did it mean? *Think, Faye, think.* Drawing a blank, I threw the letters on the floor in frustration. I sighed and glanced outside. I could see Hazel leaving cabin three and heading toward cabin two. Cyrus, Thomas, Asher, Stern, Cary, and Alex followed her, carrying their blankets, sleeping bags and other materials that had accumulated in our cabin since the ghost incident. I smiled, reminding myself I didn't hate them for hating me.

I watched them peacefully from afar. I could almost hear Hazel ordering them around. They disappeared into cabin two, but not before little Bo ran out of my cabin holding a pillow over his head. He scurried behind Hazel and the others. I chuckled. The scene looked strangely familiar, as if I'd seen it a million times before. Shaking my head, I turned back to the library and my eyes landed on the children's books piled high in the mahogany shelves.

I grimaced as my jumbled mind started racing. I thought back to the first day of camp. I remembered the events, the speeches, everything that was done. Slowly — very slowly — something began to make sense, something clicked. I continued to look the books up and down, with a mixture of confusion and clarity. I walked over to one shelf in particular and ran my finger along the sides of the books neatly stacked on top of one another. Twelve different editions of *Snow White and the Seven Dwarfs*. *Snow White. A poison apple. Snow White. And her seven dwarfs.*

Then, just like that, it dawned on me.

"Oh my GOD," I murmured in disbelief, realizing my world had just changed.

I was so excited, I nearly felt sick to my stomach. The recognition had been imminent; the past thirty-seven days had led to this very moment. I stepped backward and slowly headed toward the exit. I had discovered something — something major — but some vital pieces of the puzzle remained missing. What would I do with my new breakthrough? It was too early to tell the others. I would have to be certain before I could say anything.

Just then, I caught a glimpse of myself in the mirror. The reflection surprised me. I was not used to seeing myself in that light. I looked the same, but something was different. I almost looked lovely.

"When did that happen?" I mumbled.

A million words rushed through my mind. I closed my eyes and opened them again. Nothing had changed; my reflection was still new to me. Aware that I was breathing loudly, I tried to make sense of my thoughts. I continued to look at myself in the mirror, frowning at my newfound glow.

"How about that?" I said. "Camp Milestone did its job."

39
Chapter

It didn't take me long to figure out what I needed to do. I needed answers and only one person could give them to me.

"Good morning, Cecilia," I said, surprising myself with my calm tone. It was the following morning and I was standing outside her cabin, waiting for her.

"Faye, what are you doing here?"

"May I come in?"

"No, absolutely not. You know you can't. You need to leave. Now," she said in a low voice. I had caught her off guard, precisely my intention.

"It wasn't a question, Cecilia."

I don't know where I found the bravery to call her Cecilia, but I went with it. It seemed to be working. My confidence oozed like fresh blood from an open wound. She sensed it and let me in.

"I need to speak with you," I informed her, as we walked into her cabin.

"You know I can't do that," she said.

"No, I know you *won't* do that."

Her cabin had the same layout as Chester's — large, spacious, and appealing. Naturally, her décor was different.

Her style reflected her serious character with dark walls, dark furniture, and impeccable and decent taste. On the walls, a slew of awards stood hanging, outlining her accomplishments. Cecilia had done many things in her life. She had several Good Samaritan awards and some academic awards. She was even in the local newspapers several times. One particular headline caught my eye.

"Local woman brings children's literature back into the new millennium," I read. I looked at her as she stood quietly, watching me take in all this new information.

"I'm not going to speak with you, Faye," she said, trying to regain control of our sudden role reversal.

"Yes, you will," I answered. She frowned.

"What makes you so sure?"

"I have something you want," I said, as one side of my mouth pulled up into a half smile. I was being devious but I didn't care. I knew I would get what I wanted eventually.

I could tell Cecilia was intrigued. Without saying a word, I made a small gesture toward my rash. Slowly, her eyes followed my hands and her expression turned into one of astonishment.

"I know you want to see it," I said. "I know more than you think I do."

"Is that so?" she inquired.

"Yes," I continued. "I know all of our, um ..."

Quicker than I could retrieve my lost thought, I drew a blank. *Damn.* What was that rash called again? What did Alex call it? *Darn that Hazel,* I thought, as I remembered what she had called it.

"Um," I said, "I know all of our, er, *licking bird* figures are unique."

I tried to mumble the words "licking bird," but the little noise that came out of Cecilia's mouth made me realize she'd heard what I said.

"Continue," she said, deciding not to correct me.

"I know the pattern of the rash tells you something about us."

"What do you think it tells us?" she asked coyly.

"I don't know yet," I replied, embarrassed. I could feel the dynamics of our power struggle shift. She was regaining control. I tried to fight it.

"I know a lot more than you think, Cecilia," I continued, disappointed that my voice cracked.

"Is that so?"

"Yes."

"I know about the lightning, too. I know that's how you choose us."

Cecilia took a step toward me and shook her head, her eyes narrowing in on mine. At that moment, I found her quite intimidating.

"No, no, my dear," she said earnestly. "I'm sorry to inform you that you still don't know anything. Because it is not how we choose you. It is how you are *chosen.*"

40
Chapter

Cecilia smirked. This exchange was fun for her.

"So, we are chosen," I repeated, broaching the topic cautiously. I was walking on eggshells.

"Correct."

"Exactly how are we chosen?"

"We are not certain, but we know the lightning is the beginning. We also know it cannot be faked," Cecilia explained.

"What do you mean?"

"In the past," she said, "many people attempted to lure a lightning bolt to themselves, to get hit by lightning, so they could be special like you."

What happened to them?" I asked in a low voice.

"They didn't survive, of course."

"Oh." I took a step backward.

"Is it too much for you to handle?" Cecilia tested me.

"No, I want answers. I'm ready for answers," I said, unwavering. "I know you want to see my rash and I am willing to show it to you. I just want some answers in return."

I could see her dilemma. On one hand, I — a child, really — was trying to play her. She could chew me up and spit me out for breakfast. On the other hand, her curiosity was getting the best of her. Her inquisitive side wanted to see my rash. The mystery of the pattern drove her mad. I was so close.

"What do you want to know?" she finally asked, revealing she had lost her internal struggle.

I almost said, "Everything." But I realized I couldn't outsmart her. I needed to be specific. I took a deep breath and ignored my thumping heart.

"What does, 'History repeats itself,' mean?"

"Do you know what reincarnation means?" she asked. I gulped, unsure of what to do with that question.

"Yes."

"Then there is your answer."

"So I am a reincarnation of something?" I clarified.

"You could say that."

This wasn't going to be easy; she was so cryptic.

"OK," I continued. "We are chosen, correct?"

"Mm-hmm."

"What are we chosen for, exactly?"

"I cannot tell you that," she said in a firm way that told me she wouldn't budge.

"I know it has something to do with fairy tales," I said.

"You do?" She raised one eyebrow.

"Yes, I figured that out," I said. "I get that part now. Galiana's stupid activities and punishments were a strange way for her to treat us like fairy-tale characters."

Cecilia's eyes narrowed again.

"Continue," she said.

"Well, our punishments were clues. The books in the library were a clue. The costumes in the sewing room, even her stupid theme-park speech was supposed to be a clue. But she's so ridiculous that none of it seemed important to us at the time."

I could see her suppress a smile.

"Keep going," she pressed. I took another deep breath, reminding myself to exhale.

"Melaine has been our maid for the past two months. Galiana has labeled her as Cinderella. Hazel lives with seven boys who carry her around as punishment. She is Snow White and they are her seven dwarfs. I can't believe I didn't see it before," I was gaining momentum. "Niki has been forced to sleep more than any human should because Galiana had been trying to tell us she is Sleeping Beauty."

Cecilia Chung sat down.

"So it worked?" she asked.

"What worked?"

"Galiana's method." I couldn't tell if she was happy or disappointed. She was unreadable.

"Not really. I still don't know what it means. Why is she doing this to us?"

"She did it so you can find your true calling in life," Cecilia answered.

"I don't get it," I said, feeling faint at the realization I was finally getting somewhere. I sat down and faced her, upset that my body betrayed me. "What are you saying, that Hazel *is* Snow White?"

"Precisely."

I looked to the ground in bewilderment. I knew I couldn't press the issue too much without Cecilia closing up on me.

"How is she Snow White?"

"Well, she is the modern-day Snow White. We don't live in a world of kings, queens and castles anymore, Faye. Those days are long gone. That particular Snow White lived many years ago and her story was written for the world to read. It never lost momentum because it was such a wonderful story. Nowadays, Snow White will not live in a castle. She will not necessarily be white. But her story will essentially be the same. And her story will once again change society as we know it."

"So Hazel is Snow White. The boys are her seven dwarfs. Niki is Sleeping Beauty and Melaine is Cinderella."

"Correct," she acknowledged. She was proud of me.

"And who is Benji?"

"Oh, no," she shook her head. "That's your job to find out."

"And who am I?"

"Again, you're not getting that information from me."

Cecilia had a strange way of making me feel wonderful and awful at the same time. I smiled at her, knowing her intentions were anything but malicious.

"We have a connection, Cecilia," I remarked.

"Pardon?"

The ball was in my court again. I liked catching her off guard.

"You and I. We have a connection, I feel it."

"I'm glad to hear that. I was hoping you would," she said. I had known it all along. From the moment she spoke to me on the first day of camp, I knew we shared a connection somehow. My dream only confirmed it.

"So what do I do now?" I asked.

"You know exactly what to do, Faye. You've always known." She put her hand on my lap. "It's time for you to leave now."

"I know," I said. "But I have to keep my promise."

I stood up and looked down at Cecilia as she inched forward on the couch. I turned my back toward her and lifted the back of my shirt, revealing my shimmering rash. I could feel it now, without even looking at it. It became more a part of me every day.

"Lichtenberg figure," I muttered, finally remembering the name.

"Correct," she said quietly, praising me.

"Alex knew it," I told her.

"Alex is a smart boy."

Cecilia ran her hands along the rash, as if tracing its branches into a pattern. I had expected her to gasp, to show some shock the way the other campers had, but she didn't. She stayed cool and collected, almost as if my Lichtenberg figure was exactly what she had anticipated. Almost as if she had seen it before.

"So?" I asked.

"Thank you," she said politely as she backed away.

"Thank you, too." I adjusted my shirt.

"Would you like to see mine?" she asked.

"Not particularly," I replied. "I already know it's identical to mine."

Cecilia looked stunned once more.

"You're so gifted," she said. "I'm so happy to get to know you."

I blushed.

"I'm happy to get to know you, too."

We both smiled awkwardly as I headed toward the door.

"Faye," she called after me. "This meeting stays between us. You're not to tell anyone we spoke."

"I'm no longer keeping secrets from my friends, Cecilia. That's gotten me into a load of trouble," I advised her.

"I'm sorry to hear that, but I will not admit this conversation took place if anyone asks. It never happened."

"Then we're at an impasse," I said, "because I'm not lying."

"No, we are not at an impasse. If you tell your friends we met, and I deny it, it will seem like you are lying again. You really have no choice here." I knew she was right.

"Fine, have it your way," I said. "Goodbye for now, Cecilia."

"Goodbye, Faye."

I nodded and gave her a small wave.

"Faye?" she called after me as I was closing the door.

"Yes?" I paused.

"I'm not the only one you have a connection with, you know."

"I know," I said sadly.

And I closed the door behind me.

41
Chapter

They ran outside as soon as they heard my frantic screams. I had just paddled, then walked, then swam from the other camp site. It felt as though I had completed a triathlon, but I didn't care. I had something to tell them and I was ecstatic. Judging by the looks on their faces, they were worried and most of them assumed I had been hurt. I reached them quickly, panting heavily.

"What? What's wrong?" Benji asked me as they all surrounded me.

"Are you, OK?" Melaine wondered.

"I get it." *Pant, pant.* "Well." *Pant,* "I get some of it, I think!" *Pant, wheeze.*

"What do you mean you get it?" Hazel asked.

"I figured it out." *Pant.* "I get it! I know what we're doing here!"

I took a minute to compose myself as the gang watched me. I could tell they all felt the same wave of nausea I was fighting off.

"Guys," I said more calmly as I swallowed a big breath of air. "It all makes sense. I can't believe it. I mean, I can believe it, but I can't. Think about it. History repeats itself and nothing is what it seems. I know it's hard to believe, but it's the only explanation, really. Life isn't what we thought it was. At least, our lives aren't. Can you believe it? I mean, I definitely don't have it all figured out, but this is it, I'm sure! This is crazy. Are you following me?"

"Faye," Benji said, putting his hand on my shoulder. It was the first contact we'd had in an eternity. "We're definitely not following you. What on earth are you talking about?"

"It all makes sense!" I cried out in breathless desperation. I wanted them to read my mind. I couldn't talk fast enough. "Do you really not know what I'm saying? Think about it, guys. Galiana's craziness, her stupid speeches. Ugh! Her stupid, stupid theme-park speech! What a loony! And Cecilia Chung's vague remarks. They're all hints! And Bo! No wonder, Bo! I get it! You're sleepy! Even that pink brochure is a clue! And we really have nothing in common except for the lightning storms! Don't you see?"

"Slow down there, missy," Niki said, giggling. "We're still not following you."

I shook my head, hoping it would bring some order to my chaotic thoughts. I didn't know how to string my sentences together. Even though I knew what I was saying, I was still processing everything myself. How was I going to explain? It was harder than I thought. Determined to untangle the mess, I told everyone to stay put as I fetched an apple and came back. When I returned, some of them were sitting on the steps to Hazel's cabin and the others were standing around. I started again.

"OK. Imagine something for a second. Although I'm Faye Martin and I'm a unique person, imagine that a certain aspect of my life is pre-determined. Like, I have a destiny. Now, imagine something else. Imagine someone a long time ago lived the same kind of life I am living now. Imagine it was a special and memorable life. How would we know about it? How could we possibly hear about this person who lived umpteen years ago?"

They all stared at me, lost in thought. Alex was trying

hard to come up with the answer. This game was his favorite —
a pop quiz. Impatient, I pointed to the library.

"Books?" Melaine said. "You mean books?"

"Yes!" I shouted a little too excitably. I took a deep
breath. "OK. Listen. Once upon a time, there was a beautiful
girl who lost her mother at an early age. Her father remarried
and this girl found herself missing her mother every day."

I was looking at Hazel, hoping they would all catch on.

"The rest is history, and I'm not sure how it ends for this
person, but I do know one thing: one day, her fate was changed
by a piece of fruit. A single, dark red apple," I said extending
the apple toward Hazel.

Hazel still looked confused. I didn't blame her. I wasn't
even sure I was making sense at this point.

"What are you saying?" Niki asked.

"Here's what I'm saying, guys. Listen carefully. Those
fairy tales we've all read as children, those same books that
are in the library here at Camp Milestone, er, uh — I don't
think they're make-believe. They're *biographies*, stories of real
people who lived a version of that story a long time ago. And
ever since then, more people have come and gone and lived
another version of the same story."

"I don't get it," Alex said.

"I'm saying I think, I think fairy tales are not actually,
um, tales. They are real. And we," I cleared my throat, "are
the new versions of those fairy-tale characters, and, well, I
think this camp is a set up for us, uh, for us to figure it out," I
finished, hesitantly.

Several moments of quiet followed. I examined
everyone's expressions as they processed what I'd said.

"Are you saying I'm Snow White or something?" Hazel
finally asked in an unbelieving tone as she snatched the apple
from my hand.

"Yeah, Hazel. Actually, I am."

There was another long pause.

"But I'm black!" she finally yelled.

The others snickered under their breath. She often

didn't know she was being funny, but at times, she was hilarious.

"So what?" I said with a genuine smile. "Snow White is just a name! Hazel Lane is just a name! Doesn't it make sense?"

"No!" Cyrus shouted. "I seriously think you're digging deep here, Faye. We're modern-day fairy-tale characters? That's the big secret? That's why we got hit by lightning? You're as crazy as the G-factor."

"No, she's onto something," Benji said softly. He glanced at Hazel's cabin mates. "I wouldn't have believed it if we'd never met Bo. But six plus one equals seven. Hazel has *seven* house mates," he stopped as he looked at each of them individually.

"Exactly!" I was content he'd come to my rescue. The reactions varied. Alex took a step backward, as if he was still processing information. Asher seemed relieved and happy, true to his character. Cary started blushing and Sterne was accordingly angry.

"What?" Sterne barked. "You mean I'm just a measly dwarf? I'm one of her seven dwarves? I've been lugging Hazel around the entire summer, just to discover I'm a dwarf in some messed up version of a fairy tale?"

"Not just any dwarf," Hazel chuckled. "You're Grumpy!"

We couldn't help letting out a little laugh at Sterne's expense.

"Sterne," I said. "There is nothing wrong with being a dwarf. Behind every person who makes a difference in this world, there stands a whole bunch of little people, uh, I mean, people, who supported them and helped them on their way."

I waited for Stern to reply. He didn't react to my comment. It wasn't clear whether he was still angry or if I had made him feel special again.

"And, oh, wow. I'm Sleepy," Bo declared, suppressing a yawn.

"Right you are. The new-aged Sleepy dwarf is actually a fourteen year old boy who has a twenty-five-hour sleep cycle,"

I explained.

I looked at their eager faces, knowing they were learning the most important piece of information ever. I also knew I, Faye Grace Martin, had grown up over night. Somewhere between the chores, punishments, exchanges with Benji, and big fights, I had grown up. I was still me, only altered. I had a newfound confidence and appreciation of myself. I was part of something now, something beyond my own comprehension.

"So I'm Doc," Alex chimed in. "And Cary is Bashful?"

"I'm freaking Dopey?" Cyrus interjected, as a few of us nodded. "Am I supposed to be happy? This freaking sucks! This whole thing sucks! I mean, I got hit by lightning, which bloody hurts by the way, was sent to the worst summer camp ever, was forced to do the worst chores ever, got tortured by a crazy psychopath devil woman with red hair, was made to carry Hazel, possibly the rudest Snow White, like a freaking backpack all summer, just so I could discover I'm the new Dopey? A stinking dwarf?"

His reaction was valid. We knew how he felt because we felt the same way. None of us said a word. It was crazy, absurd, infuriating. But it didn't change that it was true.

"I don't get it," Cal said. "Why did Galiana force us to do all that stuff?"

"I'm not sure," I answered. "I think she was trying to tell us something, in her twisted way. I think she fed Hazel apples to make her realize she's Snow White. And made the boys carry her around to help them understand they are her seven dwarfs. I think someone founded Camp Milestone a long time ago to help us, er," I still couldn't get used to saying it, "to help modern-day fairy-tale people discover who we are. Remember the brochure?"

"This is crazy," Cyrus pouted, but his expression showed he was starting to believe.

"I know! But listen, you guys. Once upon a time," I continued, turning to Melaine, "there was another girl who lost her mother inexplicably. Because she didn't know how special she was or how she would survive without her mother, her father sent her to a camp where the evil headmistress made her clean and do awful chores. Her name was Melaine Jacobs. But perhaps we could refer to her as Cinderella."

I pushed a strand of Melaine's over-dyed and now cinder-colored hair out of her face as she tried hard not to cry. I hugged her, wrapping my arms around her, knowing all too well I was losing my own battle with tears. Soon, Hazel and Niki joined in our emotional squeeze and we became a tangle of blubbering messes.

"Girls are such wimps," Cyrus joked, as he joined in on our embrace. Soon, we had formed one giant group hug.

"Niki," I said between sniffles as we parted gradually. "You should have been the one who was the most obvious to me, but I admit, I was stumped for a minute. I'll give you a hint. The reason that horrid woman made you sleep all the time was because, deep down, she didn't want you to miss your beauty sleep."

Niki's face was priceless at that moment. It's amazing how much more radiant someone can become in a matter of seconds.

"I'm Sleeping Beauty?" she glowed, knowing the answer. I nodded, causing several voices to cry out random remarks.

"What about me?" Cal asked in the midst of the commotion. "Who am I?"

"I'm sorry, Cal, I don't know yet."

"And me?" Benji added hopefully. I shook my head apologetically.

"I'm sorry, I still don't know. I need more time."

"And you? Who are you, Faye?" he asked me. I looked at their concerned faces.

"I don't know that, either," I sighed.

"This is so odd," Cary said, in a voice so low we barely heard him. "Do you think this is for real?"

"She's onto something," Benji said. "This camp has something to do with fairy tales. The books in the library are all fairy tales. And the stuff Galiana made us do is more than just coincidence. Faye's right, Galiana made us live out her version of these tales. And that brochure we got. 'Once upon a time' and what not? It makes sense."

Everyone started talking simultaneously. They had loads to think about. I gave them a few moments to get their thoughts out into the open before speaking again.

"You guys?" I started, "I'm really sorry about what happened before. I want you to know I honestly never said those things Galiana wrote. I know I've been secretive in the past, but I've never lied to you. I promise."

I caught some serious glares exchanged among a few of them.

"Faye, we're sorry we got mad at you," said Melaine, ashamed of her actions.

"No, it was my fault. I've been really reserved and you guys were right to doubt me. But to prove that I'll never keep secrets from you again, I want you to know I spoke to Cecilia about this."

I took a few moments to describe my encounter with Cecilia.

"We were so stupid to doubt you," Niki said after my explanation. "Will you ever forgive us?"

I smiled. No words could explain the happiness I felt upon hearing those words.

"It's OK," I said. "I'm just glad it's over."

42

Chapter

Dear Diane,

It's hard to find ways to pass the time after you've made a discovery that changes the way you look at things. You start wondering what is worth your time and what isn't. Your letters were a godsend. It's almost freaky how they all landed in my lap when I needed them the most.

I'm sorry if I don't sound like myself in this letter, but I am preoccupied. I have yet to figure out Benji's identity or mine. He's more important, of course. I can figure myself out later.

It's been an emotional time. OK, it's been an emotional time for the girls, but the boys are handling it in their own way. The jokes and wisecracks have gone through the roof. Cyrus, in particular, pokes fun at us girls every time we get sniffly. It's nice, though, because their macho attitude keeps us girls sane.

We've still seen no sign of G-Almighty anywhere. I'm sure I don't need to tell you how much easier it has been on our mental health not having her around. I am wondering if I had anything to do with her disappearing act. Although she's my least favorite person right now, I don't want to be the cause of her, well, you know. I can't even say it. Ugh.

We have a dance coming up on Sunday. We are quite excited to go because we have an idea. The idea came to us after Cal mentioned we should lie about our discovery — Oh, crap!

Diane, I have to go. I have to go talk to Cal! I'm sorry! I'll write again soon. Thanks again for everything. It felt like old times again!

Love,

Faye

43
Chapter

I had been writing my letter outside with the girls when I had my latest epiphany. I jolted upright and scanned the area for Cal. The boys were playing soccer and I caught their attention the minute I waved my arms.

"I should've known," I said, as they approached me.

"You're not gonna tell us we can do magic now, are you?" Cyrus joked.

I gave him a dirty look.

"Of course not," I said, trying not to smile. "We're still human, we're just special somehow." I turned to Cal. "So, Cal, I just realized something. Your compulsive need to lie, it's not all that altruistic, I'm sorry to say. It's probably innate."

"Can you speak in plain English please, Faye?" Thomas pleaded, followed by a huge sneeze. Alex caught on right away.

"You're Pinocchio, Cal," he explained. "You've always had the urge to cover up for us and lie to Galiana. You're Pinocchio, get it? You lie. That's your thing. And that's why Galiana loves it so much when you do that."

Cal looked at me as I nodded my head in agreement. His ears went pink and he looked to the ground.

"There's nothing to be bashful about, buddy," Cyrus

said. "That's Cary's job anyway. So you're a compulsive liar! At least you're not Thumbelina. Now *that* would be embarrassing!"

We all laughed again. Cal was relieved to learn his friends accepted him, despite his flaws. We were all happy for him. Moments later, the soccer game continued, and this time, we girls joined in.

Like I was saying, Diane, it's hard to find ways to pass your time after you've made a discovery that changes the way you look at things. What else is there to do but have fun and enjoy your life?

Lots of love,
Faye

44

Chapter

Although the gang had been leaning on each other for support, each of us wanted some time to ourselves as well. I knew exactly where to find Benji that warm, sunny afternoon when he told us glumly he wanted to be alone. As I walked up the long deck facing the never-ending Momma Lake and the island, I admired the rolling hills and acres of land surrounding me. Benji sat at the edge of the dock. He didn't notice me until I sat down beside him.

"Hey," he said. His bare feet dangled in the clear lake water.

"Hi," I grinned.

Our relationship was getting stronger each day. We still weren't the way we had been before the Galiana incident, but we were making progress. For that, I was grateful.

"I think you're right about the destiny thing, Faye."

"You do?"

"Yeah. I think each of us has a destiny and our parents sent us to Camp Milestone to figure it out. Or maybe even to live it out."

"I think so, too."

"But you know what I don't understand?" He asked me.

"Part of me is relieved to know we have a destiny. But another part of me is disappointed because that means we don't have control over anything. We might as well do nothing because what's going to happen is going to happen."

"I don't think so," I reasoned. "I think *some* things are meant to be, and those things will happen regardless. But how we get there is up to us. Otherwise, Melaine would really be named Cinderella, and she'd meet a real prince who would be looking for her based on a glass slipper. I think it's the idea that's the same, not the whole story."

"So what's Melaine's story then?" Benji asked.

"I don't know. But I bet that's what grades two and three at Camp Milestone are for," I answered.

"I'm having a hard time understanding everything. Do you think this means that everyone in the world has lived a similar life in the past?"

"Probably, I guess."

"But then how come the entire world isn't attending Camp Milestone?"

"I don't know. Maybe somehow, Chester or whoever found out those fairy tales were based on true stories and he found a way to locate us when we get struck by lightning." I paused. "But here's my question for you. How can you know about someone who lived before unless you have written proof?"

"So what you're saying is, only people who were important enough to have been written about get to know their destiny?" Benji asked.

"Maybe? It makes sense, doesn't it?"

Benji looked at me in surprise. Then, slowly, his expression faded, replaced by one of utmost seriousness.

"How do you know this stuff?"

"I don't know," I responded. It was strange. Although I had figured a bunch of stuff out, I had been saying "I don't know" a lot lately. "They're just my theories, I guess."

Benji smiled and looked at me. We locked eyes for what seemed like an eternity. In my usual fashion, I could feel

myself blushing. *Don't fall into this again*, I ordered myself.
You will only end up heartbroken again.

"I'm sorry I doubted you the other day," he blurted. He
turned his face away from me.

"It's OK. I understand why you did." *I think.*

"I really wanted to believe you. I guess I messed up."

I could tell he was upset. Benji had an amazing ability
to keep the same facial expression most of the time, but this
moment was an exception; his remorse was painted all over his
features.

"It's really OK. You're forgiven."

"I find myself apologizing a lot around you," he said
hoarsely. It was true.

"I find myself saying stupid things around you. I really
like onions," I confessed.

He laughed, showing his teeth. His thick, dirty blond
hair had grown longer since the beginning of camp. Naturally, I
loved it.

"Not only that," he said, "but people say stupid things
about you to me, too!"

"What do you mean by that?"

"Can you believe Galiana said you loved me?" he
chortled.

Oh! He thinks it's a lie. I contemplated telling him
Galiana had been right. What would be the worst that could
happen? Then, I quickly smiled at my own idiocy. I knew
exactly what the worst would be. The worst would be he
wouldn't like me back. And after the Galiana incident, I knew
what that felt like — one of the worst feelings in the world. I
couldn't tell him anything. I would just have to live my life
secretly loving him and enjoying his friendship instead. *Plus,*
I worried, *if I admit I liked him, then it would mean Galiana
had been right. Benji could infer she had been right about
everything else.*

"Pff, I know!" I said, trying to sound genuine. "What a
crock!"

I was a horrible liar. My fake enthusiasm was giving me

away. I could feel myself crashing and burning.

"Listen, I have something to tell you," I said, changing the subject. I stuck my hand in my pocket and took something out. "These might not grow if you plant them, but they definitely *taste* magical," I said extending my hand toward Benji.

I had a few of his caramel-covered coffee beans in my hand. Benji squinted, leaving a puzzled look on his face.

"I'm not following you."

"Galiana should have made you climb a *beanstalk*, not a tree."

Benji's eyes almost popped out of his head. His face broke into a huge smile and he let out a suggestive chuckle.

"You really are — something," he said with hesitation.

Something. I'm something. Could he be any more cryptic? I wasn't sure what that meant, but it sounded like a compliment. I tried hard to suppress my delight, but I knew it was futile; I couldn't stop the big grin that surfaced on my face.

"So what do you think?" I asked, wanting him to keep talking.

"What should I think? You just told me I'm Jack from *Jack and the Beanstalk*!" he joked as he buried his head in his hands.

I was happy. I was always happy when I was with him.

"There is one more thing I have to show you," I said. "But you have to stand up."

Benji stood up obediently. Pleased at how easy it had been, I mustered all of my strength and gave him a big, hearty push. Giddy, I laughed at the sight of Benji's shocked face hitting the surface of the water. This time, I didn't wait for him to surface. Instead, I turned around and ran all the way back to camp, as I cackled and yelled, "That was too much fun!"

45
Chapter

As the summer neared an end, we prepared ourselves to graduate to grade two. We decided unanimously we wanted to announce our discovery of the camp's secret at the upcoming dance. As nobody at the dance would know about the discovery we had made — especially with Galiana missing and Cecilia determined to stay mum — Melaine suggested the best way to announce our breakthrough would be by making a bold statement.

"We're really doing this? We're really going to sew?" Cal asked Melaine, the day before the dance.

"Yup," she replied.

"Um, guys, I don't know how to sew," Niki said anxiously. Cyrus walked over to her and patted her on the head.

"Don't you worry your sleepy little head about a thing. Just smile and look pretty, Niki. We'll figure it out."

The others laughed and Niki let out a giggle. She was wonderfully easygoing.

"I guess that's another thing Cinderella and I have in common. My mom was a seamstress, and after she, um, well, you know ... I basically followed in her footsteps so I could feel close to her again," Melaine explained awkwardly.

She led us to the sewing room we had discovered earlier in the summer. We had one day to make thirteen costumes. The plan was to show up late to ensure that everyone would be there. Then, in true fairy-tale fashion, we would make a grand entrance wearing the typical costumes of our fairy-tale counterparts. While everyone else would be dressed in normal formal clothing, Camp Milestone's grade one class would show up in vintage costumes and show everyone we had figured out part of the big secret.

Because the idea was Melaine's, she gladly took charge and instructed everyone. The fast learners received big tasks and the slower learners had smaller responsibilities, such as sewing on buttons or cutting fabric. I loved seeing Melaine get excited about something; it was the first time all summer she seemed to truly be in her element. In case you were wondering about my fate, we decided my dress would be the last one made because I still hadn't discovered which fairy tale character I was supposed to be. Nobody was worried though. I still had a whole day to figure it out.

The costumes looked strange at first, but it was soon obvious Melaine knew what she was doing. She had drawn sketches of the final products and they looked stunning. She was creative, talented, and, like she had said previously, a visual person. I had never realized until that moment that all fairy-tale characters had a stereotypical image.

"Should I be embarrassed to walk into a dance wearing a dwarf costume?" Cary asked, already anticipating the humiliation.

"No," Benji said. "You should be proud we figured this secret out and aren't afraid to announce it. Just pretend like it's Halloween."

"Easy for you to say, Mr. Beanstalk," Cyrus said as he put on his bonnet. We all cracked up as we looked at Cyrus the dwarf. He looked so out of place, like the Big Bad Wolf in Little Red Riding Hood's grandmother's clothing.

We continued our costume making until dawn, at which point we started falling asleep, one by one. Most of us had never realized how much work goes into creating a single costume, let alone thirteen.

It was Sunday afternoon when I woke up. The others were still sleeping. I snickered at Cyrus, who was lying on his back with a thimble on his forehead. I replayed his voice in my head: "At least you're not Thumbelina. Now *that* would be embarrassing."

Ha ha. Where is my camera? I wondered.

The costumes looked nearly done. I looked over at Benji. Part of me wanted to wake him up so we could spend time together. The more time I spent with him, the more I craved his presence. Instead, I willed myself to let him sleep. We had a long day and night ahead of us, and I had one last mission left — to figure out my own identity. I knew the only way to do that would be on my own. I sighed, blew him a secret kiss and left. As I walked out, I swallowed hard, reminding myself that perhaps "destiny" didn't have it in the cards for me to end up with Benji. After all, Jack doesn't have a wife, does he?

46

Chapter

For hours, I sat on the dock staring out at the regal Momma Lake. *Why can't I figure it out? Everyone else's came so easily to me. Why can't I see myself the same way I see them?* Surprisingly, I wasn't upset. If I had to pick one person to be in this situation, I was glad it was me. I wouldn't wish this uncertainty, this isolation, on any of my friends. Plus, I knew the answer was staring me right in the face; I just needed to open my eyes and see it.

"Why can't I figure this out?" I asked myself aloud this time.

The more time passed, the more depressed I became. I knew I was running out of time and the pressure wasn't helping me focus. I would be the only one of my friends who hadn't figured out her identity. *G-Almighty will have a field day. Faye Martin, the only one who didn't figure it out! Ugh. This could be really bad.*

I could feel my stomach turning. I didn't even know where to start looking. Somehow, it had been so clear with the others, but when it came to my own identity, my vision became cloudy. I just couldn't see myself that way.

The sound of footsteps approaching on the dock

brought me back to reality. To my surprise and relief (and adoration), it was Benji. He sat down next to me and said, "There you are," with a sigh. Dejected, I dug deep inside my heart to muster up a smile.

On any other day, Benjamin Parker looking for me and sitting next to me would have made me beam with content. But not today. Benji recognized my mood right away. In his truly considerate fashion, he didn't say another word. Instead, we sat next to each other looking at the view for what seemed like an eternity. I put my head on his shoulder, and as soon as I felt his arm around me, I let a tear trickle down my cheek. Still, Benji didn't say a word. Instead, he let me cry and think, until I had nothing left to think about.

47
Chapter

"Everyone's looking for you. Can you find the energy to walk back anytime soon?" Benji finally said to me. I couldn't find any words to reply.

"Hey," he continued. "Remember the first day, before the G-factor graced us with her presence? Miss Chung said if we ever feel lost, the answers are not far away. She was looking directly at you when she said that. Somehow, I think they knew you'd be the last one to find out. I think this is the way it's supposed to be."

"How do you remember that?" I asked, in a deep, scratchy voice.

"I, er, have a great memory when it comes to, uh, useless details," he replied awkwardly.

I gave him a half-smile. I wished I had the energy to over-analyze his response the way I usually did, but I didn't. For once, my crush took a backburner to more pressing matters.

"Don't worry," Benji said. "Everything's going to turn out perfectly. I promise. And I never break my promises."

I felt slightly better hearing those words from him.

"Thanks," I said.

"Hey, do you hear anything?" he asked me

228

mischievously, a few minutes later.

In the distance, I could hear screaming. I looked up to see a canoe far away in the lake. Three people were in the canoe, one of them standing up and waving her arms. I turned back to Benji, who looked liked he was about to burst out laughing. As the canoe slowly got closer, I deciphered the screams. It was Niki, Melaine and Hazel. Niki was the one standing up, waving haphazardly. They were all screaming my name.

"See?" Benji said. "She loves you. They all love you. What's more perfect than that?"

I smiled. He had a point. Niki was getting more and more excited the closer they got.

"She's going to tip the canoe," I said, finally letting out a little laugh. I could hear my name clearly now.

"FAAAAAAYE!" she bellowed. "FAAAYE MARTIN! FAAAYE! DON'T WORRY, FAYE!!! FAAAAYE MARTIN! WE'RE HERE FOR YOU! YOU'RE NOT ALONE!"

"Just wait until they get here. They have a surprise for you," Benji informed me.

A few minutes later, the canoe finally reached the dock. The girls disembarked, each one holding a pile of heavy books.

"What's all this?" I asked them.

"The answer to your problems," Hazel said, as she gave me a small smack on the back of the head. "That's the second time you've fallen off the face of the planet. Don't do it a third time!"

"Yes, ma'am," I answered.

Melaine and Niki gave me a hug. Like a pack of wolves, they placed themselves around me and handed me a stack of books. There were so many. As I took a closer look, I noticed they were all the different versions of fairy tales from the camp library.

"We have three hours until the dance," Niki said. "You're somewhere in these books, Faye Martin, and we're going to find you."

It was so sweet. I could hardly control the huge grin on

my face.

"I thought I'd never see that smile again," Benji whispered in my ear. Goose bumps formed over my entire body. I cleared my throat and tried to act cool.

"Where did you guys get all of these?" I asked them.

"It's actually quite amazing," Melaine noted. "For a camp that doesn't have many frills, Camp Milestone sure has all its bases covered."

"Let's see," Niki said, picking up the first book, *Hansel and Gretel*. She flipped through the pages and examined me from head to toe, as if looking at me for the first time.

"Nope," Benji said. "Impossible. She has no siblings. Who would Hansel be?"

"You're right. Next!"

They each seized a book and started reading frantically.

"What about Rapunzel?" Hazel asked.

"No," I said shaking my head. "That's definitely not me. And I may have seen Rapunzel on the island that night with Benji."

Benji nodded in agreement. Stacy's hair had been freakishly long.

We continued in that manner for hours. Before we knew it, our time ran out and we had to return to camp to get ready for the dance. In the end, I was none-the-wiser. Unfortunately for me, I was still just plain old Faye Martin who had gotten hit by lightning, gone to Camp Milestone (the worst camp in the history of camps), met her best friends in the world there, and had a giant glowing Lichtenberg rash on her back, which was an indication she was a modern-day fairy-tale character. OK, maybe not so plain.

It was just going to have to do.

For now.

48
Chapter

My self pity didn't last long. As we walked up to the great hall that Sunday night, I knew I was glowing. And no, not because of the rash! I looked quite pretty. I had on a flowered dress and some cute summer sandals. My hair looked two shades lighter than what it had been at the beginning of summer, and my skin was bronzed and smooth. I had my hair in an upsweep and Hazel did my makeup.

"This place has really changed you," Hazel said as she applied my eye shadow. "You get prettier and prettier each day." Coming from her, that meant a lot; it was hard for her to hand out compliments.

"Isn't that the pot calling the kettle black," I retorted.

The rest of the gang wore the costumes Melaine had designed. The final products were impressive. They all looked fantastic. I could tell my friends felt guilty I couldn't participate, but I insisted I was content watching them shine. I wasn't sure why, but I felt like a proud mama bird watching her chicks fly for the first time. This wasn't about me, it was about them. And I was totally fine with that.

The music was booming from inside the hall. We stood outside watching the party for a few minutes. Naturally, we were nervous.

"This is ridiculous," Sterne said.

"I can't do this," Cary said, his face turning a deep shade of red.

"You're braver than you think, Cary," I whispered. "You so can do this."

I grabbed him and pushed him toward the hall stairs. I gestured for the others to follow. I made sure everyone had gone inside before I closed the door behind me.

The hall had been decorated professionally. It looked like a scene right out of a cheesy movie with gold and silver balloons everywhere. Long drapes hung from the ceiling to the floor and an ice sculpture sat in the center of the room next to one of the many marble fountains. Waiters with bowties walked around with fancy appetizer trays as we all stood quietly in the entranceway watching the action.

"Holy smokes. Does anyone know if Chester's a millionaire?" Cyrus muttered.

The hall was swarming with people. As we scanned the room for familiar faces, the crowd slowly noticed our presence. Gasps erupted, followed by a thick hush of silence. I ducked behind my friends, making sure to stay unseen at the back of the entranceway. It was hard for me to see what was happening.

"Our parents are here!" hissed Hazel through the deafening silence.

"What's going on?" I wondered, curious.

"They're just staring at us," Thomas said quietly without moving his lips (and out came a huge sneeze).

"Come in, come in. Please, guys, come in!" called out a musical and familiar voice. It was Chester.

The gang took a few shy steps forward. I managed to find a spot in the shadows where I finally got a good view of the room. Chester stood in the middle of the hall. All of Camp Milestone's attendants were there with their families. In the back, I could see my parents, beaming with pride.

"What a wonderful night!" Chester said. "It seems, ladies and gentlemen, our entire first grade class is trying to tell us something. And I couldn't be happier! This would be the first time in Milestone's history the entire grade found out simultaneously!"

"Actually," Cyrus said, "Faye still hasn't —"

"Cyrus, shush!" Hazel, Benji and Niki growled at the same time. Chester squinted at me and smiled to himself. *Now he knows. I had hoped we could trick it out of him.*

"As I was saying, this is absolutely remarkable. I'm very proud of all of you. In the spirit of maintaining our philosophy here at Camp Milestone, I would ask each of you to come and speak to me when you have a spare minute tonight. Aside from that, you might have noticed your families are here. I'm sure you have missed them terribly and you must have a lot of catching up to do. Let the party begin!"

Chester clapped his hands and a band started playing. Immediately, my friends spread out like a fan, each honing in on their families. I followed suit and felt relieved my parents looked just the same. Immediately, they showered me with hugs and kisses. My mother fixed my hair and straightened my dress. My dad smiled sheepishly and commented on how much I had grown.

"Oh, honey, you look absolutely beautiful," my mother said. "Look at you."

"You've obviously been up to quite a bit," my father remarked, eyeing the costumes on my friends.

I filled them in on the information I hadn't written about in my letters. Despite the sadness I was trying to hide, I was overjoyed to be reunited with them. Chester was right; I had missed them terribly. As I babbled on (and on, and on!), several thoughts preoccupied me. First, let's be honest. It was a dance and I was a teenager with a crush. Would I get to dance with Benji? Would he ask me to dance, even as a friend? Or would I have to sit on the sidelines and suffer in silence like I'd always done? In the past, I had hated dances. Diane and I would go together, she'd get asked to dance all night long, and I would sit in the corner and pretend to look busy while secretly swooning over Benji. Second, I noticed each of my

friends talking to Chester individually. I watched carefully
as they pointed to me and made tons of exaggerated gestures
suggesting they were defending me. Chester's body language
was harder to decode. He shook his head a lot, but overall, he
remained indecipherable.

Later still, I introduced my friends to my parents. While
they made conversation with my mom and dad, I kept my eyes
glued to Benji. Then, I caught Chester's glance from across the
hall. He gestured for me to come over and talk to him.

"You must be very proud of Faye," Melaine said to my
parents.

"We are, thank you," my mom said humbly.

"Did you know she figured everything out by herself?"
Melaine added.

I excused myself and walked toward Chester. I didn't
know why, but I was nervous. Chester was intimidating.
Maybe it was the eyes; they looked like they belonged on
a werewolf or something. I looked back at Benji for an
encouraging glance. To my disappointment, a handful of new
and beautiful girls surrounded him. I wasn't surprised. He was
irresistible. It was only a matter of time before one of those
girls would snatch him up. They were so much more forward
and confident than I was. *Ugh.*

"Your friends have nothing but wonderful things to say
about you," Chester remarked after I said hello to him. I smiled
uneasily. "Is it true you single-handedly discovered our secret?"

I shrugged my shoulders. I had never thought of it that
way. I looked back at Benji again. Backed into a corner, he
kept chatting with the other girls. Chester continued speaking.

"Hazel's quite the character," he said. That caught my
attention.

"No pun intended, right?" I quipped curtly. Chester
seemed taken aback.

"No, none actually," he replied. "She marched up to me
and told me she doesn't agree with the way I am running the
camp. She was particularly passionate about my decision to
have Galiana as director. Do you agree with her?"

Galiana. That was a name I didn't miss. Despite my initial aversion to her name, I couldn't help wonder — where was she?

"Why do you ask?"

"I'm only curious. Hazel was adamant Galiana made your lives miserable. She said you were forced to do dangerous deeds, you never needed her and you found your way entirely on your own, with no help from Galiana. Is this true?"

Well, not entirely, unfortunately. Hazel was only partially right. Although her methods were questionable (to say the least!), Galiana helped us come to the discovery. Actually, her punishments were instrumental clues. Sleeping for Sleeping Beauty? Climbing trees for Jack? Eating apples for Snow White? Truly, it was brilliant. But we would have found out regardless, right? That's what Hazel meant. Galiana only complicated matters, didn't she? And she was outright mean! She was cruel, unkind, unforgiving and made us cry. She should be punished for that, shouldn't she? She can't get away with that. Justifying my upcoming response, I opened my mouth to answer his question when Chester spoke again.

"The truth is, Faye, I appointed Galiana because I needed to get a job done. We had been operating things a certain way for many years, and it didn't seem to be working any longer. We needed a fresh face, a new outlook on things." *Why is he telling me this?*

"Galiana is not exactly a people person," Chester pressed on. "I know this. I knew it before I asked her to take over. But she got the job done. And she did it well. I mean, look at you guys!" He said with a hint of pride. Un-freaking-believable. Galiana was actually going to getting credit for this.

"Then congratulations on a job well-done," I said, disgusted. "You must be very proud of yourself."

"You don't agree with what I'm saying?" He had picked up on my aversion.

"Why does it matter? You've obviously already made your decision and you're clearly happy with the results."

Chester stared hard at me for a moment. Uncomfortable

under his blue-eyed glare, I looked around the room. Benji continued chatting with the girls who buzzed around him like a swarm of bees. His attention was mainly focused on Stacy. *Of course, Stacy with the freakishly long hair and killer body.* Why would he want me when he could have anybody? There I went again, back down the old beaten path. *Enough,* I ordered myself. *You and Benji are friends and nothing more. Get over it.*

The other boys had gathered around the refreshments. Cyrus was showing some of the older campers his gurgling tricks and the silly way he made fart noises with his hands. Thomas' parents were giving him his new inhaler and Cal was arguing with his uncle. I wasn't surprised to see poor Bo asleep in a corner and Niki hovering around him protectively.

"There's just one more thing I wanted to tell you, Faye," Chester started again. "I'm sure you know that anyone who doesn't know their identity cannot move ahead a year here." My jaw dropped as I glared back at him in disbelief. *He can't be saying what I think he's saying.*

"You're kidding, right?" I asked.

"I'm afraid not. I wish it didn't have to be this way, but you'll have to stay back with the new campers next year until, of course, you find out who you are."

"You're, you're failing me? But why?"

Chester laughed.

"I'm not *failing* you, Faye. This isn't school. These are just camp rules. I'm sure it won't be too long until you can join the others. I mean, look at what you've done already! You'll probably figure it all out by next summer. Oh, which brings me to my next point. You have to leave earlier as well."

"What?" I sputtered.

Chester laughed again. He seemed entertained by my reactions, which made me even angrier. *Grrrr!* Why did people always find my anger so funny? Why did people never take me seriously?

"Don't worry, it's not anytime soon. You'll get to enjoy yourself and hang out with your friends for another two weeks.

But you will go home after that while the other campers stay for an extra week."

Appalled, I couldn't believe what I was hearing.

"But, but, no! You can't do this! Why?"

"You can't move on to the next year if you don't know enough about yourself. The second year at Camp Milestone is very different from the first, Faye."

"After all you said about the camp needing change and a new outlook, you're not willing to make an exception?" Chester shook his head apologetically. "But how am I supposed to stay back with new people if I know the secret? Why would you want me there if I can spoil the surprise?"

"But you won't, will you, Faye?" he said authoritatively. "I know you won't. Do you think they would believe you, if you told them? Don't you see? I would have told you the first day if I thought you would believe me. This is something you have to figure out yourselves when you're ready."

"Then tell me who I am now! I promise I'll believe you. I'm ready! I have nothing to lose."

Chester seemed to consider my desperate plea for a brief moment before deciding against it.

"I'm sorry, Faye, I can't do it. I can't break the rules for you. I don't just come up with these rules on a whim. Camp Milestone has been around for decades. We have come up with our rules and regulations after many trials and tribulations. All of this," he pointed to the hall and the people inside it, "is based on many years of exper—"

"No," I interrupted.

"No, what?" he asked me, taken aback.

"No! You're not doing this to me," I demanded. "I'm not letting you!"

"Faye —"

"No, Chester. No, no, no —"

I stopped. A few months ago, I would never have been brave enough to talk back to my elders or be my own person. But now, I did so without a moment's thought. This was my life and I was going to defend it.

"Faye, I'm sorry. It wouldn't be fair to the other campers. Now if you'll excuse me, I have to be getting back to —"

"No, wait, please," I begged him, my eyes filling with tears. I grabbed his sleeve so he couldn't move. He was wearing a suit. For once, he didn't look like an airport employee. He looked like he could run an entire camp. He was just so young.

"Are there other Camp Milestones?"

"Perhaps," he answered. I tightened my grip on his sleeve.

"Where? Which countries?" I asked.

"Faye. Enough." Chester said as he tried to stop smiling. Although he didn't want me to ask any more questions, I knew he was tickled by me. I sighed in disappointment.

"Faye, listen to me," he said, removing my clenched hand from his sleeve. "You're a bright and fantastic young girl."

"Ugh, quit patronizing me."

"I'm not patronizing you," he scolded. "Listen, will you? You *will* figure everything out eventually. Of this, I am more certain than anything. You still have two weeks of camp. That's a long time. And you can do whatever you wa—"

"What about Galiana?" I interrupted. Chester sighed.

"As I was saying, you can do whatever you want. Explore the grounds, the forest, everything. I'll even leave a trail map for you. Enjoy yourselves, have fun. That is what camp is all about. Isn't this what you've wanted all along?" he asked me, knowing all too well that it was. "The rest will come with time. If I don't see you after tonight, I look forward to seeing you again next year."

I lowered my head in defeat.

"Your parents will be leaving soon," he said. "You should say goodbye. After that, the hall is yours for however long you like. I'm sure your friends are looking forward to dancing with you."

I shrugged my shoulders in regret. Disappointed, I forced a weak smile and thanked Chester for his time. As I walked away, I looked back at him. He was hurt by my cold goodbye. I considered revoking my frigid goodbye, but I couldn't find it in me to not be so angry with him. I wanted him to make an exception for me. I wanted it badly.

~

My mom cried as she was leaving.

"Oh, sweetheart," she said. "Now you finally know what I mean when I say I am truly proud of the person you will become."

"Yes, mom. I still don't forgive you for lying to me, but now I know."

I already had forgiven them. We all forgave our parents, knowing we, too, might have to lie to our children someday. Plus, I was so lucky to have them, both of them. Melaine and Hazel would have loved to have had their mothers there that night. The guilt made me appreciate my family so much more.

My dad gave me a long hug and said he couldn't wait until I was back home. I couldn't believe they had traveled all that way so they could see me for a few hours. There aren't too many parents who would do that, I knew. I also said goodbye to my friends' parents. Melaine's and Hazel's fathers were there, and Benji's mom, as well. Predictably, Benji's dad hadn't come. I knew Benji felt let down.

After filling my friends in on the conversation I'd had with Chester, I had to calm them down. Everyone was upset at the news that I had to leave early and couldn't join them in grade two. Although I was also deeply upset, I managed to convince them I would figure it all out before next summer. I promised them I wouldn't rest until I knew who I was. There was no point in worrying over something we couldn't control. We just had to put our heads together and figure out who I was. How difficult could it be?

Chester was right about one thing. After the adults left, the party was incredible. The dance continued until we could hardly move our feet. I danced with the entire gang, minus Benji. Why not Benji? Well, it was like a comedy of errors. Every time we tried to talk to each other, one of us would get pulled away by an unsuspecting outsider, leaving our conversation interrupted. At one point, I overheard him begging Cary to help him lose his followers, not realizing Cary was the wrong person to ask. He ran away before Benji could cause him humiliation. To my relief, there were no slow songs so I didn't have to witness Benji and Stacy slow dancing. In my fantasies, I still believed I would be the girl he'd ask to dance, but in reality, I knew it was unlikely.

Niki and I spent a good portion of the night theorizing about G-Almighty's disappearing act. It was only when Benji joined us and asked us to help him hide that we forgot about Galiana.

"What's the matter, Benji?" Niki mocked him. "Who are you hiding from?"

I laughed. It was funny seeing him squirm. Moments later, he begged me to leave with him, not knowing that I wasn't going to think twice about it. Trying not to seem too eager, I agreed and we left. On the way back to our cabin, Benji struck up a conversation.

"Can you promise me something?" he asked.

"Sure, anything," I said, realizing immediately how pathetic I sounded. *Tone it down a notch, will ya?*

"Promise me we'll actually talk in school this year," he said. It was not what I expected to hear.

"I didn't think you noticed that we didn't talk before," I said, hoping he would understand what I was hinting at.

"I noticed, Faye," he replied, looking at his feet. *Oh, really?* I felt I should say something now. Maybe this was the moment for me to admit how much I liked him.

"You look really pretty tonight," he said.

Omigod. Omigod. Say it. Just say it, Faye. What do you have to lose? Go on. Say, "Benji, I like you." Go on, do it.

"Benji, I — *promise*," I said, losing my confidence. *Coward!*

I didn't know why, but I didn't feel as though I could

admit my feelings for Benji. Not after everything I'd been through. And certainly not until after I'd figured out my true identity. Plus, as an eternal romantic and lover of chivalry, I secretly hoped he'd be the one to make the first move.

"I promise, too," Benji replied. "And remember, I never break my promises."

49
Chapter

Dear Diane,

Only two days left until I'm on my way home. I just hope I don't cry too much. Don't get me wrong, I'm so excited to see you again and it will be nice to come home, but I wish I didn't have to leave like this.

The past two weeks have been the best of my life. Chester left us a map of the surrounding area and this forest must be the coolest ever. There is a natural water slide about twenty minutes away. It was made totally by nature. So you hike up the hill, sit on the top, slide all the way down, there's a fall and then you're in a little pool of lake water. I thought I would get tons of scratches and bruises, but no, it's totally safe. Needless to say, we've been there almost every day. We've really had a blast. Cecilia Chung comes and checks up on us every morning (though, let's be honest. They are so spying on us the rest of the day). Cecilia has breakfast with us most days, but that's about all. Still no sign of the Big G. And Chester apparently has his hands full with grades two and three.

What else? Oh, we've also gone swimming in Momma Lake many times. Benji has tried to push me in with my clothes on about a million times, but I've managed to get away quite successfully. Thomas has a pretty bad sunburn. I suppose that's because most of our days involve a water source somehow. I thought we would have run out of things to say after the first few days, but that hasn't been the case. I guess you never truly run out of things to say with real friends (you and I never have!). Not to mention there are thirteen of us, so there's always something to laugh at. And if we ever run out of things to say, we can count on Alex to educate us on some scientific discovery.

I can tell some of them are getting sadder as each day passes. I wonder if it's because of me. I'm having a harder time containing my misery. Even Cyrus, the joker, comes over and gives me a hug every now and then. He'll throw in an insult right after to cancel out the seriousness, of course. I better go. I will probably see you before you even get this letter, so I might as well tell you the rest in person. What a summer, eh?

Love,

Faye

P.S. Melaine's dad bought her a waterproof camera. She will be mailing all of us the pictures from the past two weeks so you'll get to see what everyone looks like!

50
Chapter

On the plane ride home, I recalled my last day of camp. Benji refused to let me sleep. He made me stay up all night with him. We ended up talking and flirting like crazy. The next morning, they all walked me to the big empty school bus, the same bus that had brought thirteen unsuspecting strangers together two months ago. The same bus driver who almost ran me over was now going to drive me back to the airport. The same seats that my friends had sat in were now empty. The bus was the same, but everything else was different. My friends were different. My relationship with Benji was different. Our entire outlook on life was different. And most of all, *I* was different in a way I didn't even understand yet.

Hazel and Melaine cried the minute they woke up. They promised a million times to stay in touch. Niki tried to keep the tears in check, but they burst out of her giant eyes as soon as the bus pulled into the circular driveway. She cried hysterically. I hugged my friends as each gave me their parting words of wisdom.

Bo: "It was great spending time with you. I'm sorry I scared you when you thought I was a ghost."

Thomas: "I know you'll figure it out, Faye. I have no

doubt at all. *Aaa-tchoo!* Could you send me some more allergy medicine?"

Asher: "There's no point in dwelling on the past. Just look forward. Everything will be great."

Sterne: "This is stupid. This whole thing is totally stupid. I hate this place."

Cary: "If you have time, but only if you have time, and only if you want to, write me. If you want. If it's OK. If you don't mind. Um, yeah. Bye."

Alex: "Let me know if you want to borrow *Physics for the Advanced High School Student*. I'm only a phone call away."

Cyrus: "Gimme a hug, woman. And try not to miss your plane. It's not going to wait for you like we did on the bus."

Hazel: "I hate this, Faye. This is all Galiana's fault. I'm really going to miss you. We'll keep in touch, right?"

Cal: "Thanks for being a great listener. I'll write."

Melaine: "Something special is going to happen for you. I can tell. And we're friends for life, Faye."

Niki: "Everyone always says they'll stay in touch and they never do. But we will, right, Faye? Please figure it out soon. We'll push Chester to let you in our year. We'll do everything we can. You can count on us."

And finally came Benji's turn.

"You promised me," he said glumly, "I don't want this just to be a summer thing."

"And you promised, too," I said. *Well, even if he doesn't love me back, at least he loves me like a friend.*

"I'll see you soon. I'll call you when I get back."

I nodded. He gave me a brief smile, and I briefly thought I saw a glimmer in his eye. As the bus started to pull away, Benji came running up and pounded on the bus driver's door, gesturing for her to open the doors one more time. The bus stopped and I stood up in anticipation.

"Sorry," he told the bus driver.

"Hurry up," she ordered angrily.

"Here," he handed me an envelope.

"What is it?"

"A note. I almost forgot to give it to you."

"Thanks." We stood staring awkwardly at each other knowing all too well we were being watched by everyone outside. "Well, I guess you should go."

"I know."

He gave me another brief hug, which I had hoped would linger long enough to satisfy me, but it didn't.

"Bye," I said, as he turned around quickly and ran off.

I snapped back to reality on the plane and wiped the tears from my cheeks. I had read Benji's note ten times already, but the lasting memory pushed me to read it once more.

Faye,

I can't believe I had ~~all night~~ all summer with you and I couldn't find the courage to tell you this in person. Now, I'm rushed for time and I have too much to say. Just know this is only the beginning. I'm excited to see you soon and I have all the faith in you and your ability to figure things out.

Also, it was great to spend time with you this summer. You're truly the salt of the earth. Again, I'm so ~~psyched~~ glad I got to spend my summer with you. To think, if you hadn't seen me helping Diane get gum out of her hair on the last day of school, you would never have gotten upset with her, and I never would have followed you to the park. Which means you would never have gotten hit by lightning and we wouldn't be here right now. I'm sorry you were the one who had to get struck, but I'm not sorry about the aftermath. This was the best summer ~~of my life~~. OK, you're leaving. I'll see you soon. Take care of yourself.

From your friend,

Benji (never to be called Benjamin by you)

P.S. ~~How about~~ ~~The reason I~~ Want to go out with me?

Once again, his words confused me. In one sentence, he seemed to be saying one thing, and in the next he was ensuring I knew we were just friends. One sentence in particular dumfounded me. Salt of the earth? What the heck did that mean? Was he trying to be mysterious on purpose? Embarrassed, I reluctantly brought up my hand to my mouth and gave it a quick lick. It was not "salty." I sighed. I would have to Google that the minute I got home. But he asked me out, right? I wasn't crazy? That last sentence meant what I thought it did? *Right?*

A few hours later — after I'd exhausted my obsession with the letter — I decided to distract myself and keep busy. Thinking about my camp friends (and Benji) was too sad to bear. I began brainstorming. I pulled out my pen and paper and started writing.

"Let's see," I mumbled to myself, thinking back to that day on the dock. "What do all fairy tales have in common? Hmm, well, they all start with 'Once upon a time.'"

I scribbled an abbreviated OUAT on the pad.

"They like the number seven a lot, I think, like the seven dwarfs. There's usually a prince involved ..." I scribbled the number seven and the word prince.

"They all end with, 'Lived happily ever after.'"

I wrote an abbreviated LHEA.

For a moment I stared silently at my scribbles. The wheels turned in my brain. *Lhea. Lhea? Omigod, LHEA!*

"Holy cow!" I said aloud. The passenger next to me looked over. "Can you believe it?" I asked her. "It makes sense. It's not What, it's OUAT! That's why Galiana wouldn't write it down. It would give it away. And it's not Leah, it's LHEA!"

"What are you talking about, dear?" The woman next to me asked, confused by my delirious ranting.

"Our song! Our stupid camp song! It all begins with 'OUAT.' That means it all begins with once upon a time! It holds us all together. It all will end with 'LHEA.' Lhea's not a person! It's an acronym for 'live happily ever after.' Don't you see?"

Thinking I was insane, the woman rolled her eyes and returned to her book. The adrenaline rush made me bounce in my chair for a few minutes. I continued to examine my scribbles as if they would jump out of the page and tell me something more.

They didn't.

"Why so quiet dear?" my neighbor asked me, several minutes later.

"Well, it's just, um, I still don't get what it means."

"I'm sure you'll figure it out in no time," the lady answered.

"Yeah …" I sat back in my seat. "That's what everyone seems to think." *Sigh.*

51
Chapter

Dear Benji (or should I say, Jack?),

Well, here I am, nice and settled. As expected, my parents were there to greet me when I got off the plane in Seattle. I missed them, I really did. A good surprise, though, was when I saw Diane also waiting anxiously at the airport. She says, "Hi," by the way.

Although it made me nauseated, I owed it to my parents (and to poor Diane, who ran around trying to help me all summer) to give tons of Camp Milestone details. But as I relived my entire summer, I couldn't help wondering what you guys were doing, and more importantly, how you guys were doing.

I'm sure you know the best part of my arrival. You guys are absolutely fabulous. The look on my face when I entered my room had to be priceless. My entire bedroom filled with giant black-and-white pictures? You guys are too much! My favorite is the life-sized pictures of us. Of course, I soon remembered they were the pictures Melaine had taken during our past two weeks at Milestone. I imagine you guys collaborated with my parents somehow during that night at the dance? All I can say is, wow. Thank you, thank you, thank you! What a great birthday present. Suddenly, home feels like home again. My room looks like a giant scrapbook. It's absolutely beautiful. If I miss you guys, I just walk up to your life-sized picture and give you a big paper hug.

Oh, which reminds me. There is a picture of you and I that Melaine must have taken when we weren't looking. Have you seen it? It's really nice. Speaking of which, I read your note and I want to thank you for what you said. Especially the salt-of-the-earth bit. I confess, I didn't actually know what that meant, but I Googled it and now I know. That's very sweet of you. Thank you and ditto!

Anyway, I don't know whose idea this surprise was, but it was the best thing ever. I will thank every one of you individually (hope you're prepared!). So thanks, Jack! I feel like you're all in my room with me. Diane also was happy because she finally got to put faces to the names.

So, this is the first letter of many more to come. My life has changed drastically in the past two months. I used to be plain old reserved and introverted Faye; nothing more, nothing less. But now I know there's much more to me. I'm a girl with an adventure. A girl with a story. A girl with a group of incredible friends. The past two months have taught me that.

And I should also tell you I finally figured out the last little secret. Drum roll please ... Thank you. Ahem.

*So did you know the name Faye (or Fée) means "fairy" in French? And did you know that in all the fairy tales we read as children, there was a common denominator? Well, until recently, neither did I. But it turns out, the common denominator is actually the **Fairy God Mother**. And did you know my full name is **Faye Grace Martin**? Are you putting this*

250

*together? I guess I need to get myself a wand, right? Now go
and call me because I am dying to hear your reaction!*

*Anyway, Benji, we still have two years left at Milestone. Two
school years and two summers to figure out what all of this
fully means. Two years to figure out how exactly to fulfill our
"incumbent" destiny. You better believe I'm going to spend
each day trying to fill in the missing pieces of the puzzle. In the
meantime, I look forward to coming home and smiling at the
pictures of my friends. And of course, counting down the days
until I can see them again.*

Lots of love,

Faye

P.S. And to answer your last question: HELL YES!

Epilogue

"Know you what it is to be a child? It is to be something
very different from
the man of today. It is to have a spirit yet streaming
from the waters of
baptism; it is to believe in love, to believe in loveliness,
to believe in
belief; it is to be so little that the elves can reach to
whisper in your ear;
it is to turn pumpkins into coaches, and mice into
horses, lowness into
loftiness, and nothing into everything, for each child
has its fairy godmother
in its own soul."

Francis
Thompson

The End

Preview

Milestones
Book 2

Once upon a time, there was a little girl who was deathly afraid of thunderstorms. She was a lovely child, with fair skin and long hair that dangled down to her waistline. She was also a brave soul. Except for this specific phobia, there is nothing she wouldn't do or try. Unfortunately, the fear of thunderstorms was so intense for our maiden, it nearly consumed her existence. Whenever a dark cloud would drift aimlessly in the sky, she would drop everything and promptly seek shelter. She became an expert at avoiding all forms of precipitation.

On this particular Saturday evening, the sky was a familiar shade of ugly. Thunder and lightning alternated repeatedly like the crashing waves of the sea. True to her petrified nature, the girl hid spinelessly in the safety of her room, under the blankets of her massive, comforting bed. Each time a bolt of lightning flashed across the night sky and lit up her surroundings, the girl shuddered and buried herself deeper into her pillow. Her hands covering her ears tightly, she let out small yelps of terror as the inevitable rumbling of thunder followed closely behind. She was totally and utterly terrified.

Only, this little girl wasn't so little. She was actually a whopping 15 years old. And in fact, she wasn't a lovely maiden with fair skin and long hair. She was me: Faye Grace Martin, your friendly neighborhood girl-next-door turned not-so-normal Fairy God Mother.

Bzzzz.

Bzzzz.

"Holy crap!" I gasped at the sudden vibration trespassing into my deep thoughts. It was my cell phone, alerting me I had a text message.

I reluctantly reached my hand out from under my blanket and started feeling around blindly on my nightstand. A chilly aura filled the air and I immediately noticed the goose-bumps on my bare arms.

Bzzzz.

Bzzzz.

"Hang the heck on," I mouthed quietly. I believed talking too loudly would disclose my location to the evil sky gods (who, by the way, were intent on destroying me via lightning strike).

I fumbled around some more, finally grabbing my phone and swiftly bringing it under the covers.

It was Diane. But I already knew that.

Are you still hiding? She wrote.

Yup, I typed back. *Can't talk right now. U know how it goes. Will call u when it's over.*

I pressed the send button firmly and placed my cell back onto the nightstand as I curled up into a little ball, shaking furiously.

BOOM!

Geez! Another intense strike followed by an earsplitting grumble. It was as if they were getting closer to me. Oh, and in case you're wondering, singing about a few of my favorite things doesn't help at all in situations like these. Actually, I had tried every trick in the book to get rid of this miserable phobia, but it's actually quite hard (read: impossible) to be cured of a curse that truly exists. No, really. I was totally cursed. I had absolutely no doubt something — or some*one* — was trying to kill me. Their weapon of choice was a high-voltage bolt of electricity.

Bzzzz.

Bzzzz.

My heart stopped in my chest and I jumped in fear.

"Grrr, Diane! I said I can't talk right now," I whined, as if she could hear me. I grabbed my cell phone in annoyance and read the message under the blanket again.

I need u, she wrote.

Can't it wait?

No, it's urgent.

I sighed. This was so typical of Diane. She was one of those high-maintenance friends. You know those people, the ones who always need you the most when you are going through something of your own? Yeah, that was Diane all right. She was the prettiest girl in school and accustomed to getting her way. I was probably the only person who had ever told her "no." Although, even I didn't do it that often. I normally wanted to be there for her in a heartbeat, but as I said, she always had the worst timing imaginable. She knew how I felt about lightning, yet here she was, telling me she needed me for something.

What's up? I wrote.

I'm on a mission. I need u 2 help me.

A mission. Why was I not surprised?

What's the mission? I'll only help u after this stinkin' storm's over.

NO. I need the storm.

Why?

Because I want to go to Camp Milestone, too.

Forgetting everything, I abruptly sat up in my bed and sighed deeply, frustrated we'd come back to this same argument again. Simultaneously, I caught a glimpse of my own anxious reflection in the mirror as a lightning bolt lit up my room. Here's comes the thunder, I knew. But I didn't care this time.

WHAT? I typed a few seconds after my hands had stopped shaking. She'd caught me off guard, but I probably shouldn't have been so surprised. How many times did we have to go over this?

C'mon, Faye. Just help me with this.

NO!!!!!!!!!! I typed angrily, knowing enough exclamation marks didn't exist to adequately portray my adamancy. *Are you crazy? It's absurd!*

Ugh. This argument was stupid. Why were we even texting? This was most definitely phone-conversation material. Furious, I violently pounded the numbers on my cell phone, then waited impatiently as the phone rang. My muscles tensed and my vision clouded.

"Pick up. Pick up. Pick up. Pi— Diane! What the hell are you thinking? Are you absolutely nuts?"

"Faye, quit freaking out. It makes so much sense. Don't you want me at Camp Milestone with you?"

"It's not that easy. You don't understand. You'll get killed. It's not like getting shocked, you know. It's like dying!"

"So you don't want me at camp with you?" she accused.

BOOM! I trembled again and sunk back under the blankets.

Argh! Why was she being so annoying? And why was I so pathetic when it came to thunderstorms?

"Of course, I want you to come to Camp Milestone," I said accommodatingly. "It's just, well, I want you to live, too."

"I won't die," she said. This willful ignorance further infuriated me.

"Diane!" I shrieked, my tone filled with rage. "It's lightning! You are so going to die. Now get your butt back to your house and quit being immature. We'll talk about this tomorrow. We'll find some other way for you to get to Camp Milestone, OK? I promise. Hello? You still there?"

It was not what she wanted to hear. We'd hashed over this argument for a year now. Thankfully, I had prevailed every time because she was secretly afraid of getting hit. Frankly, I didn't blame her. I don't know if surviving a lightning strike was actually a good thing or not. I know the pain made you want to die, if you survived.

"Yeah," she sighed huskily. "I'm here."

"You know I'm right, Di. Just let this go. Please."

"Fine. You're right."

"Thank you," I said as my body relaxed. "Now I need to go hide. Can we talk about this tomorrow?"

"Okay," she answered glumly.

We said our goodbyes and hung up. To my surprise, guilt overwhelmed me as I slumped further into my sheets. Why did I feel like I was betraying her? I was only protecting her. So why did I feel like such a bad friend? I wished I could help her, but I knew there was no way. It's not like I made up the rules or anything.

You see, as I mentioned previously, I'm not exactly normal. In this crazy and mysterious world, an elite few get struck by lightning and survive without a scratch. OK, that's not entirely true. They do get a particular "scratch" or rash called a Lichtenberg figure, which somehow symbolizes their hidden identity as a modern-day fairy-tale character. Are you following me? I know it's hard to imagine, but it's true. Fairy tales exist. As in here. Now. In this world. They could be your best friend, your neighbor, your mother. They could be *you*.

How do I know? Well, not only did it happen to me last year, but to a bunch of my friends, too. Yup, I'm best friends with Cinderella, Snow White and her seven dwarfs, Pinocchio, and Sleeping Beauty. And I'm their Fairy God Mother or "FGM," if you will. We discovered this secret world after attending Camp Milestone last summer. Camp Milestone is the worst and best camp ever. It's run by a guy named Chester, who may just be the modern Mother Goose and whose purpose in life is to help us "Milestonees" fulfill our fairy-tale destinies.

Bzzzz.

Bzzzz.

"Are you friggin' kidding me?" I bellowed. She had texted me again.

I'm going 2 the park. Either you're with me or against me.

OMG. I am so against u. You're kidding, right?
BOOM!

"Ugh!" My body tensed up again and I quickly collected myself. This night officially sucked. I know what you must be thinking. If I've been hit by lightning once and the godmother in me has been turned on, then why am I still afraid of it? I wish I could explain, but I can't. It's a sense I have, that I'm just supposed to get hit by lightning over and over again until I'm dead. Like they are attracted to me or something. It's a phobia, OK? It's not supposed to be rational.

Am not kidding, F. This is happening. Deal with it.

U r going 2 get killed! U r going 2 get killed. U r going to 2 get killed!!!

Maybe if I repeated it obsessively, the message would sink into her bullheaded brain. She had officially lost it.

I waited impatiently for a response. Tapping my feet and wringing my hands, it didn't take me long to grow more frustrated. It was as though a steel fist had clutched my throat. She was acting like a child. You don't just want to get hit by lightning. You avoid it, like the plague.

I redialed her number; she didn't answer. *Wonderful.* She was fully ignoring me now. How mature.

I began to type again, my fingers leaving little prints on my phone.

Why aren't u answering your phone?

A few moments passed silently. Finally, she wrote.

Cause this is happening. I'll be at the park. Come if you care.

NO!! U R being stupid! Stupid, stupid, stupid!!

I dialed her again, knowing all too well she wouldn't answer. God she was just so dense. And stubborn!

Diane, please, I pleaded in desperation. *I don't want to lose you.*

Thankfully, this got her attention.

Ur not gonna lose me. Especially if you get down here and help me out.

What? Down here? Was she there already? Was she serious this time? I rolled my eyes, leaned back and smacked the back of my head against my bed post.

I'm not helping u kill yourself, I wrote back reluctantly. I suspected she was playing chicken, which meant I had to find it in me to out-stubborn her. I hated this game.

The next few minutes of silence felt like an eternity. On one hand, I wanted to be a good friend, run out my front door, and stop her from making the biggest mistake of her life. On the other hand, I was so mad at her. She was being so typically Diane — selfish and self-involved.

"C'mon, ring. Buzz. Do something," I willed my cell phone.

Bzzzz.

Bzzzz.

I smiled and sighed. Thank goodness. She had come to her senses. I clicked on the "Read Message" button.

Do I have to use an all-metal shovel or can it have some wood on it, too?

Oh, crap! I sprang up from my bed, threw the sheets off and scrambled to find my shoes.

"She's crazy. She's freaking crazy!" I yelled in a haze of fury and panic.

My eyes surveyed my room. I located my Converse shoes and came to a halt. The last time I'd worn those shoes, life had taken a dramatic and unexpected turn for me. Did I dare wear them again? Diane's life was in jeopardy. Yeah, I dared. Hysterically, I dialed her number one last time. Of course, she didn't pick up.

Instead, she texted me one last message.

Ok. Am ready. Next time u see me, I'll be a fairy-tale character, too. Can I pick who I want to be? I want to be the Princess and the Pea.

I don't know what exactly happened next, I just know I had somehow made it out into the rain and I was running as fast as my legs could take me. And yes, I was wearing those Converse.

Destiny.

Again.

I just couldn't escape it.

Panting heavily, I continued to dial Diane's cell phone number. I made myself run faster and faster still. I needed to get there. I heard another rumble above me. I didn't care. Screw the lightning. Screw the storm. Screw everything. This was a matter of life and death.

I ran up the hill and entered the park, the infamous park. I had tried so hard to avoid it — and just like that, I was back. There it was again. The same place I'd been to a year ago, and then a million times over in my dreams and nightmares. The old drive-in theater, the wide open field, the big oak tree that sacrificed a few of its branches in tragedy. Standing in the middle, like a delicate movie star, was my stupid best friend, holding a shovel toward the sky.

"Diane!" I called out, but my voice stuck in my throat. My breathing accelerated and suddenly, the atmosphere got quiet. I kept racing toward her and then I slid on the wet grass, falling on all fours. Undeterred, I rose up, continuing my mad dash. She looked so innocent, yet her frail silhouette gave her away; she was scared to death.

Suddenly, doom crept over me and I croaked. The sky was charging up. My eyes grew wider and my pupils dilated as the backdrop darkened further. It was going to happen. I knew it. The lightning was going to strike her any second. I had to make it. *Keep running. Keep running.* I was almost there. Just a little further.

"Diane!" I shouted feverishly.

Then, just as I approached her from behind, I looked up and caught the flash in slow motion. There it was. Just like before. Zigzagging purposefully toward its destination.

"NOOOOOOOO!" I screamed, as I lunged forward.

But it was too late.

Samira Armin Hodges lives in Texas with her husband and two dogs. She is a Pediatrician by day and a Young Adult author by night. Milestones is her debut novel and the first of the Camp Milestone trilogy.